DIAMANTE' PUBLICATIONS PRESENTS

MA'DAM BY NIGHT, SECRETARY BY DAY

INKED BY

K.S. OLIVER & B. ABBY

Edited by Brandi Jefferson

Cover Designed by Aija Monique of AMB Branding

Published by Diamante' Publications, LLC

www.diamantepublications.com

DEDICATION FROM KS

To my husband B, I can't tell you how much of an honor it is to be able to pen your very first novel with you. Thank you for always choosing me. It's been nearly a decade and you never cease to amaze me with your many hidden talents. This is only the beginning. #GOTYOUR6

To our children (KS) Kwan & Shaun. We did it again. I can't thank the two of you enough for teaching me every day about what it is to truly love unconditionally.

To my brothers Ajmal F. Acklin, and Jarvis M. Jones (S.I.P).

Last but not least to my baby brother Khayree Y. Acklin I had the pleasure of being involved in 19 years of your life before you were taken away. I can't believe that I won't get that call from you today saying hey sis your book dropped yet? That's ok I know I am making you proud of me. My birthday will never be the same but I promise to keep reaching towards the top just like you would have wanted me to.

***I now have the best angels in the business. I feel untouchable. ***

DEDICATION FROM B. ABBY

I would like to dedicate this book to my Wife. Ebonee' Abby, you gave me the vision to continue to push forward. From the first day that message came through on Myspace we've been friends and now we had the opportunity to do something different. #BESELFLESS. I appreciate you more than you will ever know. After 9 years of being your husband you are now my codefendant in the book game too. There is nothing we can't conquer together.

To my mother Dorothy Rose Abby and my sister Claudette Davis, I have been blessed with not one but two amazing women that were able to mold me into the man that I am today. There are not enough words in the English language to express how much I appreciate you both.

To Kwan and Shaun (KS), I'm very thankful that I got out of the military and now I have the opportunity to raise and teach you the daily lessons of manhood and brotherhood. You two are a daily lesson and I always welcome the challenge. #YAHHH

To Khayree Y. Acklin, lil bro I love you. We had a few years to rock together on Earth, just note; you will forever rock with me in my heart lil homie.

ACKNOWLEDGEMENTS FROM KS

I want to first thank God for keeping me and blessing me with the ability to write a story. I've been through it all and some, but it has only humbled me and made me even stronger. I am made of bricks now.

To my parents (Clarine & C.O) and my grandparents (Mary & Woody Oliver), mother-in-law Rose Abby, sister-in-law Claudette Davis, stepdad Leroy White and stepmom Desiree Thornton- Oliver. Thank you for everything. You have supported me in everything I have set out to do. I appreciate each of you and the unique things that you bring out of me.

Thank you to my day 1's, LeTorri Mitchell, Latrice Burns, LaChaun Tucker, Nadia Brown & Karessa Martin.

To my brothers from another Jacorey Oneal, Jeremiah Jones and Rashad Bligen. I love y'all down. Time flies and the sky is the limit. Hold your head up and keep going it's almost over.

S/O to the Literary Ladies of the ATL Kenni York, Kierra Petty, and Nika Michelle. Thank you for always being there when I needed you and when I didn't. My sisters in Lit and boy do we act the part. We don't always get along but I love you all.

Thank you to all of my readers. Special S/O to Brandi Jefferson, Audrey Hargraves, Priscilla Murray, Pamela Johnson Ward, Angelina Butler, and Natasha Hill. I couldn't do this without y'all constant support.

Diamonds are forever and so is my team. S/O to Diamante' Publications. Diamond, Janae M. Robinson, Shatika Turner, B. Abby, Tavon Wilson, Vette Wilson, Willie

LeBlanc and Vonda Roche' thanks to all of you for the constant support.

ACKNOWLEDGEMENTS FROM B. ABBY

I want to first thank God for giving me the talent of writing. After spending 8 ½ years in the military I have learned that there is no limit to success.

To my father Ed Lee I never missed out on anything and I will forever appreciate you for that. Thank you for being there even when you didn't have to be.

Christopher "MD" Abby you are my big brother and my best friend. You have always been there for me no matter what. You are the glue that keeps us all together and I have always looked up to you. I appreciate that big dawg. Thank you

To my brother Andre Abby we have come a long way, the sky is the limit and I am looking for a door to the moon. And to my baby brother Travelle "Trey" Stone we have been through it all. You taught me what it was to have someone look up to my every move. I am proud of who you have become.

To my other brother from another Eric "Jeff' Abby I have always looked up to you and it has always been a sight to see. Thanks for being a great example of a man.

Woody "Big Dawg" Oliver from the time we met it has always been love and respect. You have been there through my worst times and my best. I appreciate you always being supportive no matter what and trusting me with your baby for life.

Marco Andujar from day one you always kept me laughing and on my toes. Who would have thought a text from "the good pastor" would make us so close.

Last but not least to my godmother Inez Smith Williams, mama anytime I needed you whether it was to talk or listen you were there no questions asked and I will forever be grateful.

Special S/O to Christopher "Mr. Clean" Young, Kevin Bailey, Sorrell Thompson, Sean Banks, Todd Simmons,

Jason "Listen to Listen" Hallmon, Sam Monroe, Woo Hood, Esean Rose, Kenya Abby, Nika Michelle, Kenni York and to all of my veterans, keep y'all heads up. We've won wars around the world, and we will win this one too...Anyone I forgot charge it to my head not my heart.

Diamonds are forever and so is my team. S/O to Diamante' Publications. KS Oliver, King Diamond, Janae M. Robinson, Shatika Turner, Tavon Wilson, Vette Wilson, Willie LeBlanc and Vonda Roche'; thanks to all of you for the constant support and what you bring to the vault.

CHAPTER 1

Today just isn't my day. I hate waking up out of my bed to apprise someone else. How about someone apprise me one time? I can't believe 9 out of 10 people don't follow what they want to do to get them ahead, but would rather wait on someone else to do it for them and stay stagnated. We only have one shot in this world. You can either swing the bat a lot of times and miss, or you can swing the bat zero times, not try and lose.

I guess I get it from my momma. Haha. That's funny. I don't know where that stupid song came from. Mom, you've been a big inspiration in my life. I can't think of one day where I don't think about you and wish you were here with me. I really love you and look forward to seeing you when I come home. Also, tell Dad I said hello. Me and Lawrence talk about you guys all the time and we promise to come to visit you when the military gives me time off. On another note, a little update on my job... I do paralegal work and I make sure that everyone has good representation. Only thing I don't like for real for real is getting up at freaking 5 am to go running on somebodies track to stay in shape. You can keep that type of stuff. I could never get use to that

You know we weren't built like that. Haha. Well, I hope we get down there sooner and not later to see y'all.

Love Candace,

***

"Hello Ms. Shirley, how was your weekend?"

Ms. Shirley naturally turned around with a huge smile on her face. When she saw who was speaking to her, the huge smile instantly vanished and a frown appeared in its place.

"Hello Ms. Williams," the deep voice ranged out, "What were you doing when I walked in?"

"I was writing a letter to my mother and father."

"Well, you know you can't be in here doing your own personal business. You will have to handle that on your lunch break. Okay?" Her nose tooted up as if she smelled something disgusting. Her disdain for Candace was apparent and mutual.

"Sounds good," Candace replied with a sarcastic response. Her mind raged with ultimate thoughts of slapping the shit out of her for even asking or replying as such.

"Ms. Williams, you need to watch that attitude because this is a place of business and not your home. I just asked if you could refrain from writing and doing your personal business in the confines of this office. Surely you understand the concept of office and business etiquette," Ms. Shirley responded, slightly raising her voice and speaking in that condescending tone that irked Candace to no end.

Woosah, Candace coached herself into a calm state of mind. I have to keep my cool before I do something that I might actually regret.

Ms. Shirley was pretty cool for the most part. Initially, Candace assumed that they'd have that kind of relationship where they'd bump heads from day one, but as long as she stayed out of the older woman's way things were typically all good. In fact, Candace kinda respected her a little bit, but she was tripping today. She was the kind of woman that got her way around the office and nobody really bothered her at all.

Some may have considered it a free pass, but if that was the case then Ms. Shirley had enough free passes to take the entire Georgia football team on a vacation to the Disney World Theme Park.

Standing about 5'11 with long brownish and gray hair, beautiful creole brown skin, and a thick New Orleans accent, Ms. Shirley's strong demeanor demanded attention when she walked in the room. She was respected by everyone in the office, even the senior partners and board members. Her hair was laid at all times, which meant she had a faithful stylist on standby at all cost. The law was what she knew best and she played no games when it came down to it. Rumor had it that she used to be a big time, special prosecutor back in the day in Louisiana, but at some point someone threatened to take out her entire family if she didn't dismiss all charges against the lieutenant of Beltran Cartel and his associates.

Luckily her family talked her out of it because she was willing to go to war with them even after they supposedly kidnapped her 6 year old granddaughter while at school. After several weeks of going back and forth, she finally negotiated and gave in to the organization. Fortunately and unfortunately she got a lot of respect from outsiders but zero from her family. Her daughter exiled her from any future events and the Department of Justice Protection program relocated them to unknown locations; the daughter in California and Ms. Shirley to Arizona where she was given a paralegal position there in the office. Perhaps it was because the department ran the entire drug interdiction task force out here and they wanted to keep her involved in what she knew best. But, that was neither here or there. They needed to send that old hag back to the south or something.

"Ms. Williams," Ms. Shirley's voice faded as she reached her office.

"Yes ma'am." Candace rolled her eyes wishing that the woman would just go on about her business and leave her alone so they could both get on with their work day in peace.

"Did you file the formal continuance with the court for Williams, Johnson, Benjamin, Rose, and Robinson on Friday?"

Candace answered immediately, "Yes ma'am, I did it on Friday and put a copy on your desk so you and Lieutenant Johnson can go over it before the 9 am conference call."

Satisfied with the answer she'd received; Ms. Shirley turned around and walked into her office.

Just as Candace began searching for the latest entertainment news on her Facebook news feed, KC came in and whispered in her ear. Frightened by his presence, she popped him on the chest, "Boy, don't be scaring me like that."

KC began to laugh outrageously loud. Ms. Shirley then stepped out of her office and cleared her throat. KC looked up and greeted Ms. Shirley, then ran over to give her a hug.

"I need y'all to stop," Ms. Shirley told him. She smiled abruptly until she saw Candace looking at her. With her warning issued, she reentered her office.

"What do I have today?" KC asked, getting down to business.

Candace handed him a list of appointments before he headed towards his office.

"What do you have scheduled for lunch?" KC inquired, stopping short of his office door. He toyed with the thought of possibly taking her out for lunch once again.

"Nothing. I'll probably grab something simple from downstairs in the cafeteria," Candace replied.

"Okay. Figure out what we are going to eat for lunch and instant message me on my computer," KC said, jumping the gun by telling her they were going out together verses asking her. "None of that stuff from South Side restaurant though, because that stuff had my stomach hotter than a two dollar whore on a Friday afternoon the last time we ate there."

"Ha, ha, ha." Candace laughed as she covered her mouth to prevent making Ms. Shirley stick her head out and reprimand her once again. "Boy, you are stupid, but don't try to play my people like that."

The phone began to ring. Candace pointed at the extension, signaling that she was about to discontinue their conversation just before she picked up the receiver.

"Hello, Jackson and Duncan...Yes, sir. I'm doing well. Best as I can at this moment...Well, thank you, sir." Candace spoke with a huge smile on her face. Her eyes lifted and fell upon KC as he continued to listen to her end of the conversation. Disappointment was blanketed over his entire face. On the inside, Candace was tickled by the man's jealousy. "Just a second, I'll transfer you to him." She placed the call on hold and smiled at KC sweetly. "Hey, you have a call on line three. It's Mr. Jackson. He seems kinda pissed."

The frown disappeared when he found out that it was his supervisor that she'd been flirting with on the other end of the phone. "No, he's okay. We are planning this eight year celebration of life for his crew that he lost on a combat mission in Iraq," he explained to her. "Three of them died from an IED blast by the Taliban. Hold on, I will tell you about it later. Lemme grab the call. He actually said I reminded him of his first troop while he was on the east side. Can you tell Ms. Shirley to meet me in the conference room in about twenty minutes so we can knock out this teleconference?" KC asked before disappearing in his office to pick up his extension.

"Okay, I got you," Candace called out after him. She picked up the phone to dial but at that moment Ms. Shirley appeared at the doorway of her office.

"What do you have for me, Ms. Williams?" Ms. Shirley asked in her usual deep tone.

"KC asked for you to meet him in the conference room for the nine o'clock conference."

"Yes, I heard him when he told you," Ms. Shirley spoke as she turned to go back inside her office.

What the fuck is up with this chick? She is starting to get on my last nerves. Always being snazzy and shit. Man, I hate that bullshit.

As thoughts and aggression rang through Candace's mind, a loud noise caught her attention forcing her to notice Mr. Jackson running down the hall.

He was a sexy ass older man, about late 30's, early 40's. He resembled Idris Elba, but with a few less pounds. When it came to physical activities, he was the best of the best for his age. He was always the first to get selected because of his passion for winning and having fun. That was probably because he played college football on the 1992 Alabama

Crimson Tide championship team as the starting defensive back.

"Are you okay, sir?" Candace asked, putting on her best look of sincerity and speaking in her sexiest yet most professional tone of concern.

"Yes, yes. I'm okay. Where is my little fly swatter? This darn summer weather is really starting to annoy the hell out of me. By the way, what are you working on?"

"I'm updating the system and then I will be printing contracts to mail off. Is there anything else that you may need for me to do?"

He smiled at her, really impressed with her efficiency. "I just want you to know that you are doing a wonderful job overall," he spoke with genuine gratitude. "If we can create some time later on today and place you on my schedule that would be awesome. I would like to sit down with you and develop some professional or career goals for you."

"Thank you, sir. I really do appreciate that. I also appreciate the opportunity you've given me by entrusting me with this job," Candace said, laying it on thick as she rummaged through the supply cabinet to her left and then handed him the swatter he'd been in search of.

"You came highly recommended from KC and let me tell you, one thing I do know about KC is that if nothing else when it comes down to business and law he's crisp. He's been recognized on several different levels and he's an amazing listener so I really value his opinion when it comes down to a lot of things. I can definitely tell you that.

"Did anyone tell you about the time that he sat in on one of the biggest capital murder cases we have ever had?" Mr. Jackson beamed proudly as he began to remember the story.

"No, sir."

"Well ask him later for the details. It's one hell of a story. Gotta get back to my office. I have my wife on the phone. I just had to get this fly swatter before I go berserk on these flies. Nice chatting with you. I look forward to sitting down with you."

"I look forward to sitting down with you as well, sir." Her eye brow raised slightly as she got a final good look of the sexy older gentleman.

"Ok. Cool. Look at my schedule and let's pencil in a good time for next week No matter what day it is, besides Tuesday." He held up the fly swatter. "Thanks."

Candace smiled sweetly, thinking about the things she could do with an older man like Mr. Jackson that had nothing at all to do with the mediocre office career goals that he probably had in mind for her. Her thoughts were evaded by the buzzing her personal cell. Candace's eyes darted over to Ms. Shirley's office door quickly before snatching the phone out of her desk drawer and glancing at the LED screen. She shook her head, pursed her lips, and sent the call to voicemail.

"Not right now, Leal," she whispered. "Not outside of 'office' hours. You can wait." She replaced the phone in the drawer and made a mental note to handle the piece of side business indicated by the receipt of the incoming call. She sighed and returned her focus to her computer screen. "Back to the day life." She flexed the muscles in her neck and tried to shake off the fatigue that simmered in her bones. How the hell had she gotten to this place in her life?

***

ONE YEAR AGO

"Hey L," Candace said in tired voice as she entered the room. Her eyes jumped from him to the scantily dressed hoochie sprawled all over him as if their asses were laid out on a couch that they owned in a house that they paid for.

"What's up, sis?"

"How was school today?" she asked him, wincing from the lyrics that blared loudly in her ear as she tried to hold it together.

"You already know a nigga didn't want to go. It was aight though. Shit, I didn't want to go in the first place."

"First off, don't be cursing like you grown because you not," she said as she knocked his shoes off of the coffee table and onto the floor, no longer in the mood to play nonchalant, cool ass sister. Her eyes narrowed in on him intently, taking in his appearance and demeanor while paying special attention to his facial expression. "Where's your homework at? Ms. Wilson texted me at work and said that you've been on your bullshit again. Haven't we talked about that?"

Candace didn't bother to give him an opportunity to answer. She was tired and fed up and the last thing she wanted to do was babysit his old enough to know better ass. "Why you up in here with this music all fucking loud and shit with these nasty ass little girls in here while I'm not here, Lawrence?" She rolled her eyes at the chick who had the audacity to look offended "You have just about fifteen seconds to get this lil' girl out my face or I'm going to turn up on your ass right after I beat hers," she said, pointing at the girl who was now trembling as the truth of an impending ass whooping dawned on her.

"Damn, sis, you on that bullshit," L snapped back. "You don't even give a nigga a chance to try to explain and shit. You just start taking another motherfucker's side over you own brother. Now, that's that shit I don't like."

"No, this is going to be something that you don't like," Candace advised as she reached over L and popped the little girl in the mouth. "Didn't I tell your little ass to get the fuck out of my house? THOT hours are over. Get the hell on."

The chick's hands instantly flew up to her face and she screamed out in pain. "Owww. What the hell?" Her heart raced, not knowing what other afflictions the crazy woman was about to place upon her.

"Aye man, Keisha get the fuck out of here shawty," L hollered, jumping up and snatching the girl to her feet as if he was annoyed. "What the fuck you still here for man? You see she ain't playing."

Keisha stared at L wide-eyed. "That's just it? You ain't gon' stand up for me?"

Candace lurched forward as if she was going to swing again, but L stood in between the two females.

"Man, is you serious? I gotta live here and yo' moms and pops shoul' ain't letting a nigga parlay up in they spot. Just bounce man. I'ma hit you later."

Keisha opened her mouth to speak, but seeing Candace's angry glare over L's shoulder she thought better of it. "That's fucked up," she mumbled under her breath as she reached down to grab her knock-off Gucci purse from the couch before storming out of the front door.

The moment the lock caught on the closed door, L burst out laughing. "Aye, that was pretty dope, sis. I thought that bitch was never going to leave."

Candace clutched at her chest and her eyes grew wide. She was unable to speak and felt her air passage constricting. "

"What's wrong?" L asked, frowning with concern.

"I-I-I.... can't... breathe," she struggled to say.

"Do you have your inhaler?"

Candace nodded. "Yea. In....in...purse."

"What?"

"Innnnn myyyy purse," she hissed as she pointed at her black exterior leather purse with burgundy interior design inside.

L grabbed the bag and began to look through it. To be a Michael Kors or MK for short, it had a lot of pockets. L fumbled trying to search them all. "Ughhhhh!!!! Which pocket is it in?" He began to panic during his attempt to locate the inhaler. The last thing he wanted was to see his sister suffering. His fingertips touched something small and hard and he wrapped is hand around it securely, pulling the pump out with a sense of accomplishment. "Here it go. Here you go, sis."

Taking the inhaler from his hands and quickly giving herself relief was everything. Breathe...Breathe, she thought as she sat on the edge of the sofa.

"You ight, sis?"

She exhaled loudly. "Yea. I'm ight."

"You played that shit off right though," L said, relieved that everything was all good. He sunk down on the couch beside Candace and kicked his feet up on the table. "You the real MVP for that shit."

Candace looked over at him and scowled. "That was how I felt for real, boy! You have to get yourself together, bro. As you can see, I can't keep trying to help you out all the time. First you were with Aunt Robyn and you didn't like that, so you convinced me to come get your ass. Now you are on that same bullshit. I can't deal with this shit right now. You and your bullshit gon' be the death of me."

"So what the hell you want me to do? Learn? Ha! You can have that bullshit. We can get this money."

"What the hell's that supposed to mean?"

L folded his arms behind his head like he was resting on a lounging chair out on the beach "Shit, it meant what I said it means. I don't have time to be hearing this shit right now."

Without giving it a second thought, Candace smacked L in the face with a sting that brought tears to his eyes. He jumped upright from the shock and the impact of her blow but didn't dare raise a hand to his flesh and blood. They stared each other in the eyes, each huffing and gasping for air yet for different reasons.

"Nigga, are you fucking serious?" Candace snapped. "You need to take your ass to school and learn something. Don't be giving these punk ass motherfuckers ammo to come to my job or even call me for that much. We already know Aunt Robyn didn't have your best interest at heart. Right?"

"Yea," L mumbled through clenched jaws.

"Exactly, so why have you been acting crazy out here then?" She waited for him to give her an explanation.

L hesitated before responding. His mind was wrapped around one thing and one thing only: the fact that she'd slapped him. He could give two shits about what she was saying. None of it phased him in the least bit but he'd be damned if he allowed anyone to disrespect him, no matter who it was. That shit just wasn't going to fly. "Sis, you lucky as fuck right now," he finally said.

"Why?" she asked challengingly. I know he don't think he 'bout to sit up here and get buck with me, she thought.

"I love you, but don't ever put your hand in my face again." His expression was stone hard as he tried to lay the law down.

Smack! Candace wasn't having it. He could talk that tough shit with any and everybody else, but they were cut from the same cloth and she definitely wasn't about to let his ass punk her in her own house.

L jumped up in Candace's face with his fist balled up like he was ready to knuckle up.

Although her chest felt tight and she wanted to sit still, Candace rose to her feet daring him to follow through with his threat. "What?" she asked. "What are you going to do? You all big and bad. Do something about it then."

The steam and fire from L's temper was apparent as he visualized himself punching Candace in the face and throwing her unto the ground. He was breathing hard and hot tears started to run down his face from his anger. He gritted his teeth and tried his best not to act out his aggression. "Didn't I tell you not to hit me anymore, sis?" he cried out.

Candace just shook her head. "Well, if I didn't care about your lil dumb ass, I wouldn't try to knock some sense into you." She stared at him, taking in the hurt that radiated from his being. "You have to realize, we're all we have. You know Aunt Robyn didn't care about you. And what would Mom and Dad say if they saw you acting like this. Huh? I'm trying to save you from yourself." She paused, wondering if she was getting through to him. "You hear me talking to you, right?"

Still breathing hard, L just stood there in anger with no response. He didn't wanna hear about how nobody cared about him. He didn't need to be reminded of how disappointed his parents would be in him. He definitely didn't need his sister putting her hands on him and not giving him the respect he deserved as a man.

"What would Mom think about you having your pants all the way down your butt? With all of these tattoos and girls running around here like you are some mack daddy or some shit. Or how you think Dad would feel with the amount of disrespect that you are showing your teachers and other adults? Not to mention you jumping in my face like you just did. You know he wouldn't go for that nonsense, right? They are both probably turning over in their graves looking at all the disrespect and havoc you are creating." She stared at him once more and waited yet still got no response. "I know you hear me talking you Lawrence.

L's chest rose and fell as he spat out his rebuttal. "But you hit me in my fucking face!"

"Didn't I just tell you stop all of that damn cursing? You are not grown at all little boy."

"And I specifically told yo' ass not to hit me in my face no more but you went and did it again any fuckin' way."

Candace was done. She wasn't feeling her best and it was clear that L was in one of his rigid moods where nothing she did or said was going to sink in at the moment. It was time to exercise some tougher love that he'd maybe understand a little better. "Nigga, get the fuck out of my house then. You feel like that and you all grown and shit, go fuck up and chase coochie outside my house."

He was feeling himself. "Fuck your house! I don't have to stay here. I got plenty of places to go." He snatched up his shoes and didn't bother to throw her another glance as he fled out of the door. Fuck this shit, he thought. No self-respecting man would ever let a woman punk him, no matter who it was. He felt convinced in his decision to stand up for himself and let her be on that bullshit by herself. No way was he sticking around to be treated like some little boy as she kept referring to him. *I'ma go get this money,* he thought. *I'ma show her ass that I ain't 'bout that bullshit she talking.*

***

2006 -Atlanta, GA

"That's a pretty color on you," Aunt Robyn said she stood behind Candace, staring at her reflection in the mirror of the dressing table.

Candace was experimenting with the different eye shadows and lip sticks that Aunt Robyn seemed to keep in abundance. She always marveled over how the other girls that came and went through the house looked brand new once they stepped out of Aunt Robyn's private dressing room.

That said a lot seeing as though most of them had bags under their puffy red eyes and sometimes marks on their faces and necks which Candace couldn't explain and never dared to ask them about. She was 16 years old and knew a thing or two; mostly importantly she knew when not to stick her nose in business that she wasn't invited in to.

Aunt Robyn took a sip of the brute bubbling in her champagne glass. The rose pink polish on her nails caught Candace's attention before her eyes followed the trail down to the diamond ring shining on Robyn's ring finger. From there, Candace glanced up at the diamonds hugging her aunt's neck and daggling from her ears. They were a testament to the fine life that Aunt Robyn had made for herself.

Considering her aunt's position in life, Candace sighed and then her eyes darted up to meet Robyn's. Aunt Robyn smiled, fully aware of her niece's desire to have more in life than what she was accustomed to before she and her brother ended up in her custody. She placed her right hand on Candace's shoulder and smiled at her in the mirror. "I know," she said.

Candace's nose wrinkled. "Huh?"

"I know how you're feeling right now."

Candace was practically an orphan, given the demise of her parents, and had very few friends outside of her kid brother whom she felt a great sense of responsibility for. She doubted that Aunt Robyn had a clue as to what any of that felt like.

"You and I are a lot alike, Candace," Robyn went on

"We are?"

"Mmmhmmm. You see, you and I have exquisite taste, beautiful features, and an iron will to survive."

Candace considered the comparison.

"Your mom, she wasn't like us. She never understood my maverick behavior...my creative, albeit different, ways of trying to obtain success."

Candace grew uncomfortable at the mention of her mother.

Robyn squeezed her shoulder. "But I see a lot of you in me, Candace. You're a woman now. Well, almost...and soon you'll be out of school and need to be able to forge your own way in life. You can't sit here forever sponging off of me, you know?"

Candace grimaced as she replaced the cap on the lipstick tube she'd been holding. "I wouldn't dream of it," she responded.

"Now, don't take offense," Robyn told her, giving Candace her best look of genuineness. "I just want to prepare you for life, dear, and not handicap you. Now, in order to be a success, you have to start investing in yourself early." She reached around and cupped Candace's chin, forcing the girl to peer into her own eyes in the glass. "You're already doing that by learning to make yourself presentable. Now, you must grasp and understand the value of who you are and what you have."

"Huh?"

"Remember, you're a woman, dear," Robyn said condescendingly. "And as a woman you hold the greatest power known to man."

"I do?" Candace stared at her reflection trying to get a glimpse of whatever it was that her aunt saw in her.

"Of course you do. Now's the time to realize that and start capitalizing off of it...starting tonight," she added quickly, taking another sip of her champagne.

"What?"

Aunt Robyn dropped her hand and turned away; heading to her special closet to pull out a little slip dress that she felt would fit and compliment Candace's budding curves well. She was short a girl tonight and needed to keep a particular Senator happy, one who made sure that the law enforcement didn't disturb her, her clients, or her girls; one who preferred making visits to her estate where she often received special guests for special reasons.

She took the dress off of the hanger, returned to Candace's side, and urged her to stand up. "Come on; let's get you out of that thing."

The thing she was referring to was the oversized t-shirt that Candace wore to bed. It had once belonged to her father and she kept it around because it gave her a slight sense of comfort.

Aunt Robyn helped Candace into the light gray slip dress which exposed Candace's cleavage and came just above her thighs. Candace turned to look at herself in the mirror and wondered where on earth her aunt expected her to go in that get up.

"Why are you putting this on me?" Candace finally asked. She turned to look at her aunt. "What are you sending me to do?" Warning bells went off in her head as memories of eight or more girls' images flashed in her mind; each made up,

each scantily dressed, and each regarding Aunt Robyn as if she herself was God.

"You're not going anywhere but downstairs, honey," Aunt Robyn explained. "I'm expecting company and you are going to entertain him," she advised, pointing her finger at Candace.

For some time now, Candace had tried to dismiss her assumptions, but she was smart enough to know exactly how Aunt Robyn had come into this fortune she so eagerly bragged about. Candace shook her head. "No," she whispered, the moment feeling all too surreal. "No, I can't."

Gone was Aunt Robyn's fake tone of compassion. "You can and you will," she snapped. She took in Candace's trembling and the look of fear creeping upon her face. "If you want to live here...if you want to live a happy, peaceful existence under my roof then you will do as I say...otherwise you and your brother can be history for all I care. It isn't cheap taking care of two children and trying to keep up my lifestyle. The last thing I'm going to do is let my misfortune of being your only surviving relative end up being the cause of my downfall." She took another sip of her drink and raised a brow as she continued to study Candace's face. "So, you'll wipe that childish expression off of your cute little face and take your ass downstairs and entertain."

Candace fought back the tears that stung her eyes. "Entertain how?" she asked meekly.

Aunt Robyn smiled slyly. "However he wants you to."

Fear slapped Candace in the face. Her chest rose and fell as she realized that she was practically being whored out by her guardian. This couldn't be right. Was this happening to her other female classmates? Was there anyone that could save her from this new age slavery she was being forced into? The answer was no; no one was going to save her because outside of Aunt Robyn and her brother Lawrence, Candace had no one else.

Aunt Robyn ushered Candace towards the door as she spoke softly in her ear. "If he wants you to tell a joke, tell a joke. If he wants to tell you a joke, laugh! If he wants to discuss politics, you better conjure up whatever that school is teaching you and spit out something relevant. If he wants to dance, turn on the stereo and sway those hips. If he wants to see what's under your dress...you better show him."

Candace hesitated just at the threshold. There it was; Aunt Robyn had confirmed her nightmare is so many words and all Candace wanted to do was scream. "No," she protested again, shaking her head. "Please...please don't make me do this."

Aunt Robyn wasn't moved. "I don't have time for this. You're not a child anymore, Candace. Your mother may have sheltered you but I very well will not. Now's the time for you to grow up, little girl. This is real life and in real life there's a million things we don't want to do but simply have no choice. Here," she shoved her champagne glass into Candace's trembling hands. "Sip this. It'll take the edge off."

Candace knew that she shouldn't consume the alcohol but with what she was being told she had to do, she figured she might as well go the distance. As she sipped the acidic beverage, the taste was foreign to her palate but she soon adapted to it. Her parents would flip over in the graves knowing how their daughter was being coerced down such a turbulent life path. Candace began to chug the champagne, hoping that it would soon take some effect over her body and wash away the sting of hurt and humiliation that was settling within her spirit.

"Come on," Aunt Robyn coaxed. "Time is money."

It was always about at the bottom line with her; when it came to her coins she was efficient and no nonsense. Candace was getting a valuable education on this night and in return, Aunt Robyn would end up with a sizable profit.

The two females reached the door of the private room on the main floor of the split level house that Aunt Robyn never allowed anyone but her employees to go into from time to time. They hadn't been there with Aunt Robyn long, but both Candace and Lawrence had longed to find out what went on behind that closed door. Now that she was being forced to partake in the action, Candace no longer cared to have anything to do with the private room.

Aunt Robyn snatched the glass from Candace's hand and glared at her. "Stand up straight, present yourself like a lady, and don't fuck this up."

Present myself like a lady, Candace thought. How the hell was she supposed to do that when ultimately she was being expected to turn a trick? She opened her mouth to protest once more but Aunt Robyn wasn't hearing it.

"Shut it," Robyn hissed, her hand lingering on the doorknob. "Now get in there and do your job."

"This...this isn't my job," Candace whispered, her eyes wide and pleading. "I don't... I-I-I don't know what I'm doing. I've never...I've never had—"

Aunt Robyn didn't care to hear her niece's excuses. She simply placed a finger over the girl's mouth, and issued her a stern look before correcting her own posture and opening the door. "Senator Bradley," she called out gaily. "So sorry for the wait, my love, but trust me when I say it'll be well worth it." She turned and motioned for Candace to step forward.

Reluctantly, Candace did so and stared at the man who would be the first to violate her and experience her essence. Candace avoided eye contact with her aunt; it was useless. She'd tried to tell the woman that she was virgin and had no clue how to perform the tasks expected of her, but it was clear that Aunt Robyn could give less than two fucks.

"I brought you my prized possession tonight," Aunt Robyn advise the senator. "My pride and joy. I'm sure she'll treat you well."

Senator Bradley's large belly jumped up and down as he laughed. "I like that about you, Robyn. You always know how to make a man feel special." He eyed Candace, crossed the room, and reached out to grab her hand. "Mmmm mmm. You're some kinda pretty. I can't wait to get to know you."

Candace felt the vile rise her throat as the lust was unmistakable in the man's eyes. Behind her, she heard the door close as Aunt Robyn left her to fend for herself with no care at all for her well-being or the disturbia the entire situation filled her with. Candace wanted to cry, but her tears were frozen solid by fear as the Senator wasted no time disposing of her borrowed nightie and exploring regions of her body she'd never before shared. She was in hell and in hell there were no such thing as a hero.

***

2015 –Tucson, Arizona

"What's up, Ms. Candace? This is Keisha; we met earlier at your house."

Candace sat up, shook her head free of the memory that had pushed her into a depressing trance, and instantly got pissed again. "What the fuck you want lil girl? L's ass ain't here and the way I see it you and I ain't got nothing to discuss." She moved to hang up the phone.

"It's about Loco," Keisha called out, getting her attention.

"Lil girl, who the hell is Loco?" Candace sat up on the side of her bed and stared at the wall hoping that her intuition was wrong and that she could go ahead and hang up on this chick. "Lawrence?" she asked, praying that nothing had happened to her hot-headed ass brother.

"Yes ma'am. He's headed to the hospital. He got shot pretty bad in the arm and he made me promise to contact you even after the incident that happened earlier."

Candace was in panic. "Where were y'all at? What the hell happened?"

"We were on the south side looking for some weed when one of the local jump boys jumped out and shot Loco one time in the shoulder. He tried to rob us. I pulled off just in time before they were able to do anything more or steal the car. We on the way to the hospital now. He's bleeding kinda bad."

"Oh my God. Okay...Okay..." Her mind was flipping through thoughts quickly as she rose to get dressed. "What hospital are you headed to?"

"Northwest Medical Center."

"Aight...okay baby. Go on, I'm headed there now. Keep me updated with all the information that you know before I get there though."

After disconnecting the call, she scrambled about to get her belongings so she could meet Keisha and L. "Where the fuck is my keys?" She searched in total disarray as she started to fall over the table from the two bottles of red wine she had ingested while waiting for Lawrence to come in from their argument.

***

"How did I get here?"

Her head was spinning and her eyes could barely focus to make out anything around her. Her ears were ringing and she placed her hands over them as she tried to collect her thoughts and emotions.

"Ma'am, you are going to be okay?" an unfamiliar voice asked her. "Do you know where you are?"

"I'm...I'm...headed to the hospital." She had to think about it. That had really happened, right? Wasn't she supposed to be going there to see about Lawrence? She tried to again to open her eyes and at least get a good look at whomever was speaking to her, but the task was damn near impossible. She felt as if she'd faint at any moment as the world seemed to be whirling around her at rapid speed.

"What's your name?" the stranger asked.

"My name?" What was it? She had to think about it. "It's...it's Candace. My name is Candace," she replied, shaking her head in a daze.

"Hi Candace, my name is Rodney. Don't worry, I've got you, okay?"

Got me? What the hell are you going to do with me? Why do you have me? She couldn't make sense of what was going on.

"Hello 911? I need you to send an ambulance ASAP... to...Benson...Highwayyyyy....there's been a major car accident.

CHAPTER 2

"Ma'am, it's going be alright. Stay calm. Help is on the way to for you, okay?"

She was just about sick of hearing Rodney coaxing her to calm down and telling her that everything was going to be okay. Everything was most certainly not okay.

She coughed loudly. "I have to get to the hospital for my brother," she insisted. Another loud bout of coughing ensued as she tried to move from the seated position that she was in. "Lllll!!!" she screamed out as if her brother was in earshot and could hear her. "Get out of my way, dude," she instructed the Good Samaritan as she pushed the man away and promptly fell over.

"Sir? Are you there?" the dispatcher asked, still on the line.

"Yes I'm here," Rodney informed her. "Jenny, bring the first aid kit from the trunk NOW!" the man screamed out to the women sitting frighteningly in the passenger seat of his car.

"Does she have any type of ID or anything in her possession?" the dispatcher asked.

"I'm unsure at this time. She appears to have a laceration to the right side of her forehead. Looks pretty bad... and she also has a loud cough, possibly a punctured lung from the sound of it." Rodney watched as the frantic woman moved about. "Ma'am, it's going to be alright. Please stay calm." In full multi-task mode, he switched his attention over to his companion. "Jennyyyyyyyyyyy! I need that first aid kit now....Hurry up!"

"And what is your name, sir?" the dispatcher asked.

"My name is Rodney. I'm with the Pima....Hold...hold...hold..." He couldn't concentrate on the phone call because of the injured woman's failure to remain still. "Ma'am, you can't walk right now. I'm going to need you to rest. Help is on the way."

Candace wasn't trying to hear him. "I have to get to the hospital for my brother. Lllll....." Her body doubled over as she dry coughed so hard that he knocked her back down to the ground. She stumbled to stand up once more. "I have to go sir," she tried to explain breathlessly. "Like now! My brother is in the hos..." The cough gobbled up the last syllables of her word as she leaned over from the impact. Blood started to come out of her mouth and drip down onto the asphalt.

Rodney became nervous. "Ma'am, I'm going to need you to relax. Just relax for me okay?' he insisted. "Help is on the way." He was feeding her the same line all the while wondering where the hell this infamous help was when they needed them the most. "Hurry up Jenny, I need you hurry up with the kit!" He refocused his attention on Candace. "Do you feel any pain, ma'am?"

Candace stood still for a moment and realized that she wasn't in the best condition. "Yeah," she admitted. "I have some pain in..." The coughing ensued once more and rendered her speechless for a few seconds. "...in my side," she finally let out as she sat and leaned back against dented metal.

"Stay awake for me please," Rodney urged as he got closer and tried to take a look at her face, examining her forehead.

"Have you been drinking ma'am?" he inquired due to the hint of alcohol he detected on her breath as a result of her mouth standing open as she gasped for all the air that her lungs could take in.

"Quit touching me, dude. I don't fucking know you."

In the distance they could hear the sirens he'd been anticipating.

Rodney let out a sigh of relief. "Help is on the way, ma'am," he said once more. "Come on. Stay awake for me, Candace. Candace! Come on stay awake for me. Okay? Can you hear my voice?"

Consciousness was becoming a thing of the past as Candace began to slip away. Rodney's screams began to turn into mere whispers as she leaned back and allowed the darkness to welcome her. The sirens were getting closer as Candace was getting further away from lucidness.

"Candace, wake up. Wake up!" Rodney was beginning to panic. His palms were damp and sweat poured down his forehead as he tried to jar the woman back to consciousness. "You gotta stay awake. Candace! Candace! You can't do this, okay. Remember, you gotta get to your brother." He was trying to connect with her, to bring her back by appealing to her memory.

"Hey, here's the kit," Jenny said breathlessly as she ran up beside Rodney with the little red bag.

Rodney snatched it from her and quickly jumped into action. "Come on, Candace. Stay with me." He removed Candace's Army Advance tee shirt with a pair of scissors to attempt to relieve the air inside her of chest. The garment was only helping to restrict her breathing. He could see the swelling of her chest as more and more oxygen became trapped inside of it.

"Stay with me, Candace," Rodney continued to beg. "You know what? Duct tape is very magical. I see you were in the Army. What a coinkydink? I was in the Navy. I served a couple of years back in 2004 as a corpsman." He pulled out a sharp needle from his kit before sterilizing it with an alcohol pad. "You see this? I had to use these a couple of times in Iraq. When I first learned this I was a new recruit in Corpsman Training, right?" He took a deep breath and punctured a hole into the frail woman's chest between her second and third rib just enough to get to the space where the air was trapped. A little of the tension was released and now the task was to keep the chest cavity from filling right back up with the air that wasn't able to be properly released.

"Funny thing is, I was scared of needles," Rodney went on reminiscing as he worked. "This asshole, Petty Officer Andujar, a little short Puerto Rican dude, but who also had a funny side to him...one thing he would always tell me was that if you are scared of something so small as needle, then how do you expect me to entrust you in my Navy to take care of my fellow service members? 'See I don't need you to be in my Navy,' he told me. 'You need to be in my Navy.'" Rodney tore hard at the duct tape, covering the puncture wound on only three sides in an effort to funnel out the air from Candace's chest. "I hated that fool," he said, sweat dripping into his eyes and blending with the tears of fear that gathered in the corners. "But eventually I loved him because he pushed me out of my comfort zone."

Candace gasped for breath as Rodney's handiwork managed to give her some relief from the air restriction she'd been suffering from.

Rodney said a quick, silent prayer and smiled down at the woman. "Welcome back," he said as Candace looked around in a daze.

The sirens ceased just as the ambulance pulled up behind Rodney's vehicle. Doors flung open and immediately an EMT technician ran up to them.

"How are you doing, sir?" the short and stout paramedic asked. "How is she doing?"

Rodney looked up at the medical emergency team with a look of exasperation. He couldn't have been happier to see them if it was his own life at stake. "She appears to be stable now. I had to do a pneumothorax decompression to release the air from her lungs and chest."

"Good job, sir," the short tech stated. He took a knee and looked at Candace. "Ma'am, how are you doing? My name is Jason." Jason was light-skinned and appeared to about 5'6 with freckles on around his nose which made him look very young. "I'll be taking care of you today. Can you hear me okay?"

Candace responded with a head nod because at this time, she knew that it behooved her to listen and pay attention to the professionals. She still had no recollection of what was going on, but she knew that she was in bad shape. Thoughts of Lawrence filled her mind as she tried to focus on what was being said to her. *Focus*, she chided herself. *The sooner you get yourself seen about the sooner you can get to him. All things in time.*

***

"Ma'am, you are in stable condition," the young African American doctor wearing the white coat spoke as he checked her vitals and monitored the breathing machine upon entering the room. He looked quite young to be a doctor, especially an emergency surgeon to say the least.

"My name is Dr. Samuels," he advised. "You had a close call there but we caught you in time and you will recover well. You're at Northwest Medical Center. We had to go in and conduct an emergency surgery when you arrived last night to correct your collapsed lung. Also, your blood pressure continued to drop. But, we gave you fludrocortisone to get your pressure up and everything is fine now. How are you feeling?"

Candace was looking the young doctor up and down from the moment he crossed the threshold and came into her direct line of vision. She watched his every move, smitten with the image before her. She stared at his 5'9 frame before exiting her thoughts and getting back to reality with a thumbs up in response to the question that he asked her because the words simply wouldn't materialize for her to be vocal.

He smiled at her, no stranger to such looks from his female patients. "Also, you have a couple of people out in the waiting room that would like to speak with you. Sgt. Smith from Pima County Sheriff Department and Allison Smith, your supervisor or something like that."

Candace grimaced, not really wanting to be bothered with anyone but knowing that she had no choice.

"Alright," the doctor said, patting her arm reassuringly. "I hope you have a great day. Buzz us if you have a questions or need any type of assistance.

Just as Dr. Samuels opened the door, he signaled for the two detectives and her supervisor to enter the room.

"Hey Doc, can she take the mask off right now so we can answer a few questions?" Candace could see through the crack in the door as a fat old white man inquired.

"Her vitals are okay but don't ask too many questions," the doctor insisted. "We don't want her BP to lower again from fatigue or a depressive response to the discussion. Try to keep your questions to a minimum or we'll have to ask you to leave and come back on a later time. Cool?' Dr. Samuels responded.

"Cool beans," the fat detective responded, trying to sound hip as he thanked the doctor. Fatso led the pack into the room where Candace regarded them with cold, hard stares.

"How you feeling?" Sgt. Allison Smith asked as she approached Candace's bedside.

"Why am I here? I had an accident, right? Why wasn't I taken to 355th Medical Center?"

"You don't really wanna be on base right now," the other woman whispered, cutting her eyes over at the officers across the room."

"Well, hello, Ms. Williams. My name is Sgt. Hanson and this is my partner Deputy Sanders," the fat guy said, introducing himself and his peer. "We don't want to take up too much of your time, but we need to ask you a few questions related to the car accident."

Candace responded after looking over at Deputy Sanders and her best friend and supervisor standing to the right of her. "Okay."

"Ms. Williams, are you comfortable with your supervisor being here?" Sgt. Hanson asked.

Candace shrugged. She didn't understand have any opposition to Allison be there and even welcomed her presence if it gave her the comfort to get through the interrogation. The sooner they got this over with, the better. "Yes. We're good."

"Great. Okay, first question," Sgt. Sanders announced, getting right to it. "On the night of the incident, where were you headed?"

Candace drew a blank. For the first time since coming to and being aware of her surroundings, she realized that she had no actual recollection of what had transpired. "Umm...I'm...I'm not sure."

"Were you forced off the road at any time during the night?"

"Uh...no. I mean, not that I can remember." That was really saying much considering she didn't remember much to begin with.

"Okay..." Sgt. Sanders was growing impatient given the fact that they seemed to be getting nowhere. "Was anybody in the car with you when you were driving?"

"No."

"Could you tell us anything that you do remember from that night?" Deputy Hanson interjected. "Anything will help us at this point."

Candace laid her head back against the standard sized, medium firmness of the pillows on her hospital bed. She closed her eyes briefly and tried her best to replay the night before in her mind. "I remember..." her voice trailed off as the two law officials hung on her every word hoping to get something useful out of her. "I remember... I was sitting at home listening to music, waiting on my little brother to come back and...Wait!" she called out, interrupting her own thoughts. She sat up straight and felt panic race through her body. "Where is Lawrence?" Keisha's phone call was coming back to her and a sense of urgency took over her emotions.

The detectives shared a perplexed glance as they watched her fumble about.

"No, I'm not doing this. Let me out of here," Candace insisted as she started taking off the heart rate monitor and other the other devices that were hooked to her body. "Where is L at? Tell me where he is!"

"Relax girl, relax," Allison spoke up. "Lawrence is fine. He is standing outside the door in the lobby with some little girl."

Candace assumed that the little girl Allison was referring to was Keisha, Lawrence's hoochie of the week. She took a deep breath and focused her attention on Allison as she spoke. "I need to see him. I need to see him right now! Where he at?" Not getting a quick enough response and dead set on laying eyes on her brother, Candace continued to fumble with the chords dangling from her body in an attempt to free herself and get within Lawrence's presence.

Needing Candace to stay put and not wanting to distress her any more than she already was, Allison scurried over to the door and peered out. “Lawrence!!! Come here, hunny,” Ally summoned

Lawrence soon entered with his arm in a sling. Lawrence’s 5’10 height made him tower over the short 5’6 Ally. Raised in Miami, the light skinned short lady was spicy was well worth the wait for any man looking to snatch her up. Unfortunately for the single guys she often encountered—hell, the married scumbags too— she’d gotten snatched up on a tour to Iraq back in 2007. While she was home on her R & R with her love, Terrell, they got married and she got knocked up. The Army was super pissed at her but they couldn’t do anything because the couple had conceived within the confines of marriage. They put Terrell on vehicle commander duty and Allison went back to her station where she had the baby just as Terrell returned home after enduring multiple near death experiences.

A machine began to beep uncontrollably as Candace collapsed against her bed pillows. She was overwhelmed with emotion while looking at the boy that could have very well been her own son. She was relieved to see that he was only in a sling and not laid out somewhere in a body bag. The flurry of what-ifs began to plague her and she had to remind herself to be grateful for the fact that her brother was alive and well after all.

“Hey, y’all have to get out of here,” a nurse said as she hurriedly entered the room and took notice of the machine that was going off. “Y’all are lowering Ms. Williams’ blood pressure. We can’t have this right now. Besides, it’s too many of you in here at one time.”

"But Ma'am, we still a have few questions to ask Ms. Williams," Sgt. Sanders insisted, fixated on getting what he'd come for.

"Well unfortunately y'all will not be asking Ms. Williams those questions today." The nurse stuck to her guns, not caring that the two men standing before her bore badges and guns. She had a job to do and she wasn't about to let them cause her a position on this shift.

Sgt. Sanders gritted his teeth. "You're interfering with a criminal investigation here. Now if you'll just give us another five minutes—"

"Criminal investigation?" Allison asked, unsure of what he meant by that.

The young nurse decided to hit the panic button to ensure that everything went smoothly since she had dealt with a bad situation concerning Sgt. Sanders in the past after a drive-by shooting on the south side near her house. She swore to never forgive him for the cruel and inhumane embarrassment that he caused her neighborhood. He had tried to apologize on several occasions when he needed her for other cases at the hospital, but she gave him zero words. As a result of the continued aggravation she received from him, her supervisor ended up having to speak with his captain throwing around the threat of harassment charges if he didn't fall back.

"In about 45 seconds, this room will be swarming with security. And if that doesn't work for y'all, do know that I will making a formal, official complaint with your captain," the nurse advised with her hands on her hips. "So I would advise each of you to leave this area right now." She was clad in her cute light pink sweater, pink Air Max Sequent, and her long curly hair landed near the center portion of her back. She had some class to her uniform, because the blue scrubs hugged her body tightly, which forced her bottoms to fit perfectly. She was hell on wheels and looked the part.

"Come on, Hanson, this one right here is starting stuff again," Sgt. Sanders said, giving her a look of disgust though in fact he knew she wasn't playing.

"Ms. Williams, here's my card," Detective Hanson spoke boldly before exiting behind his co-worker. "We need to speak with you ASAP to clear up all of these questions." He nodded his head at the nurse and walked out as Allison and Lawrence bid their goodbyes and promised they'd be back soon.

***

48 hours later

"Are you okay? I got you a couple of days off to clear you head. You know we have to go down to Pima County Sheriff's Office to make that statement though, right?" Ally spoke in a direct voice.

Candace closed her eyes. "Yeah, I know. Right now it's all just a blur in my head. Like I said before, I was at home. I had about one or two glasses of wine. The lil girl called and said that Lawrence got shot and I ran out of the door. Then the next thing I know I'm laid up in the hospital with chords dangling from me, machines hooked up to me, and detectives firing questions at me."

Allison patted her friend's hand. "Make sure you get home and try to get some rest because Capt. Phillips set up a statement with the ADA on tomorrow to clear up this mess. We have your back. The whole office has your back. Even your bff." Allison couldn't hold in her laughter. She was tickled by her own joke and the way that Candace's eyes popped open to glare at her the moment the statement was out.

"Really, Ally?" Although she wasn't the least bit amused by her bestie's joke, her question was more so in regards to the task she'd just been issued. "I just got out of the damn hospital and everyone's already drilling me. I don't remember much from what happened that night to begin with but y'all want me to pull all of that crap together and give some bull shit statement just 'cause? Where's the compassion?"

Ally's laughter subsided and she quickly gave Candace a surprised, bold look before responding. "No bitch, I don't think you understand how bad this actually is. I'm not talking as Sgt. Smith; I'm talking as your girl. I'm keeping it one hundred with you. I'm going to need you to pull it together. I can back you but you gonna have to work to save your own ass here. Oh, and for the record... don't ever come at me sideways about nothing. Period. You know I'm right there to ride for you."

"I hear you," Candace sighed, realizing the truth in Allison's words. "I just need a minute though."

"You know I love your punk ass," Allison said, turning the corner to pull up in front of Candace's yard. "You are my motherfucking sister and I gotta make sure you're straight." She slowed the car down and parked with her eyes glued to the front of Candace's house. "Who the hell you have in front of your house? Why the fuck is all of that yellow tape up?"

"I'm not sure," Candace replied, wondering what else could be going wrong in her life.

"Stay here," Allison instructed Candace as she slipped from the driver's seat and headed towards the driveway.

Sgt. Sanders stepped out of his government issued vehicle to meet her as she ascended the driveway.

"Officer, do we have a problem?" Ally asked peeved that the men would be blatantly stalking Candace the way they were.

"Yes, I would like to see Ms. Williams," Sgt. Sanders responded.

"Why exactly would you like to see her? My captain spoke with your lieutenant on yesterday and it was agreed that she would come in tomorrow to make a statement."

"Well ma'am, that word didn't get passed down to me so her bad." He let out a little chuckle and shrugged his shoulders.

Allison was less than pleased by the way he was disrespecting her. "Really? So you are laughing in my face? You are a fucking idiot. I can't wait to see the stupid look plastered on your fat ass face tomorrow."

"Frankly Miss, this is a matter that does not concern you."

"What do you mean that this matter doesn't concern me? That is my solider." Allison was now heated.

"Good for you," Sgt. Sanders stated sarcastically. He focused his attention on Candace. "Ms. Williams, if you will," he called out, approaching Allison's car. "We're not intending to make a scene here."

"I demand that you get the hell out of her and leave her alone!" Allison blared, all self-control nearly thrown out of the window.

"If you'd just please step out of the car, Ms. Williams," Sgt. Sanders said, standing beside the car and raising his voice over Ally's to get his point across.

"What does she need to see you for? Is she under arrest? Do you have a freaking warrant?"

"This matter does not concern you, ma'am," the officer expressed to Allison once again. "Ms. Williams, I need for you to step out of the vehicle, now!" He banged on the roof of the car, his agitation showing along with the vein that was popping out of the side of his neck.

"You are rude as fuck dude," Ally screamed, astonished by the man's behavior.

Candace opened the door and walked over up to Officer Sanders. Before she could speak, he whipped out his black shiny handcuffs and secured one of the bracelets around her small wrist.

"Ms. Candace Williams, you are under arrest for reckless driving," he informed her.

"What the hell?" Allison let at, surprised that this was happening when she'd been so certain that they'd bought Candace enough time to piece together a feasible story in order to prevent this very occurrence.

"You have the right to remain silent," Sgt. Sanders continued, ignoring Allison's outburst. "Anything you say can and will be used against you in a court of law. You have the right to an attorney. If you cannot afford an attorney, one will be provided for you. Do you understand the rights I have just read to you?"

Candace looked to Allison pleadingly but her friend was at a loss for words and ideas. She scanned the neighborhood surveying the many faces staring at her from their own yards and windows. The entire scene was embarrassing. Her head was pounding and her mind was racing. All she wanted was to get the hell out of sight and have a moment to think this whole thing through.

"Yes," she finally answered, with no other response readily coming to mind.

***

"Hello, Specialist Williams. We brought you in today because you were involved in a major car accident that nearly took your life. Do you understand that?" the official in front of her asked.

"Yes, ma'am."

"Also, the fact that you were driving this vehicle has put major strain upon us by bringing unnecessary scrutiny to the US military. Do you understand that?"

Candace swallowed hard. "Yes ma'am."

"We have here your toxicology results from that night. You'll get a copy of this report which hasn't been altered or tampered. Do you understand that?

Her body temperature rose. "Yes ma'am." Candace was on autopilot. What else could she do aside from acquiesce to the things being told to her?"

The captain handed the report over to Allison, who was situated in a chair to the left of Candace. She tore open the envelope and her eyes poured over the verbiage with large, deep eyes of disappointment before reading the results aloud.

"Specialist Williams, your results are as follows," she began, trying her best to choke back her emotions. "Blood Alcohol Content .21 milligrams and large amount of Vavrin."

"What is Vavrin?" Captain Phillips asked.

"Caffeine pills to keep me alert during the daytime because I can't sleep at night," Candace explained.

"How long have you had that problem?"

"I've had it for quite some time now."

"We're facing some serious issues here. You're going to have to be more specific with me, Specialist," the captain urged.

Candace laced her fingers together and rested her hands on top of the steel table they were sitting at. She wasn't fond of the interrogation she was enduring or the implications that were lingering within the silence of the words they weren't saying to her directly. "I think I have been like this for about five or six months now.

"How often do you get sleep?"

"I only get about three to four hours of sleep a night."

"Okay. What else? Is there anything else you've noticed about your condition?"

She looked over at the Allison's woeful eyes and felt sorry for putting every through such an upheaval. "Well, I find myself waking up from cold sweats and thinking about some of the things I've been through."

"And how often do you have these episodes?" the captain probed.

"Maybe about two to three times a month. But, when I start thinking about some of my battle buddies that didn't make it, it kinda messes with me a lot more."

"I see. Have you ever asked for help or gotten treatment for these issues?

Candace shook her head. "No, I haven't. I tried to make myself feel normal...like everyone else." She lowered her head in shame.

Captain Phillips looked up from the notes he'd been making. "I'm sorry you have to go through all of this. We never knew. We'll will try to fight for you as much as possible. I'm going to make a couple of phone calls and see if I can use some of my connects. But, I have to ask you these questions before we leave. Standard procedures. When I ask you these questions, I want you to give a firm answer, not just a yes or no." He took a deep breath. "Okay....So here we go. Are you suicidal?"

Candace's brow knitted as she gave a serious facial expression. "No. I am not suicidal."

"Are you homicidal?"

"No, I am not homicidal."

The captain studied her for a moment as if trying to decide whether or not she believed her. "Okay, Sgt. Smith, if you don't have anything..."

"I don't," Allison replied, staring down at the toxicology report.

"Very well. Sgt. Williams, we'll stay in contact through your supervisor. Get some rest." Captain Phillips stood to depart.

***

Candace fingered the label on the bottle of Raspberry Smirnoff sitting on the table in front of her. It was half empty. The cork was resting on the floor in the same place that it had landed in when she first opened the bottle. No glass was in sight; she'd been drinking straight out of the bottle. The fate of her career was dangling in the balance and she didn't know what else she could do aside from pray, drink, and wait. Her spirit wouldn't allow her to offer up her worries to the Lord, but she felt confident that he knew the troubles of heart. The best she could do now was drown her sorrows in the alcohol and sit still until further notice. The sitting still part was killing her; the not knowing what to expect was fueling every left of the bottle to take another sip. Candace was a mess.

Buzz, buzz. The vibrating of her phone on the table jarred her. She wasn't expecting any calls and assumed that the only person who'd been contacting her was Allison. Her stomach knotted up with anxiety and for a moment she just stared at the phone. Quickly, realizing that the call would soon transfer to voicemail, she snatched it up and stared at the CALLER ID. The number itself was unfamiliar, but the area code she was completely acquainted with.

Reluctantly, she answered the phone and spoke guardedly. "Hello?" Even that one word came sounding slurred.

"Don't you sound like a ton of bricks have landed on you?"

"What do you want?" Candace asked, still toying with the Smirnoff label.

"What? Your auntie can't call and check on your well-being?"

"How loving of you."

"Sarcasm?"

"You know it," Candace replied, taking a swig from the bottle.

"Listen, sweetie, I know you've got a little trouble where you are."

Candace's eyebrow rose. "And what do you know about my troubles?"

"I hear things."

"Do you?"

"Indeed I do. Desperation causes you to make some unstable decisions, doesn't it? I'd think that you'd be scared straight from drinking. You certainly never seemed to take a liking to spirits before as I can recall."

"Things change," Candace shot back, holding her Smirnoff tightly in her hand.

"Truer words have never been spoken."

"Is there a point to this phone call?"

"You think you're going to skate out of this unscathed? The military doesn't take kindly to their own going out into the civilian word and making a mockery of what it is to be a serviceperson. Where's your integrity? Where's your sense of morale? Where's your common sense?"

"The military takes care of their own," Candace said. "If you know so much, then you'd know I'm a damn good solider. There's no way they could ever over look that just because of one mistake."

"One mistake that could have taken a life...just like your parents'."

Robyn's words cut like a knife in Candace's heart. Her bottom lip began to tremble and she felt like a teenage girl all over again, falling apart over the sudden and tragic loss of both of her parents. She hated hearing Robyn make reference to her folks or their accident. She always sounded so dry, so unfeeling whenever she discussed it. Deep down, Candace was sure that Robyn felt as if her parents had deserved what they'd gotten. But that wasn't true. No one deserved to die so horribly. Candace wouldn't have wished the whole horrid experience upon anyone, even her worst enemy.

"I'm a good solider," she repeated, snot now dripping from her nose and tears burning her eyes. "I'm a good person. They know that. I'm going to be just fine."

"You're going to be unemployed," Robyn stated pointedly. "You might want to start preparing yourself for that reality. What are you going to do with yourself? Had you stuck with me in the first place you wouldn't even be in this position."

Candace lowered her head on the cool, oak table. "No, I'd be in all kinds of positions. Ungodly positions." She closed her eyes, trying to avoid the memories that were jumping at her; the visuals of her young, limber, curvy body bent, twisted, and turned in many ways in the darkness of a room whose scent of stale cigarettes, cheap whiskey, and cologne was so vivid that she could almost smell it now. "I'm good," she said. "I'm good."

Robyn's sarcastic laughter made Candace want to reach through the phone and rip out her tongue.

"You're drunk," Robyn said. "Too drunk to listen to me. Too drunk to realize that you're losing, dear. It's the white man's military and he certainly doesn't want any drunk, black, woman making his military look bad. You have some choices to make, Candace, dear. You better sober up and get smart before it's too late. You know my number if and when you're ready."

The line went dead before Candace could muster up a response. She left the phone fall from her hand as she continued to rest her head on the dining room table. She was too buzzed to focus on the warning her aunt had issued. Even if she'd been sober she would have dismissed it as a bunch of bullshit anyway. It was just like Aunt Robyn to try to coerce her into defiling her body and her dignity for the sake of a dollar. Instead, Candace stared straight ahead at the dining room wall seeing images of her younger self scrubbing away at her body under a steaming hot shower, desperate to wipe away all traces of the John that her aunt had forced upon her. A tear trickled down the side of her face and began to make a muddle on the table. No greater hell had ever been known to her.

***

Sgt. Allison Smith had known that there was something up with Candace, but she hadn't quite been able to put her finger on it until the sit-down with the Captain. Knowing how hard it was for Candace to be so candid and feeling some kind of what regarding what the woman was going through, Allison felt it was her responsibility to fight for her subordinate and friend. She did all that she could to have the charges wiped clean so as not to taint Candace's reputation or the company's. Candace was a highly decorated soldier and she had never gotten into any type of trouble in the past. Her stellar record and their relationship worked in Candace's favor as Allison and the captain called in all the favors they could to help make this entire situation go away. Officials at the top, those up for re-elections and appointments, were looking to make an example out of servicemen who dared step out of line. But if they could help it, Candace wouldn't be that scapegoat today.

After long consideration by their unit leadership, all of their efforts materialized into a satisfactory decision. They were successful in getting the charges against Candace dropped and clearing up her record before public embarrassment by way of media exploitation occurred. Candace was grateful that Allison was in her corner. Their liaison was probably one of the best things that had happened to her. At work, the duo kept up a professional relationship, being sure not to cross boundaries within the eye sight of their peers, but off base they were more like sisters. This level of comfort that they'd created between them made it easy for one to express herself freely with the other. No subject was taboo and no sugarcoating ever went on should ever one of them need to be checked. This being true, Allison had no problem being candid with Candace regarding the meeting she'd just left after she changed her clothes in the master bathroom.

Allison pulled and tugged until she was free of her sharp Class A uniform. It looked pretty snug in some places because she had just had her second baby about eight months ago. Unfortunately, not all of the baby weight had gone away as quickly as she would have liked. But, Allison still turned heads with her nice breasts and mean curves that she'd acquired courtesy of the latest pregnancy.

"Candace, get up girl. We need to talk," Allison called out as she exited the bathroom and tossed her duffle bag to the floor.

Candace stirred but said nothing. She felt like shit. She'd been practically grilled for as long as she could remember, hadn't gotten any sleep at all since these whole mess began, and was decidedly sick and tired of discussing the situation to death. At this point, she was ready to accept whatever her superiors handed down to her so long as she could just get on the road to getting past it all.

"So in talking to Colonel Shepherd and First Sgt. Woo, we made a deal. You know you're my bitch right?" Allison asked, playfully hitting Candace's comforter covered leg as she took a seat on the side of her friend's bed. "Shit yo' ass up and listen to what I have to say. You listening?"

Candace wasn't sure she really wanted to hear what kind of compromise Allison had gotten her into, but whether she wanted to or not she knew that Allison wasn't going to leave her alone until they hashed out all of the details.

Allison shoved her lightly. "Aye, I'm talking to you!"

"Ally, I'm listening damn. What they say?"

Allison sucked her teeth and stared at her friend hard. "You better be listening because I just put my sixteen year career and my family's lives in your hands, so you need to get this shit right."

This sounded serious. Candace sat up, stretched her neck, and crossed her arms to giving Allison her full attention. She listened hard and intently, not wanting to miss a single detail. She had zero intentions of fucking up her best friend's family life or career, especially since she was the godmother of Ally's beautiful baby girl Hailey. Hailey was a miracle baby with big beautiful blue eyes and a gorgeous mixed complexion. Ally had gone seven whole months before finding out that she was pregnant after her doctors had long since convinced her that she couldn't have any more kids. Allison and her family meant the world to Candace. Aside from L, they were all she really had and she'd fly to the edges of the earth to make sure those she considered family were well taken care of.

"So here's the deal bitch, you have to do a thirty day in-patient PTSD treatment program, a one week substance abuse program, and go two weeks with half pay. Cool?"

Fuck, she thought at the mention of her income being cut for half a month. "Yeah, that's cool," she replied, knowing full well that she was grateful that she wasn't facing jail time and losing her job altogether."

Ally reaffirmed, "Bitch, I'm not playing with you. You will have your ass in those programs and you will not, I repeat, you will NOT fuck up." Allison reached over and grabbed the television remote, immediately flipping CNN.

Candace smiled and leaned over to hug her sister from another mother. "Thank you," she said. "I promise to be on my best behavior and you won't have one issue outta me."

Allison squeezed her girl back. She was also grateful to know that Candace's career had been spared. She wanted to go into depth about the PTSD she was suffering from yet had never mentioned to her before, but thought better of it. She also didn't mention that the PTSD program was her idea that she'd placed on the table as a bargaining tool when trying to clear Candace's name. She loved her and didn't want to see Candace spiral downward when there was help available to her. She'd worked too hard for it to all end in such a negative way. If Allison could help it, she'd make sure that Candace had all the support and resources she need to stay ahead in life and continue to be successful.

"You know I love you, right bitch?" Allison asked, pulling back from their embrace.

"Yeah, yeah. I love you too." Candace smiled but the grin quickly vanished as her own image popped up on the television screen. "What the hell?" She snatched the remote from Allison and turned up the volume.

"Lobbyists are seeking answers this week regarding the military's tolerance for illegal activity...crimes being committed by their soldiers outside of the military bases yet being covered up by military officials," the news anchor reported. "Sources reveal that Specialist Candace Williams stationed at the Davis-Monthan Air Force Base in Arizona was recently arrested for a DUI. Although she was apprehended by local law enforcement, she was handed over to her officials at Davis who we're told have tirelessly pulled strings to clear the soldiers' record. Upon investigating these allegations our discovery team learned that Williams has prior history of DUI, but not how you would think. In 2006 Williams' parents Patricia and Lawrence Williams II were victims of a hideous hit and run DUI accident. Anonymous sources reported seeing a swaying vehicle zooming down the road on the night of the incident. Both husband and wife were rammed off of the side of an overpass on Panola Road where the impact sent their vehicle surging onto the sidewalk and through the guard rails causing the car to dangle over I-20 before ultimately falling onto the thankfully empty westbound side of the highway due to the unbalanced position of the vehicle as it lingered over the edge. "The Williams' were dead upon impact, their modest sedan totaled, and the drunken driver that sent them over the edge was never found or identified. Questions are being raised as to what the message the military is sending by allowing its soldiers to commit potentially dangerous acts and walk away free with merely a pat on the back. What kind of

actions are being requested? We have no clear answer for that as of yet but certainly it's not a topic that will be buried any longer. Tax payers won't like the fact that their tax dollars are being used to pay these individuals to wreak havoc on society and then get a mere sentence to rehab as a means of just punishment. Officials at Davis-Monthan are being undulated with demands from top officials to learn just how many other scandals have been swept under the rug and how many soldiers are walking around free when they should be serving time for crimes either unreported or simply not acted upon. This has sparked a discussion between the country's legislature and the justice department. From here we can expect a full investigation pertaining to military protocol with regards to unlawful activity. Visit us on Facebook to let us know your thoughts on military men being considered invincible in the eyes of the law. We'd love to hear the citizens' input on this matter."

Allison snatched the remote from Candace and shut off the television. She looked over at her friend, immediately sensing her horror and embarrassment. "Don't you listen to them. Don't you dare let this discourage you. We've worked this out and you're going to be fine. Do you hear me?"

Candace covered her mouth. "That was a national news broadcast," she said, shakily. "With my face plastered on the screen. Everyone's going to know."

"You can't worry about that, Candace. Come on, don't you fall apart on me."

Candace looked over at her friend. "There's no way I'm going to get out of this unscathed," she stated, her aunt's words coming back to her. "If they start investigating the department and cracking down on the base's dirty little secrets, what's going to happen to me?"

Allison dropped the remote on the bed and grabbed Candace by her shoulders. "Listen to me, this too shall pass. Is it damning publicity? Yes. But what's done is done. We've already worked this out and you're gonna fly straight and keep your fuckin' nose clean. So long as you do your part, don't talk to anyone about what's happened, and have some faith this shit will blow over. Do you hear me? Do you hear me?"

Candace nodded as large tears dropped from her eyes. She wanted to believe Allison, but she couldn't ignore the fear that was now placed in her heart.

***

Candace packed up Lawrence's things for a week and gave it to Ally before they headed to Lawrence's school to give him the news. He was surprised to see them waiting for him outside of the main building once school was over. He'd planned to get up with his boys and maybe holler at Keisha, but seeing his sister and her bestie posted up made it very clear that his plans were shot to hell.

"What's this?" he asked as he approached them walking with his own unique swagger despite the brace that still cradled his arm. "A nigga gotta be chaperoned home after school now?"

"Maybe that's what you need to keep your ass out of trouble," Candace shot back.

"Say the word and we can make it happen," Allison co-signed.

"Man, y'all tripping," Lawrence said, shaking his head at the two women.

"Uh-huh and you're on one," Candace told him. She pointed to the back seat of Allison's car. "Get in."

"Do I got a choice?"

"Did I make it a question or did I give you a command? Get your ass in the car."

Lawrence huffed but settled himself into the back seat of Allison's car as the other two hopped in the front. Soon they were pulling away from the school and heading down the street away from the chaos and commotion of after-school shenanigans.

"I need to talk to you," Candace said, looking down at her hands and praying for the strength she was going to need in order to endure upcoming separation.

"So talk," her brother replied.

Candace shifted slightly in her seat so that she could look at him. His handsome face reminded her so much of her father, a man who was probably looking down at them both and shaking his head at the moment. "You gotta go for a while."

Lawrence sucked his teeth and shot her an angry look. "The fuck? So you ambushing me? Picking me up to sweep me away and drop my ass off somewhere like some damn orphan. Man, you coulda just left me alone to do me. What? You giving me back to Aunt Robyn?"

Candace flinched at the verbal daggered he'd just pierced her heart with. There was no way in hell that she'd ever hand custody of L back over to their trifling ass aunt. "Why don't you shut up sometimes and listen? I'm not dropping you off just somewhere. You're gonna stay with Ally for a lil' while. At least I know she and her husband will keep your ass in check."

Lawrence waved her off. "I don't need nobody checking nothing 'round this way. I'm good."

She looked at the sling around his left arm. "You good?" she asked him. "Being good got your ass shot right? Don't think that I've overlooked that very important issue just because of this other mess I'm dealing with."

"I lived. It's no biggie."

"No biggie?" she squealed. "No biggie? You coulda been killed, L! I was rushing outta the house to come see about your ass when..." Her words trailed off as she caught herself before she truly laid into him.

But Lawrence knew where she was headed with her train of thought. "So what? You blaming me for your accident? It's my fault that you was out there drunk?"

"I wasn't drunk and don't you come at me like that," Candace snapped. She took a deep breath. "I'm not blaming you for what happened. I take full responsibility for my actions. I wish you'd do the damn same. But that's neither here nor there right now. I gotta go into this program for work for a while, that's why I'm leaving you with Ally."

"I ain't trying to be nobody's burden, man," Lawrence stated, turning away and staring out of the window so that his sister wouldn't see the hurt in his eyes. Even though she tried to gloss over it, he knew that it was his fault that she'd been out that night racing to get to his side. It ate him up inside to know that he could have been killed that night as well as his sister. It also hurt to know that he was being passed off to yet another adult in the wake of a difficult situation. Maybe Candace couldn't help the fact that she had to go away, but it didn't lessen the blow for him any more to know that he once again had to be a squatter in someone else's home who probably didn't really want him there to begin with.

"You're not a burden, L," Allison said gently, completely aware of his past living situations. "Trust me, on that. You're like family."

"Family will fuck you over quick," he retorted.

Candace felt the brunt of his statement. "This isn't the same," she told him. "This won't be like the situation with Aunt Robyn. And it's temporary. You'll be back home before you know it." She studied his silhouette for a moment, noticing the tightness of his jaw line. "And once this is all over you better promise me that all of your bullshit will be behind us. I want to keep this family together...you and I, I mean. But you gotta do your part too, L. I know I've got some issues right now that have nothing to do with you and maybe sometimes I come down a little too hard on you because of it...but I'm working on that. I just need you to do your part and tighten the hell up if you want this shit to work. Deal?"

Lawrence swallowed back the lump in his throat. He wasn't in the mood for the emotional moment that was occurring in the unescapable confines of the moving car. Candace talked a good game and at the end of the day, she really was all that he had. Could he trust her? Should he trust her? Did he have a choice? "Aight," he mumbled. "I'ma do better, man. But for real for real, Candace...respect goes a long way, man. I'ma need you to show me some respect if you want that shit back and keep ya' hands off me."

She opened her mouth to snap and thought better of it. He was right. She didn't really need to get physical with him in order to get her point across. Her aggression was just another sign of the other shit she was dealing with mentally and he didn't deserve to be used as a punching bag. "Alright," she said, turning back around to face the front of the car. "Things will get better. You'll see. We got this." As she said the words she realized that she desperately wanted to believe them and needed the proclamation to prove true for both of their sake.

CHAPTER 3
TOUGH BREAKS

Although she had no clue what to expect, Candace surprisingly knocked the treatment program out like it was a breeze. She complied with everything asked of her, participated in activities, and ended up receiving recommendations from the director and head nurse practitioner. Things started looking up for her as she realized that her time was dwindling down and soon she'd be back to her regular life. The migraines she developed were a major drawback in the whole experience, but she figured it was a small sacrifice since she had been through so much over the last couple of months.

Before she knew it, she was back in the full swing of things. Her work performance was A+ again and her brother-sister relationship was getting back on track. All was well, but in life just when it seems like everything is good, something bad pops up. The occurrence of this phenomenon in her life nearly crushed Candace.

"Let's get that mile in Williams," Sgt. Daily encouraged her as she reached the track at the far end of base.

It was time for her annual fitness exam. If it wasn't a requirement and a necessity for her to pass if she wanted to move up in rank, Candace would have certainly canceled the appointment. Her temples were throbbing horribly. All day she'd been functioning while enduring the trying migraine. Though she'd grown use to the on again, off again pain, today it just seemed to be unusually relentless. But, she had responsibilities and following everything she'd gone through earlier in the year, there was no room for her to show weakness or draw attention to herself.

Mind over matter, she mentally pressed herself. *You got this*. She'd done this physical fitness test many times. Usually it was a piece of cake. *Just get on with it and it'll be over before you know it*, she thought. So she'd listened to herself. She'd managed to get through the initial areas of the exam and now the mile run was the last stretch. She was almost home free.

Candace took a deep breath, creased her brow as a result of the pain, and stared down at the ground as the testing Sargent readied his clock.

"Go!" he prompted.

Immediately, she began to sprint at her own pace, knowing that darting initially would only tire her before she'd gotten through the first lap around the track. It was all about endurance and pace. As her legs continued to rhythmically carry her forward and the wind whipped around her, Candace began to feel lighter and lighter. *Shit, I got this*, she thought. *I'm practically floating on air*. She was moving at a steady speedy but suddenly the images in front of her began to get blurry. She squeezed her eyes shut tightly and opened them again, hoping that her vision would clear. Her attempt failed. She shook her head, trying to shake off whatever it was that was causing her sight issues. It's almost over, it's almost over.

By the time she bent the curve to begin her last lap the blur faded to darkness and the light feeling she'd experienced intensified. Practically in slow motion, Candace's body toggled to the ground collapsing in a heap in mid-lap. She tried to run on a mild migraine and passed out on the last lap. Others who were out on field for testing and regular physical training took notice of her and hurried over to assist.

Sgt. Dailey reached her first. "Call 911!" he shouted out to anyone who was listening as he dropped to his knees and began to take her vitals.

Candace body was limp but a faint pulse existed. Sgt. Dailey maneuvered her head to rest in her lap as he tried to get her to regain consciousness. Another soldier handed him a bottle of water which he squirted on her thinking that maybe she'd fallen out from heat exhaustion and needed to cool down. Nothing seemed to work.

Soon, sirens grew near and a paramedic team was on the scene. Candace was holstered onto a gurney, placed into the ambulance, and rushed to the nearest hospital. During the ride, she came too and nearly panicked herself right into a heart attack upon seeing the emergency tech staring back at her.

"What's happening?" she asked, looking around and realizing that she was in the back of an ambulance. "What happened? Where are you taking me?"

"Ma'am, you passed out while taking a PT test," the nice, young Hispanic paramedic explained to her. "We're transporting you to the ER so that you can be seen about. Please relax for me."

How could she relax? One minute she was finishing her PT Test and the next minute she was being carted off to the hospital. The last time she'd been hospitalized she'd undergone surgery and suffered the humiliation of having her personal life, habits, and issues placed on front street. Candace was in no mood to relive that kind of drama.

"I'm fine," she insisted.

The tech was paying her no mind as he charted her vitals.

"I said I'm fine!" she hollered, trying to sit upright. The strain of her migraine overpowered her temper and forced her to lean back, close her eyes, and touch her temples with the tips of her fingers.

"I really need you to relax," the tech advised again. "We don't want your blood pressure being altered."

So despite her trepidation, she was whisked off to the hospital. Her direct superior was notified upon her arrival to the emergency room. An attending doctor wasted no time in popping into her exam room and rattling off the list of tests that they were going to perform as a result of her confession about the migraines. Hours and multiple tests later, the medical staff came up with nothing to explain the constant migraines or her recent loss of consciousness. Candace was disheartened. If they couldn't figure out what was wrong with her, how on earth would they be able to figure out how to fix it? She worried that her peers and superiors would start to view her as weak and inferior because of the plethora of issues she seemed to having surrounding her lately. It didn't look good and now she had this unknown condition documented on her records. What else could possibly go wrong?

***

The answer came sooner than she'd ever imagined. After weeks of constant visits to the doctor, an alleged remedy drug was finally discovered. They tried to convince her that this medication was the best bet she had in combating any further episodes. The hope was that it would eventually kill the problem altogether or at least give her the ability to maintain. So she began to take the little wonder drug and no sooner than it got in her blood stream good, Candace began to feel the constant changes it produced. Each month her body suffered more and more and her mentally stability was becoming questionable. She no longer felt she had control over her life given the old wounds she was trying to overcome, the DUI scandal she was still trying to live down, the exile from her extended family, and now this medical issue that she just couldn't seem to shake.

She'd been summoned to Allison's office. The work day was half over and she was dying to get out of her uniform so that she could relax and maybe have a drink. It wasn't a great idea, but the thought was tempting. She tapped lightly on the half opened door before entering the office. "You wanted to see me?" she asked. Her interest was piqued when she saw Captain Phillips perched upon Allison's desk and Allison's face screwed up in a scowl as she stood beside him. "What's going on?"

"Close the door," Captain Phillips requested.

She did as instructed and then stood awkwardly before her superiors. "What's going on?" she repeated her question.

"We commend you for going through the PTSD program and staying strong through all of the whole ordeal surrounding your arrest. Your counselors also commended you grandly for your impressive improvement and compliance." Captain Phillips gripped the edge of the desk tightly behind him as he spoke. "But the order came down for higher up that we simply cannot tolerate such dangerous criminal activity without some solid reprimand."

"What?" Candace's eyes widened. "I was reprimanded. I did everything that was asked of me. I shipped my brother off so that I could attend that program, sir. I've never been in any other legal trouble. What more can I do to prove that I'm a decent person and a solid soldier?"

"Your dedication to the military isn't in question."

"No? But my human decency is huh?"

"Candace," Allison spoke up, trying to deter Candace from going in on her boss.

"No Ally," Candace snapped, forgetting all about protocol and respect. She eyed Captain Phillips. "So what are you saying? What more is going to be done to me?"

"Unfortunately, we're going to have to let you go."

His words resounded throughout the room and Candace felt her legs grow weak. "Let me go?" she repeated, shaking her head. "You...y-y-you can't do that."

"Believe me, if we could avoid this we would have. We tried. Sgt. Smith here especially pulled out all the stops trying to get the decision over turned."

Candace still couldn't believe it. "But the Colonel...he signed off on it before...he agreed—"

"Things have changed," the captain cut her off. "And it's beyond any of our control on this level. They're tightening up and trying to assure that we're running a straight and narrow department here.

Candace's mind immediately reverted back to the CNN newscast that painted her out to be the scapegoat for the military's untouchable persona. It was clear to her what was going on and she didn't like it one bit. "I'm being made an example out of after all, huh? Despite bending over backwards to prove that I belong here, doing everything that was asked of me, I'm still being tossed out on my ass."

"Specialist, you'll watch your verbiage in this office," Captain Phillips snapped.

Candace was unfazed. "A little media hype and the Army turns on me and for what? For the higher ups to save their asses."

"That's enough."

"God forbid any of you risk your positions to save mine."

"That's not fair to say," Allison spoke up. "Like Captain said, we stuck our necks out for you."

"Yeah? And how far did it go?"

"How dare you question me like that? You know I'd never take our welfare lightly."

"This isn't personal," Captain Phillips intervened. "You can't see it that way."

"You're right. It's political," Candace retorted. "Political bullshit...*Sir*."

The captain's displeasure was evident in his facial expression. He looked over to Allison and nodded. In turn, Allison picked up an envelope from her desk and handed it to Candace.

Candace snatched it and looked down at the seal. "What's this?"

"You're being discharged," Allison explained. "To keep a low profile and to avoid making matters any more difficult for you than they already are, you're being honorable discharged.

Actually, there's a whole list of individuals that have been put up for early release. You were placed at the top of the list."

"Is that supposed to make me feel better?" Candace asked. "What am I supposed to do now?"

Allison was hurting on the inside but she couldn't let her emotions get the best of her in front of her boss. She had to keep it as professional as possible at least until later. "I've included a stellar letter of recommendation and a list of sources from Military OneSource regarding ex-military employment assistance."

"We wish you the best," Captain Phillips stated. "And we truly hate to see you go."

Candace stared at him blankly, fighting the urge to maw him in the face.

"Discharge instructions are inside the envelope," Allison said softly. "I'm so sorry."

Candace nodded, realizing that in a matter of seconds her life had changed. "So am I," she replied, snatching off her patches and throwing them on the office chair to her right before exiting the office.

***

Candace felt as if she was on the verge of another major breakdown, so she packed up her and Lawrence's clothes the following Friday afternoon and headed to check Lawrence out of school early. He was more than thrilled to be getting out of what he felt was prison. Excitedly, he hopped into the car and gave Candace a kiss on the jaw. "What up, sis?"

She looked at him and beamed. He was quite possibly the only joy she had in life. Besides his occasional school disciplinary issues, Ally had told her that during her absence

Lawrence had stayed on point and even helped around the house as much as possible. She could see a change in him—his mannerisms, his behavior, his outlook on certain things all seemed to be evolving.

"I figured we needed a little getaway so I booked us a rental for a few days," she told him.

"That's what the fuck I'm talking about," he gushed, punching the air energetically as they headed for the interstate. "I'm tired of these whack, black, fake people in Tucson."

"Hey, watch your damn mouth, boy," Candace scolded him, realizing that some things just never changed.

"My bad, sis. I was just expressing my feelingggggggs!!! Every thang gonna be alright...expressing your feelings. Everything gonna be alright," Lawrence sang playfully.

Candace laughed until she started to cough outrageously. "Boy, you are stupid as hell," she said as she gasped for air and clutched the steering wheel tightly. "You know I missed you a lot when I was gone right?" she asked, taking side glances at him as her hysteria subsided. "You were the only thing that kept me going, knowing that mom and dad weren't here to take care of us and that we are all we have...knowing that I had to pull it together...for us."

Lawrence didn't reply though he shared her sentiment. When she'd returned for him it was the best feeling in the world, knowing that he could rely on her to be there for him and that he could trust her word. It meant everything to know that someone genuinely cared for him and that he wasn't alone.

Candace pursed her lips together and contemplated over her next words. She didn't want to lie to him, but she didn't want to worry him either. They were all they had in this world really and she felt she owed it to her brother to be honest with him no matter what. "So, here's the deal," she said slowly, getting his attention. "Things are going to change."

"Okay."

"I was discharged earlier in the week."

The confession lingered in the air for a moment before Lawrence responded. "As in fired?"

"Right."

"So then, can we really afford to be going on this lil' trip?"

"We're okay," she told him. "I don't want you worrying about our financial stability. Let me handle that. You just focus on staying out of trouble and finishing school."

"Seriously sis, if you need me to make some moves I—"

Candace shot him a heated look. "L, don't make me kick your ass. I'm serious! I've got this. Don't go doing anything stupid. Promise me."

"I just want to help."

"Promise me!" she demanded.

Lawrence exhaled loudly. "Okay. I promise. Whatever you say sis, I got ya' back."

Soon they arrived at the Crowne Plaza where Candace expediently checked them in. As they headed for the elevators, excited about their little get away, her eyes met some familiar hazel brown pupils accompanied by nicely structured light skin face. It was like love at first sight all over again. No words were spoken as the two sized each other up before falling into each other's arms as if propelled by magnets. Not knowing what the hell was going on; Lawrence cleared his throat hoping to remind the two that they were not alone.

Candace snapped back to reality. "Oh...ummm...L-L-Lawrence...uhhh." She was stuttering and all, which had Lawrence wondering who this cat was for real. Candace took a deep breath and tried to break the mesmerizing stare that she shared with the God-like creature standing before her. To help, she took a step back to place some space between them because even the scent of his cologne was driving her crazy. "Uhh... L, this is Sean," she tried again to make the formal introduction. With her senses about her, she was better able to speak. "Sean this is L, my little brother."

Lawrence gave Sean a head nod as he gave the man a once over. *Where the hell she get him from,* he wondered.

Sean returned the gesture before redirecting his attention to Candace. "What's up, love? How've you been?"

Candace blushed, remembering the comfort of his embrace and the power of his lips as she watched them part while he spoke. "I've been well," she lied. "Sorry I wasn't able to give you my contact info before leaving. I sorta had to get out of that place fast."

"Well, we gotta make some time to catch up. I'd be lying if I said I didn't miss you."

"I'd be lying if I said that I wasn't glad to hear that."

Not feeling the sappy lines they were throwing each other, Lawrence dropped the keys on the floor to get their attention in hopes that it would speed up the boring convo and bring it to an end.

Candace shot her brother a look of annoyance while Sean merely ignored the young man.

"Are you here with anyone?" Candace asked him, secretly praying that his answer would be no and that she would get the opportunity to experience the wonders of his touch on a more personal, intimate level later on.

Sean replied quickly, "Yeah. A few buddies of mine just got in but we aren't doing anything until later."

"So then you're free to join us for dinner in the hotel's restaurant at 5:30," Candace said slyly.

He smiled at her seductively. "You've got yourself a date, pretty lady." His hand lingered on the right side of her face for a moment as he closed the gap between them. "So I'll meet you there at 5:30."

"We'll be there," Candace replied softly, longing to feel his lips against hers.

Much to her chagrin, he departed with only a kiss to her forehead. She turned and watched him head toward the exit as Lawrence grew impatient and moved on towards the elevators. As they waited for the doors to open, he couldn't contain his curiosity.

"Who was that, yo?" he asked bluntly.

"An old friend," Candace answered as the doors parted for them. "And don't be so rude next time."

"Obviously it's an old friend," Lawrence commented. "That much I can tell. You still floating on that cloud or what?"

Candace's face scrunched up and she punched him in the shoulder. "Hush! I met him right before I left Iraq. He was one of new guys I met in my unit right before I came back home to take care of your big headed self. We're peers or at least we were."

Lawrence looked at Candace's glazed over eyes and shook his head knowingly. “Looks to me like it’s a tad more than just that,” he said in a calm voice. “Well, whateva you do sis, don't make me body him.”

Candace rolled her eyes although she was touched by the endearing way that her younger brother was trying to look out for her. “Boy, chill out.”

As they entered the room, they were met by a gush of cool air as their five star experience awaited them. A unique assortment of chocolates and fruit sat in a nicely decorated basket on the table in the small dining area. The room smelled sweet as the breeze flew in through the sheer curtains covering the cracked patio doors. Lawrence hurriedly claimed one of the grandiose bedrooms as his, dropping his bags at the threshold of the room and shoveling through them to retrieve appropriate clothing. A much needed shower and relaxation was in order before heading downstairs to have what he was sure would be an awkward dinner with his sister and her friend. The thought of watching them make googly eyes at each other as he tried to digest his entrée didn’t exactly appeal to Lawrence but it was a small price he’d have to pay in exchange for the lavish weekend that his sister had planned for them.

Candace said nothing as she entered her room and took in the simplistic beauty of the boudoir. Everything was white from the carpeting, to the linen, and right down to the complimentary robe draped across the bottom of her bed with her day-spa package envelope nestled on top of it. She took a deep breath and felt her body loosen up a little for the first time in a long time. *Here’s the part where you actually relax,* she thought, fingering the plush pillows that decorated her bed. *Just relax.*

***

Candace sauntered carelessly from the elevator. The long sheer panels of her elegant white dress with the halter top flew behind her with the wind of her gait while showing off her figure in a major way. Her walk, her poise, her look in general read model. It was her confidence that sometimes waivered. Just as she looked up and moved to walk inside of the restaurant, she noticed Sean waving his hand in the air from the far corner of the room. She instantly started smiling and her heart began to pound so loudly that she just knew those she passed by could hear it. Her eyes couldn't help but trail over every bit of his muscular frame as she grew closer to him. Moisture began to formulate between her legs at the mere sight of him. She had no clue how she was going to manage to control herself once seated beside him when she was damn near about to have an orgasm just from looking at him across the room.

Sean wore an all-white silk Armani casual suit with the top of his shirt open. With his chest partially exposed, Candace's mind ran wild with thoughts of running her hands over his tight, well-defined six-pack. Lord, this man took sexy to a whole new level with the way he presented himself. He had to know that he was like water to a cactus with the way he stood there in all his undeniable sensualness—a necessity to quench the thirst of an obvious drought. Unconsciously, Candace licked her lips as if she'd just savored the nectar of his kiss—call it anticipation if you will—and then sucked in her breath as Sean rounded the table to greet her with a heart-fluttering embrace. She prayed that he couldn't feel the erratic beating of her heart through her chest as she buried herself inside of his arms. The genuine Arabic oil that emanated from his neck flew up her nose and lured her to nestle closer to him. She was even more aware of her juices seeping and felt she'd made the right judgment call by throwing on a pair of thin red lace boy shorts, otherwise her secret would have been out because the floor would have surely been dampened underneath her and Sean would have been privy to just how hot his mere presence made her.

"Where's your little brother?" Sean asked, ending their embrace just a moment sooner than Candace would have liked.

"He wasn't feeling well after coming in from the pool earlier, so he told me to head out with you." It was a lie, but only a partial one. Lawrence had insisted that she go alone but she knew that it was because he sensed the attraction between her and Sean and didn't want to feel like the third wheel.

"Sorry to hear that," Sean said sympathetically as he pulled out her chair for her.

I'm not, she thought as she took her seat. Had Lawrence been present it would have lessened the chances of Sean getting to see the lace undies she was sporting. "Well, he made me promise to tell you, don't make him have to find you and body you."

Sean laughed and the corners of his eyes wrinkled up in the sexiest way. "If I had a sister like you, I would say the same thing."

They shared a chuckle and busied about peering over the menu. The moment filled Candace with a sense of dejavu. “Hmmm,” she purred.

“What is it?” Sean asked, looking up at her over his menu with those soulful eyes.

She smiled sweetly. “This just reminds me of our standing lunch dates we use to have back in the day.”

“Tuesdays and Thursdays,” Sean said, quickly recollecting. “I remember them well.”

“I miss that...the time we spent together.”

Sean didn’t reply right away.

Candace noticed the way he stared at her and suddenly she felt guarded. Was she allowing herself to get all caught up in past feelings only to find that she was alone in longing for a recap? She corrected her posture in her chair, crossed her legs under the table, and stared down at her menu. *So much for having him relax my body,* she thought.

"Why didn’t you tell me?” he asked, never looking away from her.

Candace glanced up confusedly. “Huh?”

“Why didn’t you tell me that you were leaving? You felt so sincere about what we had, the time we shared...but you ended it abruptly.”

She should have known that an explanation would be requested but the thought that it would come before they were even able to order drinks never crossed her mind. She’d been so surprised to see him again after all of this time that the reason for their separation wasn’t nearly as important to her as their reunion.

“I thought I’d done something wrong when we last saw one another,” Sean went on when Candace didn’t respond. “The last thing I remember is me putting you to sleep. The way you were laid out so peacefully...it seemed like everything was perfect.”

Candace smiled but felt a little uncomfortable talking about their one night stand that occurred on her last deployment—their most intimate, engaging experience. “Well, if I remember the course of events correctly, I was the one that put *you* to sleep and had you sucking on your thumb.”

They both laughed. There was a little truth in her joke and each of them knew it.

“But seriously,” she said, bringing them back to the topic at hand. “It wasn't like that, boo.” She could remember the incident as if it had just occurred the day before. “First Sgt. Michaels caught me walking coming out of the shower the next morning when I left your room. He ordered me to get dressed and report to his office. By the time I got to his office, the wheels were already in motion. He informed me that I had to get back home immediately because my aunt was found guilty of three federal charges and they didn't want me to miss any critical proceedings regarding me taking primary custody of L.”

“What?” Sean asked in astonishment.

“Yeah, it was a lot. I wanted to let you know, but you weren't at the normal lunch meet up spot that Thursday and my flight was scheduled for that afternoon.”

Sean nodded and sat down his menu. His entire vibe changed as understanding and remembrance took him back to a sea of emotions that made him nauseous. “Yea, yea, I remember that day. They had us block off this IED blast that killed four locals and two soldiers."

Candace watched as anguish washed over his face and he gripped his chair tightly, his knuckles turning colors as he tried to push the painful memories and heavy thoughts out of his mental. She knew what that was like, that feeling of post-helplessness and sorrow. She also remembered the somber feeling she'd had the day she'd boarded her plane to return to the states, not knowing if she'd ever lay eyes on the sexy specimen of a man that had her nose wide open back then and her heart taking leaps and making flips inside of her chest even now.

She suggested that they go ahead and order as a means of trying to lighten the mood and change the subject. As the night progressed, they made light conversation and enjoyed the back and forth banter that they kept up. In a matter of hours, they'd settled back into the romantic comfortableness that they'd first created years ago while stationed clear across the world. The more they engaged, the more Candace continued to envision wrapping her thick legs around his chocolate waist once again. The fantasy was almost as delicious to her as the memory of the real deal. *It's going down*, she thought. There was just no way that she could let his ass get away from her twice.

CHAPTER 4
INTERRUPTIONS

The existence of their private alliance seemed like it had just developed and budded yesterday. She pleasantly recalled the gentility of his touch and the way that he'd once caused her body to spasm uncontrollably. The memories made Candace shutter; she could almost feel him inside of her again. After all, he was the last man to make her clitoris feel like a drum at the battle of the bands. She continued to harbor her private thoughts, praying that she wasn't being transparent in her desires by way of her facial expressions and body language. Then again, maybe showing a little intent was just the move to make to ensure that the quality time they were spending didn't end any time soon.

Suddenly, her little fantasies were halted when Sean excused himself from the table in search of the restroom. During his absence, Candace took the opportunity to freshen up her lip gloss, joust her hair, and exhale. Her body was full of sexual tension that mounted the longer she sat across from the man of her dreams. As Sean returned, Candace noticed the change in his demeanor. The lightheartedness was replaced with an air of slight seriousness.

"Everything okay?" Candace asked.

He nodded as he took his seat. "Yea, I'm good." Sean let out a deep sigh and looked over at her as she stared back at him expectantly. "Look, I have something to be up front with you about."

Here it comes, she thought. *The moment when all of my hopes come crashing down and reality slaps me in the face.* She just knew that any chance of them rekindling their old flame was about to be shot to hell with the admission of whatever his confession was about to me. That's the way her life seemed to be going—every time things looked good and promising a setback occurred.

"I'd be lying if I said that I haven't enjoyed this reconnection between you and I," he told her.

Candace smiled, unsure of how she should feel given the fact that she had no clue what he was about to come back with. "So have I," she assured him.

"I just feel like I have to let you know that I...I have a three-year-old daughter."

She let the news sink in and felt herself release a breath she hadn't realized she'd been holding on to so hard. Visions of him admitting to being married or gay had filled her head from the time he uttered the words 'I have to let you know'. Him having a kid had been the very least of her worries.

"So you aren't married?" she asked for clarity.

"No," Sean replied. "My divorce was finalized two months ago."

A thought occurred to her and she almost didn't want to ask the question. "Were you married while we were in Iraq?"

"No, I met her shortly after my unit got back."

Candace looked relieved.

"We didn't last long at all," he spat out, laying his feelings out on the table. I'm glad someone sent me a stupid fucking video of her and another solider getting it in while I was on the last leg of my recent deployment." He shook his head in disgust. "Shit was humiliating. But, the custody battle was the worst though. We actually just finalized the custody after a sixteen months of going back and forth because they live in Columbia, South Carolina. Her trifling self moved shortly after we separated. So now I gotta fly out to Atlanta and we meet at her cousin's house so I can visit with my daughter or pick her up." Sean paused for a moment, looking dead into Candace's eyes with hurt flashing in his own "No, you know what was really the worst part of it all? They were getting busy in *my* $2, 000 bed with my daughter just down the hall."

Candace grimaced. The chick had balls to do some grimy shit like that. She could see the anger in his face and wished that she could erase all of his pain and sordid memories. "Do you have a picture of her? Your daughter I mean," Candace asked. It was a slick way to redirect his mind from negative to positive. She had seen Ally use it on several occasions with some of the soldiers in the unit, refocusing them on that which they loved to calm them down—their pride and joy; their family. It worked every single time.

Upon first sight of the photo, Candace fell in love with the little girl. "What's her name?"

"Shanelle," Sean replied.

After studying the picture for a few more moments, Candace handed it back and shifted the conversation once more. "So what do you have planned or scheduled for the night?'

"The guys and I are headed to a little party if you would like to come."

"Hmmmm". She considered it but realized that she needed to check on L prior to leaving. "Sure. Just give me a minute to pop upstairs."

He nodded. "I completely understand." Sean signaled the waitress and asked for check. Candace entered her purse and retrieved two crisp twenty dollar bills. "Tell her to keep the change, okay?" she insisted, handing the cash to Sean. "I'm gonna run to the little girls room."

She needed the brief separation to give herself a moment to think clearly. Going to this party with him would buy her a few more hours of time in his company. Hopefully it would lead to a night of reliving the passion they'd once created. She pulled herself together, took a good look at herself in the mirror over the sink in the ladies' room and knew without a doubt that she was ready to feel him all over her, probing every inch of her body.

Upon returning to the table she found her forty bucks resting among their empty dishes and soiled table linen. Sean's face donned that same serious look he'd had as he'd informed her about his daughter. She was perplexed. What could be the problem now?

"Please don't try me like that anymore," he said slowly and deliberately. "I'm not one of those guys that lets females pay for their meal."

Candace seemed surprised but was quite relieved. Since during her time in Sacramento, she'd only come across thirsty and cheap soldiers. Paying her own way had become a norm so she did it without so much as a thought now. It felt good to know that she was in the presence of a true gentleman.

Officially checked and having no qualms about it, Candace retrieved the forty dollars with a smile.

Satisfied, Sean rose from the table and the couple headed to the elevator. The doors opened for them and they entered together. Candace pressed the Level 5 button. No sooner than the doors touched again and the elevator began to rise, Sean grabbed her by the waist and pulled her close to him leaving no space between them. Her breathe was taken away as his thick lips pressed against her and his tongue forcing her mouth to receive it. He kissed her passionately like he had angrily missed her, and wanted to let her feel just how much. His hands roamed her curves as her arms wrapped around his neck, locking there with no desire to ever let him go. Surprisingly, "Drake's Hot Line Bling" played in the background but neither of them notice as they were immersed in the heat of the moment.

Sean's hands slid down over her hips down her thighs before inching up slowly and pulling the fabric of her dress upward as well. He longed to feel the warmth and softness of her skin. Candace wanted nothing more than to welcome him to the playground that constituted her body. *Pull it up,* she mentally cheered him on. *Pull it up, tear it off me. Whatever!*

Ding! The elevator stopped at Level 3 and Candace's head began to spin as they quickly withdrew from their embrace. Immediately, she went about smoothing down her dress while trying not to make eye contact with the person that had just joined them in the elevator.

"What's going on, Sean?" the man asked a jovial tone to his voice as he eyed the couple suspiciously. He noticed the heavy breathing, the flushed look on Candace's face, and of course the bit of shine upon Sean's lips which he could only guess came from the woman's lip gloss. "Who do we have here?"

"Jon, this is Candace," Sean said quickly, pressing the button to hurriedly close the doors of the elevator so that they could get to their designated floor. "Candace, this is Jon. He's one of the new guys I told you about earlier." He focused on his buddy who was grinning knowingly. "Hey Jon, you guys can go ahead and head out to the party. I'm going to catch Uber with Candace."

Finally, the elevator stopped at level 5. As Sean and Candace got off, Sean and Jon shook hands and said their goodbyes. Candace was glad to be away from his friend but wished for more alone time to finish what they'd started in the elevator. She let herself into the hotel suite and Sean followed behind, lingering near the door. Candace crossed the floor of the living area and peeped her head inside of L's room. There he was resting on the bed.

Candace smiled at him. "You good for the night? You hungry?" she asked, realizing that she hadn't brought him back a plate.

"I'm straight," he replied. He noticed her rushed demeanor and sat up on his bed to peer over her shoulder out into the living area. He could only see the brother's head but he knew good and well who it was and what was up. "Where you headed?" he asked his sister, settling back against the pillows

"With Sean to a party."

L gave Candace a weird look.

Candace spoke up, stopping him before he could utter a word. "I know, I know, bro." She cocked her head to the side hoping that he'd cut her some slack and just let her have this moment. "So you good?" she reaffirmed.

They both noticed an additional presence. Candace turned around to come face to face with Sean. Lawrence looked over and glared at the muscular man. "Bruh, you better take care of my sister."

Sean could do nothing but respect the request and concern. "I got her, man."

Candace crossed the room and walked to L, placing a kiss on his jaw. "Don't leave the suite and don't open the door for any reason," she instructed him.

Lawrence didn't reply.

Candace turned to leave the room and stopped at the door as another thought occurred to her. "Don't stay up all night either. We're going sightseeing at ten in the morning."

Lawrence nodded and kept his focus on the television in front of him.

Candace smiled, pulled his door up, and together she and Sean exited the suite. They walked down the hallway quietly before entering the elevator once more. Candace stepped inside and pressed the Lobby button just as Sean reached over to hit the level 4 button. Candace looked in Sean's face with a bit of surprise.

"I have to go by the room to freshen up a little bit," he explained.

Candace didn't object. In fact, she'd been hoping for the opportunity for them to be alone and get physically reacquainted with one another. Him delaying their arrival to the party simply told her that he too wanted the chance to get a little more active. During the brief elevator ride, they kept a respectable distance from one another though each could feel the heat of attraction that permeated between them. Candace's thoughts were filled with dirty little scenarios that flickered one after the other, but all included her wrapped around Sean's body completely naked. Once again her womanhood dripped as she ached for Sean just as she had several times over the years while caressing herself on long lonely nights.

The doors opened and they both exited on level 4. As they entered his room, Sean went towards his bed to grab the remote and then turned the channel to ESPN. He then took his shirt off and exposed his dark chocolate muscles. By the look of it, Sean definitely did a lot of work on keeping up his physique. Before heading towards the bathroom, he reached out for a hug. Candace was hesitant to comply because she knew exactly what it would lead to. She had fantasied about this man for so long and now there he was right in front of her. Suddenly, she felt shy and inadequate.

"Boy put on a shirt," Candace told him, not because she didn't want the inevitable to occur, but because she wanted to make certain that he was completely in and wouldn't regret the decision to travel back in time with her. "Do you know what you're doing?"

Sean gave Candace a look of innocence for a few moments, before turning around to retrieve his shirt before taking a couple of slow steps towards the open bathroom door. No he didn't, Candace thought. She blinked rapidly, watching as his back faced her in his escape to the bathroom. She wasn't about to let the chance to feel him slip through her fingers. Who knew if either of them would have the nerve to spark things up after he came out of the bathroom? Who knew if they'd ever even see one another again after this mini vacation was over for her? She couldn't leave their fate to chance. She couldn't deny herself the very thing she felt she needed at this moment; the very thing she'd been wanting from the moment she boarded that plane years ago to return to the states leaving her prince charming behind.

Candace dashed forward and grabbed him by the back of his pants. Sean turned to face her with lust in his eyes. She pulled him close to her. Yes, her body was screaming for his expert love-making skills, but even more so she'd been waiting a very long time to give him the payback that he deserved. She'd played it out in her mind almost as much as she'd imagined their passionate trysts—the revenge that she had thought about multiple times over the years. Now, she was finally getting the opportunity to return the favor of what he had done to her.

Candace pushed Sean onto the bed before he could manage to pin her down. In shock, he partially laid back looking up at her in awe while wondering what she planned to do with the air of power she'd just assumed. Seductively, Candace stood on the side of the bed and removed the white dress from her curvy body. Sean was paying attention to her every movement. His look ensured her that he too had been awaiting this very opportunity for a long time. She had him practically salivating at the thought of being reminded of what her pussy tasted like.

Slowly, so that he could be sure to get an eyeful of her curves in the lace red panties with the matching bra, she climbed up on the bed, and maneuvered her thick thighs over Sean's stomach to straddle him. She noticed that Sean was trying to readjust his pants and manhood prior to her sitting down, but she quickly pushed his hands away. Giving him a sinister smile, she lowered her upper body to bring her face closer to his. The feel of his warm breath as he anticipated her next move made Candace tingle. She placed her lips against Sean's chocolate soft lips, taking her time to explore his mouth while he caressed her ass. The more she kissed him, the more she felt her clit throbbing against his already rock solid manhood, the bulge that he'd tried to get control of before she took over his body.

Her kissing exploration ventured downward to Sean's neck. She felt his member jump through his slacks and knew that she'd found a sensitive, hot spot. He gripped her as tightly, trying to contain himself because he didn't want to move to fast. She was driving him insane with the way her tongue danced across his skin. Her body pressed firmly against his as she began to gently caress his arm. The feel of the swell of her full breasts against his chest only made him hungrier for her. Sean slipped his hands through the legs of her boy shorts in order to have skin to skin contact with her round ass. He moaned as she sucked on his neck ruthlessly and reached behind her to slap one of his hands away before he could slide it between her legs to get a sample feel of the moisture seeping between them.

Her mouth moved up to his ear and she whispered her words softly between teasing flicks of her tongue against the

circumference of his ear.
"This...is...for...making...me...cum...six...times...the last time."

Yes, he'd gotten the best of her during their overseas episode, sending her body into orbit and making it damn near impossible for any other man to hold a candle to his performance. Even more than she desired to have him satisfy her craving for him, she longed to make him feel as helpless against her spell as he'd made her feel. She needed him to be so into her that his every waking moment would be filled with nothing but memories and flashbacks of how she put it on him. She needed him to need her the way she'd developed a permanent longing for him. Payback was a bitch—a bitch in red lace panties.

Excited and unable to succumb to this domineering role she was acting out, Sean flipped Candace over onto her back. He heard her suck in her breath with pleasure as he buried his face into her cleavage and began to kiss the tops of her luscious breasts while fondling the covered remnants of them through the fabric of her bra. His kissing became a light nibble which escalated to an intense sucking only to end with him desperately devouring the sweetness of her flesh. She hoisted herself upward so that he could reach around and unsnap the hook, freeing her mounds which he promptly popped into his mouth, one after the other.

Candace moaned excitedly, feeling the bliss that his mouth and roaming hands provided her with. Her arms enveloped his neck, her hands caressed his head, and her legs squirmed relentlessly as her body temperature rose off of the charts. Concentrating his mouth upon her right nipple, Sean's left hand trailed down the space the between her breasts, down her flat stomach where his fingers circled her innie for a moment, and then down to the warm area between her thighs. She parted her legs slightly, not wanting to appear too eager but definitely ready for him to feel the center of her being.

There was no question about her attraction to him or her intentions for the evening as his fingers were met by the juices that soaked clear through her underwear. He moaned deeply as he increased the pressure of his suckling. Her physiological response to his touch had him ready to dive in. She was much wetter than he remembered her being the first time around. He slipped his hand inside of her drenched panties and felt the bareness of her lower region. Sean probed around, feeling his way like a blind man as he caressed her fat outer lips followed by her pulsating clit. He pulled away from her breast and noticed the rise and fall of her chest as Candace's desire escalated. She was beautiful, every inch of her, and he wanted to taste it all.

She saw the fire in his eyes and knew that Sean was ready to set her body ablaze. *I'm supposed to be in control*, she reminded herself as she tried to guide his head back to her breasts. But it was too late. Sean was a man on a mission as he placed tiny kisses along the same route his hand had previously taken until his face came into contact with her womanhood. With Candace's hands resting on his head, Sean mercilessly ripped the thin fabric of her panties away from her body. The move was sexy and erotic; Candace shivered from the excitement of the moment. He lowered his head without giving her the opportunity to brace herself, smelling the sweetness of her natural essence as he enclosed as much of her pussy within his mouth as he could.

"Oh my God!" she exclaimed, gripping his head tightly. It was a sensation that she'd never quite experienced before and her body had no way of preparing for the shock he was putting her in.

Sean slurped and sucked, dining on her juices and devouring her as if she was his last meal. He made deliberate, long strokes against her entire genital area with his tongue making Candace flinch and call out each and every time. She didn't want him to stop, which was good because he had no intentions of doing so. She spread her legs wide, using her body language to beg him to push her further into the throes of ecstasy. The improved access to her pussy was a cue to Sean to dive deeper. His strong, massive hands held her thighs in place as he drove his tongue into her opening as far as his expand could reach. He darted in and out, orally screwing her as she trembled uncontrollable from the pleasure of it all.

"S-S-Sean!" she screamed out in a stutter. "W-w-what are you doing to me?"

He released his grasp on her left thigh and began to massage her clit in a steady, circular motion as he continued tonguing her now insanely drenched pussy. Candace's head flung back against the pillow top mattress as she arched her back and thrust her hips to match his rhythm. She was on the brink of busting a nut like no other. The thought of him swallowing the liquid effect of her climax made her hips rotate even faster. If she didn't control herself, the moment would be over sooner than she wanted it to. Given the way she'd been dying for this type of release, Candace wanted to make certain that their quality time lasted all night or at least until he couldn't get it up any longer.

Trying to regain some self-control despite the expert way that he fucked her with his tongue and fingers, Candace patted Sean on his head feverishly, signaling for him to let up. When he ignored her, removing his tongue from her entrance only to cover her clit and torture her with a series of quick flicks and sucking, she patted him harder. He was relentless and she was near orgasm. Candace squeezed her legs around his head and winced. Her squirming was turning him on. He knew that she was ready to explode, but he too wanted their session to continue as long as possible so he finally conceded and rose up from his position of sexual power.

As he lifted his head, Candace peered down at him. His lips were saturated with her juices and his breathing was heavy. She cocked her right index finger back and forth, requesting that he return his lips to hers. He pulled himself up and obliged the pretty woman's demand.

Hmmmm, Hmmmm. A muffled humming sound occurred from across the room, but neither of them cared to investigate it. They shared a messy, lustful kiss, each equally hungry for the other. It was time to take this encounter to the next level. Still trying to keep his lips in contact with hers as her hands caressed his face, head, and arms, Sean lowered his zipper and removed his pants and briefs, struggling to hurry and get back to the body that was waiting for him. Their kiss deepened as he towered over her body. His dick throbbed anxiously as Candace reached down to stroke the length of it.

Hmmmm, hmmmm. The pesky humming didn't let up. Candace broke their kiss, turning her head in the direction of the noise realizing that it was her cell phone going off. Whoever it was, they were determined to reach her and obviously didn't care less what she was in the middle of doing. Letting out a frustrated sigh, she wiggled away from Sean and sprinted her naked body across the room to fish the phone out of her purse.

"Candace," Sean said in disbelief. There they were having a hot and heavy moment and she hits the pause button to answer her phone. His ego was a little bruised, but his manhood stood at full attention as he observed her sexy curves in the buff.

She looked at the CALLER ID and tilted her head towards the ceiling. Rolling her eyes she sighed heavily as she clicked ACCEPT and listened to the familiar voice begin to speak before she could even issue a formal salutation.

"I need to see you and it can't wait forever so don't put me on ice." The mandate came off as arrogant as the caller expected it to.

Obligation led Candace to give her consent to the forced meeting she. "Fine," she said disappointedly as she looked over at a confused Sean. She damn near cried at the realization that she wouldn't be able to finish what they started, yet again having to walk away from the only man who'd been able to make her wet and vulnerable. "When and where?"

CHAPTER 5
WHEN YOU LEAST EXPECT IT

She sat at the bar watching the late night partygoers laughing it up and having a grand time. As she downed her second Blue Motherfucker, Candace entertained the idea of just walking out, getting in her car, and saying fuck it. Who was she to force her to come all the way down here in a timely fashion only to stand her up? It grated her skin to know that the family matriarch still felt that she had a hold over her after all of these years. *So why didn't you just stay your ass in that bed with Sean*, her conscience berated her. It was a reasonable question and if Lawrence knew that she'd not only left him alone to screw but then left her company for this bullshit meeting he'd certainly hit the roof.

Candace couldn't help but laugh. *How did it come down to this*, she thought. *How did I manage to find myself tiptoeing around my teenage little brother and not wanting him to disapprove of my actions?* But she knew it was greater than that. Any misgivings that Lawrence could possibly have about what she was doing were both understandable and to be expected. Neither of them really had a desire to have anything to do with their estranged family member given the history that stood between them. But, with her recent bout of misfortune and losing her job, she felt like she had nowhere else to turn. Leave it to her aunt to pop onto the scene the minute her back was to the wall. The phone call she'd received earlier could have very well been a curse and blessing, but knowing her aunt the latter was more likely. Still, Candace felt compelled to hear the older woman out in hopes that she wouldn't end up going the hell off in the process. Besides, she was horny and tired; a bad combination when dealing with someone you weren't too fond of.

"A lady doesn't sit in public downing liquor like some drunkard." The raspy voice that she'd come to loathe roared from behind Candace. She didn't even need to turn around to confirm that it was her.

"And what would you know about being a lady?" Candace retorted her back still turned.

"Oh honey," Robyn said, taking a seat beside Candace at the bar. "I wrote the book on it. Built a business around it even."

"Really? That's what you call them now? Your ladies?"

Robyn smiled; unfazed by the shots her niece was taking at her. "They are my ladies and I treat them with nothing but decency and respect."

"Until of course they come up short for the night, right?" Candace took a sip of her drink and felt the tension build up in her shoulders. Instantly, she knew that this meeting was a mistake. But she was there now; might as well see what the hell was up. "What are you doing in Arizona?"

"My business expands, honey," Robyn replied. "We're not restricted to just the east coast. I have contacts and clients all over. Sometimes they require special meetings."

Candace chuckled. "What? The Madam herself is making house calls?"

Robyn pointed a diamond studded, oval filed nail at Candace's face. "It's that cynicalness that has you sitting here in the middle of the night drinking your troubles away like some degenerate has been."

"Is that why you called me down here? You finished your business with whatever poor rich sap you leeched money out of tonight and decided what better way to end your evening than spending a little time insulting me, right?"

"I'm trying to help you, Candace. That's why I asked you to meet me."

"Help me?" Candace scoffed at the idea as she tossed back the rest of her drink. Robyn never cared to help anyone other than herself.

"Yes. We're family and—"

"Family?" Candace raised an eyebrow.

"...there is no shame in admitting that you need help. That's what I'm here for, honey. To help you. You and L. That's what a good aunt does."

"Wait, hold up. And just how do you think you can help us?"

Robyn looked at her as if she'd grown a third ear. "By giving you a job, dear. I mean, clearly you're going through a rough patch with the whole DUI thing. It's apparent that you have a problem so. This life wasn't meant for you. You weren't cut out for this...war, raising a kid...a teenager much less...being an average working mom so to speak."

"Ha! So you think I'm better equipped to be a whore?"

Robyn looked around disgustedly hoping that no one heard Candace's vulgar outburst. "Perception is a dangerous thing. No one is asking you to be a whore. I don't breed whores."

Candace shook her head. "Perception, huh? This isn't a glass half full, glass half empty sorta thing, Aunt Robyn. You don't breed whores?" She laughed dryly. "You could've fooled the shit out of me."

"The way I see it, you can either sit here and destroy yourself slowly but surely trying to ride that high horse of yours or you can humble yourself, come back home, and let me help you."

Candace reached into her purse and pulled out the two twenties she'd tried to give to Sean earlier. She tossed them onto the counter and stood up from her seat locking eyes with the woman she badly wanted to strangle. "Thank you for making the trip out here to let me know that you think so very little of me and my ability. Unlike you, I don't need to rely on my pussy or anyone else's to survive." She turned to walk away, pissed that she'd made the long drive from her mini vacation in paradise to sit there for Robyn's bullshit.

"You're going to wish you'd made a different decision," Robyn called out after her. "You're about to go straight into a depression over your lack of vision and bad decision making."

"And you can go straight to hell," Candace replied loudly enough over the chatter and commotion in the bar so that Robyn was sure to hear the directive. She exited the bar without looking back, wondering how the hell Robyn knew that she was now in need of employment.

It didn't matter what the woman said, there was no way that Candace was going to fall back into the trap of being under Robyn's rule. She wasn't a whore and wasn't about to be forced into being one. She had drive, ambition, and an iron will. Sure, things were a little shitty right now but she'd rather die than give Robyn the satisfaction of stealing what little self-respect and integrity she had left by turning her into a lady of the night.

***

"So where did you go last night?" Lawrence asked the next morning, entering his sister's room of their suite and studying her exhausted demeanor.

"We had dinner in the lobby restaurant and then we just talked for a while," Candace replied, grabbing a pillow to cover her eyes as her brother pulled back the hotel room curtains to let in the sunshine from the beautiful Californian sky.

"So you didn't the party you said you were going to?" he asked, skeptically fully expecting that the party was a private one most likely occurring in Sean's hotel room.

"Noooo," Candace let out, not wanting to engage in conversation when sleep was so vital.

"So you were out all night just...talking?"

"What is this? The third degree? We ate, we talked, I came back shortly after."

"You seem pretty exhausted for someone that allegedly wasn't out all night. Why didn't you wake me up when you came back? Shoot, I was starving in the middle of the night?"

"I asked you if you wanted something when I came up to check on you."

"Yeah, I wasn't hungry then. Around one something I ended up going to the vending machine and got a bag of chips and lemonade."

"You went out when you didn't even know I was back?" Candace asked, peeping around her pillow shield. "After I specifically told you not to leave the suite."

Lawrence feigned innocence. "What? A nigga was hungry. What, you wanted me to just sit here and perish?"

"You're so extra." She turned over in hopes that he'd catch the hint and give her time to sleep in a little longer.

"So, on my way back, I saw that Sean dude headed to his room when the elevators opened. Did you have fun at least? I could tell you were feeling him." Lawrence softened up a little bit, hoping that his sister would open up to him and tell him. He wanted her to be happy. Even though he didn't know Sean from the next dude, if she was happy then he was happy for her.

"To be honest with you, there wasn't really much to it," Candace said regretfully. "We reminisced, we laughed a little, he told me about his family—"

"His family? Dude's married?" Lawrence's brow rose and he immediately balled up his fists. So much for dude making his sister happy.

"Not exactly." Candace sighed. She wanted to push the memory out of her mind. Knowing that Sean was still in the hotel made her pensive. How could she explain walking out on him in the heat of the moment? How could she expect him to give her a second chance to re-spark the flame they'd had blazing so high? Sure, she could tell him the truth but the truth was so ridiculous that she was sure he'd either not believe her or come up with a slew of follow up questions that she wasn't prepared to answer. It wasn't every day that a girl had to explain to the man of her dreams that she was born into a brothel legacy.

"I'd really rather not get into," Candace stated.

"Sorry it was that bullshit, sis. The way y'all was eyeballing each other I shoul' thought I wasn't gon' see you no time soon this morning. But, don't let that shit mess up our good time," he said, trying to lift her spirits.

"I'm over it," she answered. "Nothing a couple of drinks couldn't get me through."

Lawrence frowned. "Man, Candace, why are drinking?"

"Boy, I was fine. Stop worrying."

"But you know you shouldn't be drinking though, sissy. We can't go back to how we were..." His voice trailed off as he remembered their head-butts, her accident, and them being separated in order to redeem herself in the eyes of the military.

Candace could hear the concern in his silence. She turned over, squinted in the sunlight, and reached for his hand. If only he knew how much she loved him and how dedicated she was to making sure that they had a stable life. She thought about telling him about the meeting with Aunt Robyn then thought better of it. He was just a kid—a kid who knew too much and had seen too much already. There was no sense in instilling any kind of worry in him about life with Aunt Robyn. Besides, after the way Candace had handed the witch back her feelings last night, she doubted that Aunt Robyn would dare reach out to either of them again. *Family my ass*, Candace thought, remembering the trite way in which her aunt had tried to use their blood lineage to persuade her to accept her sordid offer.

Lawrence placed his hand in Candace's and she pulled him onto the bed in a tight embrace.

"Everything's going to be okay," she told him. "I need you to trust me on that. I got us." "We're on vacation, remember? We're supposed to be relaxing. So chill...let's have fun and stop worrying so much."

Lawrence nodded. It sounded like a plan to him. "So what are we doing today?"

"What time is it?"

Lawrence turned around to look at the clock on the nightstand. "It's 9:15," he reported as he picked up the remote and turned the television on to ESPN."

"Okay," Candace replied, stretching and getting up out of bed. "Give me three minutes to get cleaned up and then we can go grab some of that complimentary breakfast before we head out sightseeing."

"Aye, can we scrap that and just hit the beach instead?"

It didn't take long for Candace to make a decision. She reached into her luggage and pulled out her swimsuit and wrap. "Get ya' ass up and get ready then," she told her brother as she headed off to the bathroom.

It didn't take her long to spruce up. By the time Candace was dressed and ready to roll, Lawrence was laid out on the sofa in the living area flipping through a magazine.

"Bout time," he complained.

"Please. It didn't take me but a minute."

"In your mind. You know how y'all females do."

Candace busied about packing her beach bag with a local attractions book, ginger from the mini bar in hopes of settling her now aching stomach, and a book that she'd been dying to read but had never gotten the free time to do so.

"If you encounter a female who doesn't take adequate time to make herself presentable, you better not fuck with her," Candace warned.

Lawrence didn't get the chance to respond before a loud knock sounded at the door, startling them both. Candace walked over and looked through the peep hole to find Sean on the other side. She hesitated before letting him in. Now wasn't the time to have a confrontation or heart to heart about what had happened the night before. She was nervous to be in the same room with him again, unsure of how he'd view her after the way she'd left him high and dry.

Slowly, she opened the door and came face to face with the man she felt destined to have to give up. "Hey," she offered meekly.

"Hey?" he asked rather than said. "That's all I get from you?"

Candace looked back over her shoulder at Lawrence as he sat straight up on the couch at the sound of Sean's voice. "Now really isn't a good time," she said.

"When is it ever? You gonna let me in?" He motioned for her to widen the door and grant him entrance.

Reluctantly, she stepped back and allowed him to come in. He stood in the middle of the living area and Candace closed the door, leaning her back against it for support as she crossed her arms.

"Are you okay?" he asked her.

"I'm great," she replied.

"You're great? Hmmmm. See, I didn't detect great with the way you ran out of there last night."

"Aye, bruh, you got some beef with my sis?" Lawrence asked, rising from his seat.

Sean turned to look at the young boy and then shook his head dismissively. "Nah, I think you've got your facts twisted. I think your sister has some underlying issue with me."

"It isn't that," Candace interjected.

"Whateva the beef is," Lawrence went on. "Whoever's got it with you, you might wanna grill that shit up and eat it, bruh, 'cause you can't come 'round her messing with my sister's emotions and shit."

"L!" Candace snapped, raising her hand to silence him. "Please...I got this okay?"

"You don't got this," he shot back. "This dude comes outta nowhere and gets your nose wide open then lays a boom on you and fucks up your whole mood."

"A boom?" Sean questioned, looking from Lawrence to Candace.

"What I tell you about your mouth, L?" Candace chided her brother. "You ain't grown; I ain't gonna keep telling you that."

"See how you handling me?" Lawrence asked. "Handled that nigga like that," he said, pointing at Sean.

Sean looked confused. "You want to tell me what exactly it is that I did wrong?" he asked Candace.

Candace crossed the room and picked up her beach bag. "Like I said, now's not really a good time."

"Yeah," Sean said, hurt laced in his tone "Looks like you guys are about to head to the beach."

"Yeah...a little family time."

"Which each?" Sean asked.

Candace hesitated before answering. "The Santa Monica Pier. We have some...uhhh...brother-sister bonding to do." She threw the last statement in to ward off any notion Sean was concocting of accompanying them.

He let out a loud breath. "Okay...okay, so when you get back—"As a confused

"Sorry to rush you," she said, cutting him off mid-sentence, "but we have to roll. We're already behind schedule with our day so...." She looked over at her brother. "L, you ready?"

Lawrence walked past Sean, opened the door to the suite, and held it open as he looked back at the duo. "Yeah. Let's hit it."

Sean caught the hint. They were getting rid of him. For whatever reason, Candace had no desire to speak to him and he was uncertain as to whether or not he'd ever get a clear answer from her as to what had gone wrong. With no other recourse, his feet fell in motion and Sean headed for the open door. "Alright then. I'll just hit you later. Maybe you'll have a free moment."

"Yeah, maybe," Candace said, not at all sounding reassuring.

Sean lingered in the doorway for a moment, but after seeing the way Lawrence glared at him he decided against giving it one more try. Silently, he exited and made his way to the elevator, feeling hurt and disappointed.

***

The Cali sun was shining as they laid back on the beach. They'd only been there for two hours and Lawrence had already had three girls bring him food and a soda on the strength of his swag. The only thing Candace could do was look and laugh. Somehow, her little brother had turned into in a charmer right in front of her eyes. He had many distinguishable qualities about him but one of his most intriguing features was his eyes. She remembered having to put him to bed as a kid and looking into his hazel browns, which were so warm and nurture to gaze into.

As Lawrence got up from his lounging chair to walk one of his admirers back to the food area, Candace noticed a sexy, 5'11, chocolate skinned guy clad in a NY fitted cap, a wife beater, and basketball shorts walking thru the sand directly in front her. She did a double take, but didn't want to make it obvious. Seeing the man with his sexy swag and appealing attire instantly made her think about Sean and the bullshit that had happened the night prior. She wanted to kick herself for ruining what could have quite possibly been her happily-ever-after.

The brotha's arms were tatted creatively and Candace couldn't overlook the bulge of his finely chiseled muscles. He caught her eyes as she tried to turn away quickly and started smiling as if he had seen an angel in the flesh. Reflexively, she acknowledged the smile with one of her own.

"What's going on?" he asked with his deep, sultry voice as he stopped right next to her while looking down at her curves perfectly displayed in her swimsuit. "I couldn't help but notice that you were over here by yourself."

Candace sized the young man up before responding. "I'm doing fabulous. Thanks for asking," she said sarcastically. "And yourself?"

"You look fabulous as well," he replied instantly, not at all turned off by her snarky response.

Candace smirked. “Hmmm...And I not actually alone. I was sitting here with my brother until just a minute ago.”

“Can a brother get a pass on his awkward segue way?” the guy asked, flashing her his stunning, white smile. “I’m just saying, I was admiring your beauty and just had to come over and meet you.”

Candace laughed at his corny honesty. Her guard lowered slightly as they eased into a pleasant conversation. Before she knew it, Lawrence was back with his possessive attitude and all.

"CeCe, who is this clown," Lawrence rang out.

“Clown?” the guy replied nonchalantly, caressing his chin between his thumb and index fingers. “You and dude about to have a problem if he insists on disrespecting me like that again.”

Both Candace and Lawrence were mildly impressed. Even though Lawrence was a teenager, he had an intimidating nature which caused most others to shy away from any kind of confrontation with him. Even Sean had held his tongue for the most part when interacting with Lawrence. Back in Atlanta while living with Aunt Robyn, L had to grow up fast. He’d earned a respected name in his old neighborhood and everyone knew the young thug to have a zero tolerance reputation. It was a lucky break for him that Robyn had run into a few issues of her own because the local police had been watching Lawrence and was closing in to arrest him on a list of federal charges, including reckless endangerment and aggravated assault. Still, not knowing Lawrence’s background and clearly not giving a fuck, this new guy wasn't the least bit fazed. He was on his grown man shit. He held his own against Lawrence off the rip and the duo simply wasn't used to that.

"You wanna address me from here on out, my name is Rico," the young guy announced. "And yours?"

Lawrence was speechless. He just stood there and sized up the chocolate skin tone, tatted, medium build man for a second.

"Well fuck it then," the guy stated, turning back to talk to Candace.

"Yo, that's my sister you talking to partna," Lawrence snapped through clenched teeth as he grabbed Rico's arm to turn him back around.

Candace stood to her feet quickly, jumping in between the two. "What the hell? L, stop! Do you hear me?" she squealed as Lawrence tried to reach around her to yank Rico. "Lawrence! I said stop it!"

"You better listen to your sister, Lawrence, before we enter into a grown man zone and you can't return," Rico responded, a mischievous smirk appearing on his face.

Lawrence stepped up angrily, forcefully shoving Candace to the side and closing the gap within the two bulls.

Candace could foresee the situation getting out of control. Her resolve was weakening and she wanted to pounce on her brother for embarrassing the shit out of them both. "Damn it, Lawrence I said stop it, now!" She raised her fist with the intent to punch him in the arm, but she'd promised not to lay hands on him and despite the hectic situation she wanted to keep her word. Besides, knocking the shit out of him while he was calling himself being protective of her wouldn't have blown over very well. If anything, it would have just sent Lawrence right over the edge and intensify his current level of aggression.

Lawrence was breathing heavily through his nostrils and was ready to give Rico the business. He quickly turned around to let his sister know that he was about to swing on her admirer but after establishing an eye contact with Candace his breathing slowed, he unballed his fists which he'd had clenched and ready for action, and he eyes, once narrow slits, widened. He saw the pleading in her eyes and the frustration painted on her face. It spoke to him and he realized that he needed to calm down. Lawrence looked back at Rico for a moment, momentarily ready to concede. Then Rico produced a smirk which set Lawrence's fire ablaze.

Lawrence's stance returned to its ready for action position and he no longer considered his sister's concern. The two bulls looked at one another menacingly, neither one of them willing to back down now. A crowd was growing but the need to stand their ground surpassed each man's fear for the ramifications that could possibly follow. Rico initiated the break of silence by winking his left eye at L. That was all the ammo Lawrence needed. Instantly, he struck Rico in his left eye never once flinching. A series of gasps, oohs, and other sounds of shock flowed through the body of spectators would couldn't take their eyes off of the scene. Candace's hand flew to her mouth and she wanted to simply sink through the sand and die right there.

Rico rubbed his face for a moment. Feeling blood as his fingertips caressed his skin, he looked Lawrence in the eyes and stated, "You've officially crossed into grown man zone and you can't return now, lil homie."

The deadly seriousness of his tone sprung Candace into action. She pulled at Lawrence's arm and then wedged herself between the men once more with her back to Rico. With her hands planted firmly against his chest, Candace pushed Lawrence backwards. "Go! Now!" she screamed out. "You don't want this."

"Damn straight, but you gon' get it today, lil nigga," Rico said abrasively, whipping out his .9mm.

The steel caught the glimmer from the sun and shined brightly in Candace's eyes as she turned around to face Rico. She opened her mouth to question his balls for pulling out a gun on a kid, despite her brother's attack against him. But, before she could speak or even rationalize her thoughts, she noticed two cops on bikes scurrying through the crowd along the boardwalk, trying to get to them.

"No, no, no," she whined. The situation was getting worse by the second. Thinking quickly on her feet, whether it made it made sense or not, she turned to face her brother who had yet to follow her instructions. "Hit me!" she encouraged him.

"What the fuck?" Lawrence shot back, both confused and disturbed.

"You stupid son-of—bitch...just...ugh!" She hauled off and lugged him with all of her might in an uppercut along his jawline.

Taken aback, Lawrence reacted by backhanding his sister in the mouth. Immediately, he was sorry for his lack of self-control.

"Shit!" Rico let out, replacing his gun in the waistband of his pants and trying to cope with what he'd just witnessed.

Candace tumbled backwards into Rico as the crowd hissed with verbal evidence of their own confusion. She could taste the blood in her mouth but didn't waste a second reacting to it. "Go!" she screamed at him again. "Get the hell on now. I'll find you later. Please." She shot a look over her shoulder to see the cops abandoning their bikes and tussling with the crowd in an effort to approach the scene. She turned back around only to see the back of Lawrence's retreating figure. *Good,* she thought. *Now to flip this situation.*

"Step aside," one of the officers called out, instructing the crowd to part so that they could assess the situation.

Candace took a quick breath and turned around to face Rico whose eyes danced with confusion. "Why did you do that? What the fuck dude?" Candace proclaimed.

Rico opened his mouth and then closed it, realizing that he was about to get fucked over right quick as Candace attempted to save her brother's ass. Any other time he'd call a chick out as psycho and defend himself against the lie she knew he was about to tell. But, he respected her loyalty to Lawrence as well as her bravery. She'd just taken one for the team just to keep her kid brother out jail. That showed guts and where he was from you couldn't do anything but respect a down-ass chick.

"Ma'am, is everything okay?" The second officer said, walking up on the duo.

Not thinking clearly, going with raw emotions, and fuming from recent events, Candace turned with an aggressive stance, meeting the concerned glares of both officers. "Yeah, we are straight. Just a lil' domestic dispute. We appreciate you for coming to make sure we didn't kill each other. Bye!" Candace replied as she turned around to eye the two officers closely. Both looked young and fresh out the academy.

"Ma'am," first officer stated firmly. He was a taller than his partner with jet black short yet spikey hair. "I'm going to need you to calm your voice down."

The second officer, plump in stature with a receding hairline placed his hands on his hips as if he was intimidating someone.

"Whatever dude," Candace responded as she sucked her teeth. They were comical to her. Common sense told her to pipe down and play the role of naïve abused girlfriend as she'd intended to, but her attitude was in high gear and the sight of the pansies in uniform only reminded her of the uniform she'd recently been stripped of.

"Since you have a lot of attitude, let me see some ID," stated the taller, light brown skin, medium build officer with the camel water pack on his back.

Rico look at Candace with a disturbed, disappointing expression as if he had something to hide. Her little tirade had drawn more attention to them than the original commotion over his scuffle with Lawrence. He hoped that her put-on didn't cost him greatly in the end.

"Sir, I need to see your ID, now!" the first officer snapped. He placed his hand on his weapon as if he felt threatened by the disturbing look Rico had just given Candace.

"Sir, unfortunately I do not have any identification on me right now," Rico stated as respectfully as he could.

The first officer pointed over to the boardwalk as his partner began to force the crowd to disburse. "Sir, I'm going to need you to step to the side over there please so we can check to see if you have any warrants, okay?"

"Under what grounds," Rico rang out, with a confusion look expressed on his face, wondering how they were going to do that when he had no idea to produce for them and he wasn't at fault for anything.

"Because he said so," the other officer cut in.

"Well, under my Fourth Amendment Rights, per the United States Constitution, dated on 1776, we have the right to refuse your seizure of our IDs," Rico shot back immediately without so much as blinking "No crime was reported, no crime was committed, and no witnesses or complaints to get statements." His eyes darted around at the few lingering passersby as if daring them to utter a word about what had gone done.

He needn't worry; although many had watched the scene very few understood what had actually transpired. Even if they wanted to snitch, they had no idea had to explain the scenario.

Candace stared at Rico blankly because she had just been hit by a brick of his knowledge. First Rico had stood up to L, which never happened, and now he'd just completely dumbfounded the two rookie cops. She wondered where this amazing man had come from and wished that they'd met under different circumstances. Just as he mentally marveled over her ability to ride or die, Candace was equally as impressed by the way he hadn't bothered to snitch on Lawrence and have him sent to juvenile detention until he was 18. The last time Lawrence had gotten into legal issues, the judge had promised that juvie was definitely his next move. Somehow, both of their unexplainable antics were saving Lawrence from the fate she feared for him.

Candace's legs and thighs started to get wet as she thought about how he had captured her interest and he didn't even know it. After a few seconds of silence, Rico asked the officers with a confident tone and a wink from his left eye, "Is that all officers?"

The officers looked at one another with puzzled expressions as the small crowd that still lingered cheered with excitement.

The shorter cop eyed Candace's busted lip. "Ma'am, you can file a formal complaint. All you gotta do is say the word and this guy will—"

Candace looked from the cops to Rico and then back to the cops. "I didn't call you down here in the first place. We're good."

Rico stepped forward and placed his arm around the small of her back. "You guys have a wonderful day," he said, urging her to turn around and walk away with him. He chuckled lightly at the irony of the about face they'd just done in the situation. "So now that we can get back to our initial conversation," he said with his arm still around her waist, "what you got planned for tonight, little ma? You know you owe me one."

Still dazed and speechless, Candace took a deep breath and then placed herself eye to eye with this new guy that she knew nothing about. True enough, he had held her down although she'd painted him out to be a woman beater. In her eyes, Rico was nothing short of amazing.

"What do I owe you?" Candace asked.

"Let's see... I smoothed over that little issue with those little toy cops that just left, plus by examining the situation, your little brother has a bad temper, so I'm going to guess that this wasn't the first time he's been in trouble. I'm going to take it even further, and make an assumption that he's currently facing some legal issues hence you making him dip and putting on ya' lil act. So, if I would've pressed charges, which I wouldn't have because it would taint my name and brand, but hypothetically *if* I had, he would currently be on an express trip to juvie." Rico smiled at her though stared deep into her eyes. "Am I correct?" He winked with his swollen eye and winced from eh pain.

Candace stared at him for a moment and then chuckled lightly. She looked down at the ground and sighed at the reality of the situation. "To be honest, you hit it right on the money. My little brother is a hot head." She looked up at him with sincere eyes. "Look, I'm sorry that he clocked you and that whole thing with the domestic issue..."

He waved her off. "Forget about it."

"I even like your swag," she went on, cocking her head to the side and looking at him seriously. "But unfortunately for you, you aren't hitting the box today or tomorrow, so don't try to use that mental psychology bullshit on me like you did those officers." She smiled at him knowingly.

Rico let out a hiss of wind through his mouth, lowered his head, and then brushed over it with his left hand as he laughed. "Dang, you know how to cut a brother down to size don't you?"

Candace laughed along with him and then took a step closer towards him. “What I can do though give you is my phone number and offer you my friendship."

He looked up at her with a glint of hope in his eyes and she winked at him.

CHAPTER 6

The entire encounter was now a blur. Candace was stunned herself by the turn of events and knew that there was no way that she could tell anyone else what had happened without them looking at her as if she was crazy. Certainly it would be difficult for anyone to understand her position and she feared that she'd be judged by her actions alone as well as the end result.

Sitting in her bedroom, she stared at the screen of her laptop in a daze. It was hard for her to think of anything but Rico. It had been three weeks since they'd last seen each other following that fateful day on the beach. Once her attraction for him was well established given the way he'd presented himself, Candace had instantly gotten over her failed opportunity with Sean. Her spirits had even been lifted regarding her discharge and trying to figure out her next career move. Having Rico around sort of made things a little easier for her to cope with. He was good for her physical, emotional, and mental health.

Ever since her mini vacation, Rico would slide up to spend the weekend with her. She loved having him around and was grateful that he always made the time to see her. When they were together things were good, but when he was away Candace was filled with thoughts of him seeded in mix emotions. She missed him, that was for sure, but she wondered what his life outside of her was like. Whenever she called him, he'd usually chat her up very briefly before telling her that he would have to call her back when he was off work. While Candace understood the fact that the man had to make a living, it concerned her that his return calls would only come in between nine and ten at night. Even then, he would talk for only a few moments before mentioning that he needed to go on for work in the morning.

Candace was skeptical. She wasn't sure if he was bullshitting her or what, but she had to be honest with herself and realize that she really didn't know him all that well to begin with. She snapped out of her daze and hit her palm on the desk. "Ugh!" she let out, mad at herself for allowing him to fuck her head up so early in the game. *But that tongue though*, she thought with a smile, remembering the way he'd pleased her over and over again with long, determined strokes the last time he'd visited. *OMG, he did that*. Just as her mind started to drift off and her hormones began to surge, a light touch on her shoulder forced Candace to jump up from her seat.

"Agggh!" she screamed, turning to come face to face with the culprit. "What the fuck!" she exclaimed, clutching her chest and leaning against the desk to keep from falling out.

"I knocked and rang the bell twice. You didn't answer so I just let myself in with the spare key," Ally explained, sitting her purse down beside Candace's laptop. "What the hell were you in here doing?"

Candace swallowed hard, turned around, and sat back down in her chair. She didn't want to get into the details of what had her so disoriented that she didn't even hear her doorbell. "Nothing," she replied flatly as she started typing on the computer.

"Nothing huh? Ally challenged. "You've been fucked up since you returned from your little trip weeks ago. Barely call, you always busy, giving me one word answers to my questions. You know I know you so I know when something's going on with you and I know you're not still salty with me about the whole discharge thing because there's a complete difference between pissed off you and distracted you." She paused and waited for Candace to fill in the silence. When her friend failed to do so, Ally crossed her arms and cocked her head to the side with an attitude. "So we keeping secrets now, bitch?"

Candace chuckled at her friend's hurt tone. It was true that they hadn't spoken much since she'd been hit with the news of being put out of the Army, but Ally was right. None of that had anything to do with their recent disconnect. "It's not like that," Candace stated. "So get out of your feelings."

Ally studied Candace's face as she tried her best to keep her focus on the computer screen and not her inquisitive friend. No matter how much she tried to hide it, Ally could see the signs written all over Candace's face. "Hmmm. Let me find out you all lovey dovey now."

Candace lightly bit her lower lip.

Allison's face lit up with excitement. "I'm right aren't I?" Ally sat on the side of Candace's bed and stared. "Girl, if you don't pour this tea up right now!" she threatened.

Candace was amused. She'd honestly missed the camaraderie between her and Allison since being removed from the military scene. She was going crazy with her private thoughts of Rico and longing for him. She wanted to talk about it and Allison was her best friend. Perhaps it was time to clue her girl in. Besides, with the way her pussy was fiending for Rico's tongue, she needed a vent session badly.

Candace turned to her friend and tried to contain the huge grin that forced its way upon her lips anyway. "Lemme tell you... When L and I went to Santa Monica, I ran into Sean," she said, starting from the beginning.

Allison's face was contorted as she searched her memory bank. "Sean, who?"

"Sean, Sean," Candace replied, staring at her friend hard. "Iraq Sean."

"Oh word!!!! Ally proclaimed, remembering the stories that Candace had told her long ago about her brief liaison with the man of topic—stories, dreams, day dreams, and even wet dreams about this supposed mystery man were in abundance where Candace was concerned.

"We ran into each other as soon as me and L got to the hotel," Candace explained. "Girl, he was still sexy as ever. He, Lawrence, and I were supposed to have dinner but it ended up just being the two of us. It was hot, girl...the tension between us. It was as if we were back in Iraq, like nothing had changed. Then he goes to the restroom and comes back all sullen and shit. I guess he'd made a call home or whatever because he chose that moment to let me know that he had a kid."

"Oh wow," Allison stated. "I'm assuming that a wife is attached to the kid."

"An ex-wife per their very recent divorce."

Allison knew how head-over-heels her friend was about this man so she treaded lightly with her next line of questioning. "Do you think that he's over it? The marriage, I mean? I'd hate to see you get all wrapped up in a guy who's still stuck on someone else and then it not work. You've already been through so much."

Candace shook her head. "No, no, no. It wasn't like that at all. I mean, what I got out of it was that he's over it and isn't too fond of the ex. That situation wasn't a make or break for us."

Allison was skeptical. How could her friend over look this man's entire mood change after whatever alleged call he'd made upon excusing himself? "I just want you to think with your head and not the space between your legs."

Candace heard the remark yet forced herself not to process it. Too often she'd been made to feel as if she was nothing but mere pussy and that she didn't have the intellect to take care of herself and make sound decisions. She didn't want to believe that Ally was now viewing her in this way. "It seemed like we were rekindling that old flame," she went on, despite the triggers that had just been set off. "He invited me to a party but instead of going, we went back to his room. Everything was good...we were both into the moment. But then...something happened and I just couldn't...I couldn't go through with it." It wasn't a lie; it just wasn't the complete truth either but Ally didn't need to know about the way she'd ran upon Robyn's beckoning.

Allison was confused. She shifted her weight on the bed and looked down at her feet. "So...you didn't fuck him?"

"No."

"But you're up in here daydreaming about fucking him?" She looked over at the computer. "What? Are you trying to find him online to get another shot at it? I mean, what happened that prevented you from going through with it?"

Candace shrugged off the last question. "Things happen. But the next day I ran into this dude named Rico at the beach. Lawrence's ole over protective ass started acting a damn fool when he saw the dude trying to holla at me. He hit the man in the face hard as fuck. Like, he just blanked out and hauled off on him."

"Really?" Allison responded while covering up her mouth. "Oh my God. What are you going to do with that boy? What the fuck is wrong with him, girl?"

"I know right. I was scared as hell. The last thing I needed was for him to catch a damn case. I tried to get him to calm down and I finally got him to get the hell on before the police came."

The drama she was hearing had Ally on pins and needles. "Oh shit! How did you do that? How'd you reel his ass in long enough to talk some sense into him?"

The memory made Candace shudder. She knew that things were about to get crazy and hoped that Allison wouldn't think to have her ass committed once she finished her story. "So I picked a fight with L real quick to get him to slug me and then I fussed him out until he went ahead and ran off."

"You did what!" Allison was astonished.

"And I tried to make it seem like Rico and I had been in some kind of domestic conflict—"

"To take the heat off of L and put it on Rico," Allison finished for her, shaking her head in disbelief.

"Right." Candace couldn't meet her friend's eyes as she continued. "So, the rent-a-cops come over and start looking us over and then asks for our ID right. I guess Rico wasn't feeling the interrogation, but he then starts rattling off this verbiage about the fourth amendment, right. Had them clowns dumb founded. He was like; we have the right to refuse your seizure of our IDs because no crime was reported and stuff. So, the cops look to the few folks that was still crowded around us and not one person moved to step forward to say what had happened. It was like everyone was mesmerized by this dude's swag."

"Mmmhhmm," Ally let out, knowing exactly where this was going.

"It was epic girl. I mean, he could have dropped dime on L real quick and painted me out to be crazy."

"He wouldn't have needed much paint for that," Ally commented jokingly as she leaned over to the right and propped herself up on Candace's bed with her elbow.

"So, I ended up giving him my phone number. I mean, what choice did I have after the way he played the role with me, you know? And later that night, he called me and we met at the bar in my hotel."

"No fear that Prince Charming was going to come down and bust up your new love affair?"

"I wasn't the least bit concerned about Sean," Candace replied dismissing her friend's sarcasm. "After getting to know one another for a while, we went out to get some fresh breeze." She leaned back her chair and smiled mischievously for affect. "...while cruising around in his fresh 2014 Red Challenger with the white leather seats and hot ass rims on it. Ha! Girl, I'm telling you...when we got in the car, the damn thing welcomed him back."

Allison laughed and shook her head. "Shut up."

"I'm so for real. He actually introduced me to the car. I was amazed at that point. What killed it was when the car system told me that my body temperature was lower than normal and asked if I would it like to heat my seat." Candace stared up at the ceiling remembering the moment as if she'd won the lottery. "Real 92.3 was playing that hot new joint by Chris Breezy, Nikki Minaj, and Meek. The radio was jamming nothing but R&B all night, so you know how I am."

Allison knew all too well. "Mmmhhmmm. Hot ass."

"We chilled for a minute from like this mountain top with the most spectacular view. And then... we started making out on his car."

"Of course you did."

"I'm telling you, he had me so hot and bothered. I was beyond ready. He started sucking my tattas and then pulled my skirt up. When he started licking on my thighs, I couldn't do anything but lay there. Then he pulled my panties to the side. Mmmm. Let me stop." She licked her lips and reminisced on the moment. Her panties were getting soaked with each second that passed by. All she wanted was for Rico to fall through and put her out of her misery.

Allison fanned herself. "Yea, you need to stop before you get me horny and I go home and rape my husband." She laughed a little trying not to think too hard about the picture that Candace had just painted.

"Girl, he did that," Candace continued. "Got me over here jonesing and I can't even focus on these damn applications."

Allison looked over at the computer and sat up straight. "How's it going?" she asked, referring to the Candace's job search.

"You know how it is...looking for a job is a job."

Allison nodded, feeling remorseful. "I'm so sorry, Candace. You know I really did all that I could."

"I know."

"I never wanted anything to happen to you. But you know that no matter what I'll always be there to help you however I can. I'll always have your best interest at heart."

Candace was in no mood to put her friend's guilt at ease. She'd long since gotten over the situation and knew that there wasn't much else that Allison could have done to come to her aid. Shit happens and she was a living, walking testament to that fact. "I know," Candace said blankly. "I know."

Allison sighed. "I'm so, so sorry. Is there anything that you and L need?"

Candace shook her head.

"You know that I'm down to give you anything you need," Allison stated. You just say the word and I got you.

Candace shot her a quick glance with raised eyebrows. "You know what I need?"

"What is it? Just tell me."

"A fuck. A good ass, hair pulling, ass slapping, multiple orgasms type of fuck. Can you deliver that?"

Allison screamed, "Eww! Sorry girl I don't get down like that honey."

Candace laughed. "Not from you, nut. From Rico."

"Wait." Allison looked at Candace long and hard. She'd listened to the story that Candace had shared never once hearing her actually admit to experiencing her new boo's love pole. But, given Candace's declaration Allison knew that her friend had been doing more than getting head. "You slut," she called out, erupting in laughter. "You've known this guy all of two minutes and already you spreading your legs?"

"Bitch, don't judge me," Candace replied, knowing full well that it was too late for that.

"So how was it?" Ally inquired for more.

"Girl, not only can he lick on the clit like a pro, but that fool can lay it down too. I have to watch his little sneaky ass though. He likes to catch me off guard with his little freak sessions. Like, he called me right after work one day and had me meet him at the Embassy Suites. When I got there, he instructed the front desk manager to escort me to his room with a cold bottle of champagne and roses. When he opened the door, he gave me a glass of champagne and a warm embrace. Music was playing in the background. I was done from there. The brother had it all planned out from go. There was no way I could deny him the goodies after that."

The two burst out into laughter over Candace's obvious infatuation with her new lover.

"He put me right to sleep and I didn't even know it. He's been here a couple of times during the week and once on the weekend. I was actually looking to go visit him this weekend, but he's been so busy with work and stuff. Every time I call him, he either has to call me back or he's in the middle of a delivery. I have sexual needs dammit! I'ma need him not to keep sending me through withdrawals like this."

Ally laughed again. "You are dick whipped, I see. Well I'm going to tell you like this," she said, laughter subsiding and her seriousness shining through her tone. "Don't always believe what a man or a woman tell you.' When you think everything is right, it's wrong and when you think everything is wrong, it's probably right. So just take that and put it in your back pocket." She gave Candace a stern look. "You wanna go down there this weekend? Fine. But don't go alone. Take somebody with you just in case. But not L or my husband's crazy asses though." Ally laughed at the thought of how either male would react if Candace's new beau got out of line.

"Hmmm, I'll figure it out," Candace promised just as her phone rang. She looked down at the CALLER ID and excitement filled her body. "This is him right here, girl." She quickly collected herself before answering the call. "What's going on, boo? How's your day going?" A brief pause ensued as she nodded her head attentively. "So you're coming down tonight?" She wiggled in her seat as she tried contain her joy.

Allison continued to watch all while hoping that this guy was on the up and up.

"Is everything ok?" Candace asked Rico. She listened to his response followed by further instruction. "Okay, I'll meet you at our regular spot. Is nine o'clock okay?" Her eyes filled with hope. "Good, I'll be there at nine. Do I need to bring anything?"

Allison began to wonder where this spot of theirs was and quickly concluded that it must be a hotel room.

"I'll see you then," Candace said into her cell before disconnecting the call." She replied.....Ok, I will be there. See you soon, she implied.

"Where there you go," Ally stated.

"What?"

"You wanted to hear from him. You wanted to see him. Now, you got what you wanted. He came through. Seems like he's alright."

"He's a good guy," Candace gushed. "See you were getting worried and shit." She continued as she looked at her phone to retrieve the time. "It's a quarter to nine now I better gone ahead and get my shit together."

"Code for freshen up that coochie," Allison said with a laugh. "Yeah, I get it." She rose to her feet and retrieved her bag. "Just promise me you'll be careful with this one. Make sure he's in it for all the right reasons and that he's willing to step up and be a man when you need help."

It was clear that Allison was concerned with Candace's financial stability and didn't want her to end up in a tragic situation and with a loser boyfriend who couldn't help her.

"It'll be fine," Candace said, dashing over to her closet to find something cute to throw on.

"Let me know how the job search goes, okay. And if you need anything, anything at all, like I told you...just ask."

Candace smiled at her friend. "Thanks, Ally. Now get the hell on. I'll be fine."

Ally took Candace's statement for what it was worth and showed herself to the door. She wanted the best for her friend and prayed that the woman would be spared from any more misfortunes.

***

Rico walked into the room and Candace met him halfway with a passionate kiss flesh against his juicy lips.

"Hold up Ma, let's not get too worked up," he said, pulling away from her embrace. "I need to holla you about something important."

A chill traveled through her body and instantly Candace remembered the night that Sean felt compelled to share his news with her. Sean's news hadn't been so bad, but the way that Rico was looking at her she didn't know what to expect.

"What's up? Why you acting so weird, Ricardo?" Candace asked with a serious tone and using his government name.

"Damn, shawty." He looked hurt. "It's like that?"

Candace failed to respond.

"Please don't call me by my government again," Rico stated politely. "I would really appreciate that. Damn," he said, taking a seat. "I feel weird as fuck right now. I've never cared about what a female thought until I met you. I mean, we've been kicking it pretty tough over the last couple of weeks and I just wanted to give you the opportunity to make the decision on your own instead of me making the decision for you."

Candace was confused. She took a seat next to him and leaned in to him. "What are you talking about? A decision about what? What is it you got to say, Rico? Just spit that shit out and stop beating around the bush." As she stared into his troubled eyes concerns of him living a double life occurred to her. *Fuck*, she thought. *Is this dude about to tell me he's married? Did he really wait until I caught feelings for him to spring this own me thinking there was a possibility that I'd be down to be his side chick?*

Rico sighed. He leaned forward resting his elbows on his knees and placing his face in his hands. "Okay, the reason why I've been so busy with work and not really able to talk at night or see you is because I have a little girl."

Dejavu sunk in and Candace leaned back already ready to go. She wasn't about to listen to another sob story about a marriage gone wrong and an unfortunate child caught in the middle.

"She's three years old with a cardiovascular disease called Atrial Septal Defect," he went on. "It's really damaged the function of her heart. Her name is Kelsey. This week she had two surgeries to replace her artery with an artificial one." His voice began to tremble as he went on. "According to her doctor, she needs a heart transplant because hers isn't pumping correctly. The artificial artery won't work long term. It's been a hard fucking week."

Candace stared at him, trying to decide how she felt. She could tell that he was devastated by the tone of his voice and the way he was now rocking back and forth as if he would break down at any moment.

"I've been trying to let go of my second hustle, you know? Go straight legit and shit."

Candace's posture tightened up. Had she just heard him correctly? "What do you mean go straight legit?"

"Real talk, I grew up on the bad side of Santa Monica and let's just say the streets was my father and my mother and eventually became my employer. As a kid, I stayed in and out of jail on gun charges and shit. When I got out on the last charge, I vowed to never go back. But the street life was all I knew. So, I pulled a couple of my childhood friends together and we started a trap in the hood. We became the plug for the hood." He stared up at the ceiling, feeling the weight of the world bearing down on him. "Shit was all fun and games, you know? An exciting life...until Kelsey was born."

Rico turned and looked at Candace, trying to appeal to her maternal instinct and hoping that she'd understand. "I felt like

I had a greater purpose. I served a more meaningful role in life. I was needed." He paused as he realized the sincerity of his own words. "So I tightened my shit up, enrolled in school to finish my GED, and knocked out a couple of semesters at UCLA. Kelsey's heart doctor recommended a reputable heart specialist center in South Carolina," he continued. "We've visited and it checks out. So Heather is going to move Kelsey to Greenville so she can get help from her parents."

"Heather," Candace repeated.

Rico nodded.

"The baby's mother," Candace rationalized.

"Yeah." He studied her face for a moment and knew exactly what was running through her mind. "Aye, that's over. On my word, you have nothing to worry about there."

Remembering the way he'd been so evasive in the evenings and insisted on mainly coming her way for visits made Candace wonder. She'd already been pensive about his shady behavior and now that she knew about Heather and Kelsey, her doubts were returning to the forefront. "Are you living with her now?"

"Heather? Hell no. Why would you even ask that?"

"Because of you not being able to talk at night. Because of you choosing to come here verses me come there."

"I told you. I been busy grinding and sitting with Kelsey in my free time." He took a deep breath to check his tone before continuing. "I'm telling you all of this because I care about you. I'm telling you all of this because I see a future with you and I was hoping that you felt the same way. If I was on some shady shit, trust that I wouldn't drop dime on myself by giving you any indication of what was going on."

Candace sat in silence, watching as he spoke and taking stock of her feelings. Either she was getting soft or Rico was for real. The look in his eyes and the sound of her voice made her believe that he was being honest and upfront with her. He was right; he didn't have to tell her all of his business like that if he was on some creep shit. She also knew that he must have genuinely cared for her, as he mentioned, to be sitting there revealing his emotions and sharing such a heart wrenching moment in his life with her. Instantly, she felt guilty for giving him the third degree about having another woman when he obviously had much greater concerns. Besides, they hadn't really made their relationship official anyway so who was she to get out of pocket over the chance of him being involved with someone else?

"I'm sorry," she said softly, reaching over and touching his arm. "I'm sorry for questioning you and I'm sorry for what you're going through with Kelsey. I know this can't be easy for you."

"It isn't," he admitted before pressing his lips together to ward off the sob that was trying to seep out. "But this place in South Carolina seems like our best bet. I've been looking at Charlotte or Atlanta as places to move to so that I can be closer to them but not like right up in Heather's face, you know?"

Candace nodded. "Understandable."

Rico grabbed her hands and looked deep into her eyes so that she could not only hear but feel his request. "I want you to come with me."

Her breathe was swept away by his declaration. Her eyes grew wide and she gripped his hand tighter, stunned that he'd made such a seriously grand offer at this point in their relationship.

"Don't be quiet," Rico insisted, examining Candace's nonverbal reactions. "What you thinking?"

"I...uh...well...I'll have to think about it."

"Of course. Who wouldn't?"

"It's all a bit much," Candace said, thinking of her lack of employment, switching L's school, and helping Rico with the care of his daughter whenever and however possible. Not to mention the fact that they'd known one another for a very short amount of time. "I'm glad that you are being such a great dad. That says a lot about your character."

Candace closed the gap between the two of them with a kiss. This time Rico didn't fight her off, but met her tongue with a forceful stroke of his.

"Damn," he said, once the moment passed. He'd felt the urgency and passion in her kiss and knew exactly what it was that she wanted. "I know I've been neglecting you Shawty, but I gotta find me some food first." He rubbed his stomach to prove how hungry he was.

"Oh, I have something you can eat alright," Candace said, bursting out in laughter.

Rico joined in, pushed her back onto the bed, and decided that maybe she was right; he could use an appetizer.

***

Lawrence sat at the kitchen table snacking on a bag of Spicy Nacho Doritos and staring at his sister as she made dinner. She wasn't herself. She hadn't been the same in days and he was beginning to wonder what was going on. Sure, he knew that being unemployed was taking its toll on her, but he feared that she was slowly spiraling into a depressed state that he wasn't sure how to bring her out of it.

"What's up with you?" he finally asked between crunches.

Candace began chopping up an onion and was oblivious to the question that had been fired at her.

"Candace!" Lawrence called out.

Startled, Candace stopped cutting and shot her head upward. "What!" she snapped back.

Lawrence laughed. "Dang, where were you?"

She sighed and returned her attention to chopping up the vegetable. "What are you talking about?" she asked lowly.

"You been walking 'round here like a zombie lately, sis. What's going on?"

She shook her head. "Nothing."

"That's how we doing it now?" Lawrence asked, raising a brow suspiciously. "We all we got remember? You can't be keeping secrets."

"No secrets. It's nothing...just...just go do your homework or something."

Lawrence sat straight up in his seat sucked his teeth loudly. "That's that bull."

Candace, still chopping away, glanced up and back down twice, trying to figure out where his attitude was stemming from. "What?"

"Yo, it's Saturday. Ain't no homework."

"Well then...I don't know. Read a book. Please...just...leave me alone. Owww!" She quickly looked down and saw the blood trickling from her left index finger. The juice from the onion and the sting of the cut itself made her wince. She dropped the knife and quickly sucked on her finger to apply pressure to stop the bleeding.

Lawrence jumped up. "You can't even focus to make dinner without cutting yourself." He hurried over to grab a paper towel from the opposite end of the counter.

After a few seconds Candace pulled her finger out of her mouth only for the crimson to drip once more. The sight of those red droplets brought tears to her eyes.

"Here," Lawrence insisted, thrusting the napkin at his sister.

Candace grabbed the paper towel and dabbed at her wound but couldn't keep her composure long enough to tend to it. She leaned against the counter top with her head down sobbing uncontrollably.

Lawrence was sure what to do. "Damn, it hurts that bad?"

She shook her head. "No...no," she replied, choking back her sobs. "It isn't that...it's just...it's everything."

He stared at her, trying to understand what it was that had her so unglued. An idea occurred to him and he quickly clenched his fists, ready for action. "It's that nigga ain't it?"

Candace didn't respond.

Lawrence's eyes bucked in response to her silence. "It is! It's that nigga!" He kicked the bottom cabinet with his left foot and swung his right fist through the air. "I told that nigga! I told that nigga! You got him in here making you shed tears and shit." Hastily, he walked away to grab Candace's cell phone off of the kitchen table. "Call him!" he insisted. "Call that nigga up so I can tell him what time it is."

Candace was so overcome with emotions that she could barely muster up the strength to set her brother straight. She shook her head frantically but only sobs continued to flow from her mouth.

It tore Lawrence to pieces to see his sister so emotional. The last time he'd seen her fall apart to this degree was when they were younger following the news of their parents' deaths. From that day forth he felt that it was his responsibility to have his sister's back and make certain that she never felt that kind of hurt and pain again. He was hot-headed when it came to the brothers that stepped to his sister, but only because he knew she had no one else to protect her heart.

"Fuck it," he said, unlocking her phone and strolling through her call lists to find Rico's number. "I'll call that nigga myself and he better hope his ass don't answer."

"No," Candace managed to get out, rounding the counter and approaching her brother. "L, no. You don't understand. Put the phone down."

Candace reached for her cell but Lawrence snatched away from her and took a step back. "I understand all I need to understand. You can't let these niggas run you like this, sis. Fuck I look like."

"It's none of your business! Gimme the damn phone."

By this point, the line had already rung twice and Lawrence was committed to giving Rico the business. He gritted at his sister, pissed that she would think it was okay to be all in her feelings over some dude that wasn't worth one of the many tears she was wasting.

"I'm making it my business," Lawrence spat out. "Get some backbone. Wipe ya' eyes, I'ma handle this."

"It's nothing for you to handle! Please, give me the phone, L!"

"Hello?" Rico's voice was now in Lawrence's ear, though his salutation was stalled as he listened to the struggle that was occurring in the background.

Candace pulled on Lawrence's arm with one hand and reached for the cell phone with the other. He held firm to the phone as he struggled to free his arm from her hold without pushing her away from him. As a result of their tussling over the phone, the microphone was away from his mouth as she spoke making it difficult for Rico to hear him. "You think you can just fuck my sister over and I'on do nothing, playboy?" he shouted out.

"L, please!" Candace cried out, not wanting any more drama to spark up between her little brother and her boyfriend.

With other choice, she slapped the phone out of Lawrence's hand causing it to fall to the floor with a crash. Both she and Lawrence watched as the back was knocked off by the impact causing the battery to drop to the floor and slide up under the kitchen table.

Lawrence glared at her. "You that hung up over that nigga that you'on want me to put him in his place for hurting you?"

"He didn't hurt me," she replied, shaking her head. It was all too much for her to deal with. Her life was one dramatic scene after the next and she wanted it all to end. "You don't...you don't know what you're talking about. You react...you always react without thinking, without listening!"

"You're walking 'round acting like ya' best friend died or some shit," he shot back. "You crying like your heart is broken or something and when I asked you if it was about dude you ain't say nothing."

"That's right," she seethed. "I didn't tell you that he did anything."

"You ain't tell me that he didn't either." He hesitated for a moment. "So what is it sis? Tell me it ain't the dude 'cause you damn shoul' ain't bitching up over no lil cut."

Candace took a deep breath and sunk down in one of the kitchen chairs. She was emotionally spent and didn't have the energy to lie or pretend to be okay. "It is about him."

Lawrence stepped closer to her and bent his knees to look down into her eyes while pointing his finger in her face. "I told you! I told you! I knew it. And you in here protecting that fool?"

"He didn't do anything wrong, L. It isn't like that."

"You crying, but he ain't do nothing wrong," Lawrence summed up the situation.

"It's complicated."

He reoccupied his seat at the table and stared at his sister. "Educate me."

She turned her head to the side to look at him for a long moment. Finally, she decided that maybe she'd feel better if she just let it all out. "He has a kid," she said. "A daughter who's sick and is moving to South Carolina."

Lawrence raised a brow. "So what you saying? Rico moving to South Carolina to be with his kid? He still getting up with the baby's mama?"

She shook her head. "No, no. It's not like that. The mama's taking the baby to Greensboro, but Rico wants to move closer to there so he can see his daughter often and be close enough to get to her if and when he needs to."

"So he's moving?" Lawrence asked again.

Candace nodded and lowered her head.

"And your heart really is broken 'cause he's leaving," Lawrence stated, trying to put two and two together.

"He asked for us to go with him," Candace said softly.

"Word?"

"At first he wasn't sure if he was gonna move somewhere in South Carolina or maybe Atlanta. He told me this about a week and a half ago. But yesterday..." Her voice trailed off and she paused to give the tears time to subside. "Yesterday he told me that he'd settled upon Atlanta."

Understanding washed over Lawrence and he felt a cold, eerie feeling creep into his body. "So, he wants us to move to Atlanta with him? We can't go back there, Candace. We can't go back. What did you tell him? Did you tell him yes?"

"I didn't tell him anything. I mean, I told him I'd think about it."

"What's to think about? If we go back there she'll find us and harass us and ain't no telling what kinda tricks that witch will pull to get in our business. You know she ain't wrapped too tight."

She considered being honest with him by letting him know that Aunt Robyn had long since found them and had been harassing her, but she didn't want to worry the child. Hell, she didn't even want to tell him about the prospect of them returning to Atlanta because she knew that it wouldn't resonate well with him given his past experiences living in the city. He had a reputation there as well as a record. The Atlanta Police wouldn't hesitate to throw the book at her brother if he made one wrong move. With Lawrence's temper and the bad influences that she knew would be likely to surround him,

Candace didn't want to chance it. There was no way she'd risk her brother's future just to chase after some man.

"I know we can't go back," Candace whispered, wiping her eyes free of moisture. "I know it."

Lawrence studied his sister's body language. She was hurting. She'd sacrificed so much to keep them together and to take care of him. At every turn he'd given her hell, yet she loved him just the same and was always putting him first. After coming back from their mini vacation he could tell that she was really feeling this Rico cat. He liked the way her eyes lit up, her mood was lifted, and she wasn't attached to a bottle frequently. He'd started feeling like Rico was doing his sister some good up until she'd recently began behaving like a depressed recluse.

Who was he to keep her from happiness? If Candace wanted to start a life with Rico then he didn't want to be the reason she had to give that up. Sure, they'd have to dodge Aunt Robyn and pray that she'd just leave them alone. That would be the hard part. But, Lawrence knew that Candace's greatest concern was keeping him out of jail. Perhaps now was the time to show his sister that he could exercise self-control and could be trusted.

"If you wanna go, we should go," he told her.

Candace turned to look at him as if she'd seen a ghost. "What?"

"If you wanna go, we should go," he repeated. "I mean, if you feel like this dude is the one for you then I want you to be happy...no matter what."

"But Aunt Robyn—"

"Forget her. It's you and me, right? We're all the family we need."

Candace's heart thudded in her chest at the possibility of being able to secure the happily-ever-after that she'd often dreamed about. "And you?"

He knew what she was asking. "I'll be on my best behavior. I promise."

"I need more than your promise, L. Once we do this shit, that's just it. You can't be getting caught up out there. You have to play it straight and stay out of the bullshit. I'm not playing with you."

"I get it. I'm telling you, you ain't gotta worry about me. I'ma go to school, come home, and find a hobby or some shit. I'm gonna do right. I swear on everything." He watched as hope filled her eyes. "I want you to be happy sis. Mom and Dad would want you to follow your heart."

At the mention of their parents she reached across the table and grabbed her brother's hand. "They would want me to look after you."

"And you do that."

"Are you sure about this?"

He nodded.

Candace smiled. "You look more and more like Dad every day. And this what you're doing for me...this selflessness, this concern for my happiness...he'd be proud of you."

Now it was Lawrence's turn to beam proudly as his eyes glazed over with tears.

"You miss them don't you?"

He nodded again. "Every day," he answered, sounding as if a frog was caught in his throat.

"Me too," Candace whispered, squeezing his hand even tighter. "Me too...but we've got each other. That's never going to change."

Lawrence lowered his head, trying his best to remember what his parents looked like. If it wasn't for the few pictures that Candace was able to savage he'd have very little recollection of their likeness. He thought about their demise, biting his lip at the memory of their totaled vehicle and the night they'd learned of the accident. "No one ever said anything to you in all these years about their DUI crash?" he asked pitifully.

Candace shook her head, not wanting to give in to the euphoric memories of their past. "No. I haven't checked in a very long time."

"Hmmm. And Aunt Robyn's never been any help. She never even seemed to care."

"To be completely honest with you, I kind of gave up on finding out anything. It's done now," she stated sadly. "We have to learn to move forward and let it go."

Even as the words escaped her mouth, Candace knew that the task was easier said than done. They'd never be able to get their parents out of their hearts and minds, which was to be expected. But trying to move past their many questions surrounding their parents' alleged accident was difficult especially when Candace had been involved of a DUI incident of her own. The memory shook Lawrence. All he wanted to do was ball up in his mother's lap right now and cry. He'd give anything to have his parents back. But it was a wish that would never come true no matter how hard he prayed for it.

Candace squeezed his hand. "We're going to be okay," she tried to assure him. "We'll move with Rico, I'll find a job, you'll stay out of trouble, and we'll stay as far away from Aunt Robyn as possible. Okay?"

Lawrence nodded his agreement.

"I've got you," Candace told him. "No matter what, I've always got you."

CHAPTER 7

"What the fuck L?" Candace was fuming. Her chest was getting tighter and tighter by the second as she tried to listen to her brother explain his position.

"Sis, I didn't have shit to do with that chick or that bitch ass dude," Lawrence protested with his hands in the air as if the gesture gave his statement more validity.

"Bro, didn't we have an agreement? Didn't we?" Her voice cracked as she tried to stay calm. "No trouble. You promised me that. I've only been at my job for two months now."

Candace had landed a position as a paralegal at a law firm after they moved the move to Atlanta. Jackson and Duncan Law Agency now signed her checks thanks to some strings that Allison was able to pull with a guy she knew from back in the day, Kadyn Carter fondly referred to around the office as KC. It was KC who had vouched for Candace making his boss Mr. Jackson feel more than confident about offering her the job; a job utilizing a skill in which she'd never acquired but had to learn quickly again thanks to her own private tutor and on the job trainer, KC.

She was settling into the job, overlooking her trifling ass supervisor, Ms. Shirley, and managing not to drown any of her small worries in booze upon returning home from work each day. She found solace in finding Rico and Lawrence at home to lift her spirits after a long day of paper pushing and errand running. The two of them were her world, but now Lawrence was fucking up the serenity of it all with his usual bullshit.

"It's alright sis," Lawrence tried to convince her. "Why you spazzing like that?"

"Spazzing like what, Lawrence?"

"Aye, come on. Chill with all that Lawrence stuff, sis," he said, offended that she was calling him by his given name verses his nickname.

"Lawrence Williams II, is that better for you?" Her attitude was off of the charts.

"Sis, chill the fuck out."

She was dismayed by the way he was speaking to her as they stood in the crowded lobby of the Atlanta Police Department. "Lawrence Williams II is my little brother, everyone!"

"Is that what we do now, CeCe?" he asked, pissed off that she was blowing his street credibility by treating him like some punk ass kid.

Their verbal sparring caught the attention of others nearby. On older woman yelled out her two cents. "Tell him, girl. Get his ass in line. These lil young boys 'round here think they have all the answers. They'on know shit."

A roar spread through the heavily populated area as others began to have their own disagreements over how the young street boys were perceived verses how the old school street folk saw things. It was clear that the prescient wasn't used to getting this much ruckus and unruly activity over such a petty debate. The area guards became unorganized, trying to silence all of the civilians while the officers manning the desks got antsy with trying to rush through whatever paperwork they were dealing with in an effort to move more people out.

Candace tried to ignore everything else that was going on around them. “What the fuck did you do?” she whispered.

Lawrence huffed, his frustration elevating because he was tired of going over and over the same predicament. “I didn't do shit. I was fucking with KP. You remember KP, right? You used to have class with his older sister back when.”

Candace thought about it for a second. "Oh Shelia’s little brother?"

“Right, right. Him! So we rolled up on this broad that he was telling me about. I’m chilling in the car breaking down a Grape White Owl to twist up some kush, listening to that Nikki & Chris Brown joint, right...all of sudden my weed fell over. I bend down to scoop my shit up but when I looked up, I seen this big ass motherfucka punch the shit out of KP. I guess it was somebody that KP’s broad knew or some shit ‘cause she was yelling for ‘em to stop and shit.”

Candace clutched her chest as she listened to Lawrence’s story unfold. Hurry up and get to the fucking point, she thought, feeling herself on the verge of losing her cool. The police department was one of the last places she wanted to be and she definitely wasn’t fond of the fact that Lawrence was the reason why she was there.

“So, KP recovered and kicked ole boy in the jewels then he bodied the dude. That shit was like, quick. He started starting stomping the fuck out of him. And then—”

“Alright, time’s up,” an officer stated, interrupting Lawrence in mid-sentence while towering over brother and sister as they sat huddled on a rickety, peeling, brown wooden bench.”

"I need a few more minutes with my sister," Lawrence said, throwing the officer a glance over his shoulder.

The officer paid no attention to Lawrence's request. To him, Lawrence was just another delinquent, another intake case, another criminal. "I said it's time to go," the burly officer barked as he firmly grabbed Lawrence by the forearm forcing him to his feet. He then looked down at Candace. "You've got to go now, Ma'am."

Lawrence tried to snatch his arm away but was unsuccessful. "Man, take ya' hands off me, playboy," he seethed.

The officer chuckled. "I see we got us a live one here. Looks like I'm gonna have fun showing you just how much of a bad ass you really are not."

Candace began to wheeze as she watched the officer place her brother in handcuffs. Lawrence had never known when to shut up even when he was staring trouble dead in the face. Candace was scared for him and her body was beginning to physically react to the stress that was mounting. "It's going to be okay, L," she said, between struggled breaths. She stood to her feet. "I'm gonna make sure I get you out. I promise." Her air passages were failing her with each word that she spoke. "I-I-I love y-y-you. Please...please be careful."

Unmoved, the officer turned Lawrence around and shoved him forward.

"What the fuck!" Lawrence exclaimed. "I know my rights, man, and I ain't no fuckin' animal. Don't be pushing on me and shit like I'm yo' kid or some shit."

"You got a lot of mouth, boy," the officer shot back, ushering him through the security checkpoint.

Lawrence stopped dead in his tracks turning to face the older man with hate in his eyes and his nostrils flaring with anger and intent. Even with his hands behind his back in the cuffs, Candace knew that his fists were bald up. She knew her brother and his temperament all too well.

"Boy?" Lawrence repeated. "I got yo' boy."

"You don't have shit," he officer told him, glaring down at him as if daring Lawrence to get out of line.

"Lawrence!" Candace called out, seeing exactly where the situation was headed. She stepped forward only to be stopped by another cop.

"Ma'am, you're not allowed beyond this point," the officer advised her.

Candace felt helpless as she looked past the officer in front of her and over at her brother as he continued to face off with his police escort. "S-s-stop!" she tried to call out. "Lawrence, plea-please. Don't do it!"

"You don't wanna make your first night more difficult than it already will be, son," the officer told Lawrence. "Save all that bravado for when you're really gonna need it."

"I'on need yo' bitch ass telling me what to do or when to do it. You ain't my daddy, nigga."

The officer grinned and stepped close enough to Lawrence so that the boy could feel the man's breath on his face. "You're in custody of the city now, boy. That makes me your damn boss, your overseer, your teacher, your puppet master, and even your got-damn daddy."

That was all the ammo that Lawrence needed to seal his fate in front of a room of officers and civilian witnesses. With as much force as he could muster up, he threw his head forward and quickly head-butted the officer dead in the nose. The officer's yelp along with a cracking sound caught everyone's attention. Only a fragment of a second passed before nearly every officer in the receiving area was toppled on Lawrence who was immediately tossed to the ground.

"Son-of-a-bitch!" the injured officer cursed, touching his hands to his face practically washing them in his own blood.

"Oh my god," Candace whispered, her eyes wide with shock. It was like watching a scene from a movie. It was a horrible sight, but she just couldn't turn away.

Lawrence struggled on the ground from the weight of the officers apprehending him. "Get off of me! Get the fuck off of me."

"You just earned yourself an extended stay for assault and battery of a law official you dumb fuck," the officer called out through the thicket of his peers surrounding them.

Several male cops yanked Lawrence up from the floor. A gash was on his own forehead from being pummeled to the ground and jumped on. His eyes frantically searched the crowd as he winced and trembled like a wounded animal being forced into captivity. The officers tried to get him to walk towards the entrance to his destiny, Lawrence's feet were planted to the ground, though unsteadily. He refused to be moved.

"Let's go!" the cop to his left called out.

Lawrence's eyes finally found Candace's.

In no mood for foolishness, the officers lifted Lawrence slightly off of the ground and carried him towards the entry way.

"Get me out sis!" Lawrence yelled as the officers man-handled him through the large, automatic, double doors. "Don't leave me in here. Get me out! Get me out!"

His pleading became in inaudible as Candace watched the doors slowly close behind her brother's retreating figure. The moment they clanged shut, reality swept her off of her feet and stole the air from her lungs. Tears were streaming down her face and she could no longer control her troubled breaths. Candace bent over, still clutching her chest as she tore through her purse in search of her inhaler. She hadn't had such a powerful asthma attack in months and knew without a doubt that stress was killing her. Finding the pump, she plopped down onto the bench and inhaled two puffs of the medication. Slowly, she felt the constriction ease up and she leaned her head back over the top of the bench. *Jesus be with us,* she thought, not knowing how she was going to deal with this situation. *I should have stayed my ass in Tucson. At least there my brother wouldn't have been five-o's target.*

***

"Babe, stop crying." Rico spoke softly. "It's going to be alright. I hate seeing you like this. What's wrong?" He'd just gotten home from a tiring day and had plans on taking a long hot shower, eating whatever she'd made for dinner, and cuddling up with the woman who had stolen his heart. But, the moment he entered their modest home and didn't smell the aroma of food he knew that something was askew.

"My, my..." Her voice cracked in between tears as she tried to voice her issues.

Rico kneeled down before her as she sat on the sofa with her face down and eyes swollen from crying. "What's wrong?"

he asked again, reaching out to wipe her face with his fingertips.

A long pause separated the two voices.

"The police...th-they...they got L on one count of terroristic threats, aggravated battery, leaving the scene of felony—"

"Damn," Rico let out, covering his mouth with his fist.

"And—"

"And?" His eyes were filled with askance wondering what the hell else the teenager could have possibly done.

"Assault of an officer."

Yep, Rico thought. *He done fucked up*. "Damn, boo," He thought about the situation for a minute before rising and taking a seat next to Candace. "It's going to be okay," he said, placing an arm lovingly around her shoulders as her body continued to shaking with crying. "What they saying 'bout bail?"

"They made his bail $50,000.00 cash or $100,000.00 on collateral." She turned to look at her lover. "He isn't supposed to be in there."

"Babe, he assaulted an officer."

"But only because he was so adamant about his innocence and the cop kept fucking with him. He didn't do anything this time. I can tell he wasn't lying this time. They got him in there with all of those rapists and murders." Candace continued to weep louder. "He's just a baby...my baby..."

"Innocent or not regarding them other charges boo, L gotta man up about the thing he did do. Assaulting an officer? That shit alone is what's gonna fuel the judge's fire."

Candace shook her head. “He didn’t mean it, Rico. He’s just scared...he’s scared.” Her sobs took over.

Rico squeezed her shoulders and kissed her forehead.

“I love him. I can’t let my baby just...just sit there.”

“I know,” Rico said soothingly. “I know, babe. We’re gonna help him. We’re gon’ do the best we can. How much do we have in the savings account?"

Since moving in together, they’d combined their finances like a true couple and Candace was the treasurer of their relationship, handling all of their expenses. She looked up for a moment before responding. “Ummm, I think about thirty-five K... but I thought that was for emergencies. I mean, isn’t Kelsey going to need meds and stuff? I don't feel right putting us in that type of a bind.”

"Babe, what do you think this is?" Rico asked.

"We can't use all of that. If we do then we won't be able to take care of anything else."

“What other choice do we have, sweetheart?" He placed his tatted hands over Candace's. "I hate seeing you cry."

She looked up into his eyes and smiled. “And here I thought you were a male chauvinist when I first met you.”

They both began to laugh despite the circumstances.

“Come on,” Rico prompted, trying to veer them back on course. “We’ll be straight no matter what, I promise.” He gave her a huge, reassuring hug and a kiss.

“Still,” Candace said softly. “We can’t use all of that money. We can’t deplete our savings like that. I mean, truthfully after we pay the bond we’ll still need to finance his legal fees.”

Rico nodded because she had a point. "Do you have any family members that you can get to contribute to it? I mean, I don't have family but if I did I'd ask for help in a heartbeat."

Candace looked down at her hands and considered it. She hadn't let Rico in on that part of her life. All he knew about was her and Lawrence so far as her family ties went. But, hearing him pose the question her mind immediately went to Aunt Robyn. It didn't help matters that she was there in Atlanta and easily accessible should she decide to reach out to her. She took a deep breath, trying to figure out whether or not it was anyone's best interest for her to approach Robyn. Did she want to have anything to do with the woman and how she made her money? Would Lawrence appreciate the help or would he rather just take his chances in jail? Would Robyn use their vulnerability as an opportunity to blackmail her into some bullshit and hold her assistance over their heads? Candace knew the answer to that one with no hesitancy. Of course her aunt would gloat every second she got about how she saved their asses once again. Who knew what price she'd have to pay in exchange for Aunt Robyn's help?

Candace slowly looked up at Rico. It was a gamble, but her spirit told her that this was a risk she'd just have to take. Her only problem would be making sure that Rico never found out the complete truth about Robyn's business. "There is this one aunt," she said softly."

"Okay. Can we hit her up?" Rico asked. "Where is she?"

"Here," she answered. "In Atlanta."

Rico's brow rose. "Word? Why didn't you say anything?"

She shrugged. "We aren't close." It wasn't a lie.

"Is she the only family y'all have?"

She nodded.

"You feel comfortable hitting her up? I mean, you think she can help?"

Candace gave a half smile. "Oh, yeah. She can help."

"Good. I say let's ask her. You want me to go with you?"

Candace shook her head. She wanted to keep him as far away from the truth as possible. "You don't have to do that." She let out a loud breath. "Ughhh!! Fucking Lawrence! How can you love someone so much and hate them at the same time when they make stupid decisions?" She rose from her seat and wiped at her eyes with the back of her hands.

"Where you going?"

"Might as well get it over with," she answered. *Let's just pray that Aunt Robyn isn't trying to impress one of her clients or anything*, she thought, not wanting to walk in on her aunt's business in full throttle.

"Where she stay?"

"I'm going to visit her little office on the south side."

Rico's face hardened. "Are you sure you want to go down there alone? Those people have no freaking sense down there."

"Yea, I'm sure. I gotta act fast. I can't just let Lawrence sit there." She grabbed her purse and took out a compact to check the damage she'd done to her face.

Rico jumped up. "I'ma go with you."

Candace held her hand up in protest. "No, please. I can handle it."

"Bullshit. I'm not letting you go to that side of town by yourself. You wanna have a heart to heart with your estranged aunt by yaself, cool. But, I'ma be right there to make sure nobody fucks with you."

She couldn't argue with that. When Rico put his foot down about something there was no changing his mind. Candace had to admit that she appreciated the way he cared for her. He was a good man. She only hoped that nothing happened during their visit to make him think any less of her.

***

"And who are you?" the desk clerk asked, pausing her nail file in mid-air as she looked up at the duo that had just walked through the stained double glass doors unexpectedly.

The look of annoyance on the receptionist's boney face didn't sit well with Candace. Neither did the grandeur of the office she'd only been in once upon returning to the states to retrieve her brother. The décor, all artsy and overly done was a testament to the money that Robyn was obviously raking in. It astounded Candace to know that her aunt had more or less obtained a storefront for her candy-shop of whores and was passing it off as a legit business with her fake sense of class in the middle of the hood.

"My name is Candace," she said as politely as she could. "I'm here to see Robyn."

"Do you have an appointment?" a flamboyantly gay guy asked as he walked up to the desk and handed the girl a folder. "Go," he told her. "File that."

The chick with the stank attitude tossed her nail file onto the desk, took the folder, and disappeared behind a door to her left.

"I don't have an appointment," Candace said. "But I'm sure she'd want to see me."

"Last name please?"

"Williams"

"Ma'am, I don't see your name on the list of visitors for Ms. Robyn today or her approved drop-ins."

"Approved drop-ins?" Candace asked. Just like Robyn to have some flunkies upfront to hamper those she was avoiding from getting to her. She shook her head at the thought.

"Sorry," the dude said, smirking at them not the least bit apologetically. "Try making an appointment for later."

"I don't have later," Candace retorted.

"And I don't have a follow up suggestion for you."

"Well how about you call her then, cuz!" Rico blurted out, not at all comfortable in the highfalutin environment with the people looking down their noses at them.

The gay dude turned his nose and pointed his finger. "No, Sir! I'm going to need you to calm down. We do not tolerate that type of tone in our place of business." He adjusted his navy blue polo shirt and his khaki pants as if it had worn him out to issue that verbal warning. "We have protocol here, hunny."

"Cuz, call your boss and tell her that her niece is at the front to see her, sweet ass nigga," Rico shot back.

The guy, standing a full 6'4 and weighing at least 275 pounds, leaned forward and glared at the man before him. "I said, *Sir*, we do not tolerate that type of tone in our place of business. Now, if you have a problem we can step out to the parking lot and fix said problem."

Just as the statement left his lips, Robyn's longtime personal assistant, Leal stepped out of a closed door and sauntered the short distance of the hall. She focused in on the scene and was surprised. "Now Candace, why are up here giving our people a hard time?

Candace turned to acknowledge the voice. "Leal!!!!!! What's up, girl?"

The two embraced in a hug and soft kisses to each side of the cheek. Leal had just started being at Robyn's beck and call when Candace had finally broken free from her aunt's hold. "You still work for Robyn, girl? Candace asked with a surprised look. She'd hoped for so much more from the girl who'd once appeared so innocent and doe eyed with nowhere to go and no one to turn to but the leech that picked her up off of the street.

Leal was about 5'9 with light skin. Candace felt that Leal was that chick that always tried to take the easy way out. She'd started out as a mere call girl but from the looks of things she'd graduated to a much higher position in Robyn's little dynasty.

"You know I'm not going anywhere," Leal replied. "Even though your aunt is a bitch at times, she's my bitch. Family's family and we're all we've got."

The two laughed but for different reasons. For Leal, it was a cool to think back on how she'd gotten to this point and how Robyn had saved her from the streets by taking her in and placing her within her organization. For Candace it was amazing to see how loyal people were to Robyn when she knew the woman was nothing but an opportunist. Robyn was Candace's flesh and blood but her loyalty to her would never be anything compared to the dedication and devotion in Leal's heart.

Rico cleared his throat as he eyed the feisty assistant still standing at the desk. He was more than willing to take the guy up on his offer.

Candace looked backward and gave Rico a blank stare. There was no way that she was about to let him get into an altercation. They had enough problems at the moment.

"Alright, alright damn," Rico replied, backing down.

"Who is this, CeCe? Leal asked inquisitively.

Candace made a quick introduction. "Leal, Rico. Rico, Leal. Baby, me and Leal went to school together at McNair High. Have you talk to anyone since school?"

"Actually, a few of our classmates work here."

Candace was surprised. She would have never guessed that the girls she'd grown up with would actually want to build a life for themselves around loaning out their bodies. "I see you been doing nice for yourself," she commented.

"Thank you. A bitch had to work for this. I retired from the streets. I have two kids now. I put in the time so now, I'm living well."

Candace wondered how many Johns Leal had gone through before she entered retirement mode. The thought saddened her. "Congrats on the kids," she stated.

"I heard you were in the service. How was that?

Rico cleared his throat again. They'd come down there for a reason and it wasn't so that Candace could play catch-up with her old school buddy. He was feeling uncomfortable for some odd reason and simply wanted Candace to handle her business so that they could bounce.

Leal looked Rico up and down. "Girlllll, you better get your man. His rude ass."

"Mmmhmmm," the gay guy co-signed. "All kinds of rude."

"I got them, Ramon."

"Humph. Okay boo," Ramon replied as he and Rico made eye contact once more.

"Follow me girl," Leal said, turning around to access the pin code to get into the back offices. "Neither one of y'all have a gun or any sharp objects do you?"

"Yea," Rico answered. "I got my bitch with me."

Candace was slightly surprised to hear that he'd come in with his gun.

"Well, you and your *bitch* have stay out here," Leal advised, blocking the threshold and standing between Candace and Rico, "because you and your *bitch* can't come back here."

Rico looked at Candace with a blank stare. She didn't want any trouble. She also didn't want Rico to know more than he had to.

"It's okay, babe," Candace said. "You might as well wait for me in the lobby. Aunt Robyn wouldn't be too pleased to have someone new sprung on her anyway."

Rico's eyes were filled with concern. "You sure?"

She nodded. "I'll be out in a few, okay?"

Reluctantly, he conceded. "I'll be right out here if you need me."

Candace smiled lovingly as Leal allowed the door to close behind them.

"He's a charmer," Leal stated as she head to the glass door that led to the Queen Bee's throne.

"He really is," Candace shot back.

Leal lingered at the door with her hand on the knob. “Why are you here?” she asked her old friend. “I mean, you left so abruptly and with such an attitude about the whole thing so...why are you back?”

“It’s personal.”

“Is it? You know I owe this woman my life. If you’re here to make waves then let me encourage you to just turn right back around and leave now.”

Leal’s tone came off as both threatening and pleading. Candace couldn’t believe that the girl was so caught up under Robyn’s spell that she’d step to her the way she was. Leal was obviously naïve to Robyn’s treacherous side. All the same, she Candace wasn’t about to be punked by one of her aunt’s slaves.

“I have family business to discuss with her,” Candace explained. “Nothing more, nothing less.”

Leal looked at her for a long moment trying to decide whether or not she believed the girl. Finally, she turned the knob and entered the office. “Robyn, you have a special guest.”

Robyn spun around in her chair to look at her assistant. “Did I ask for a special guest?”

“No, but I asked to see you, so don’t take it out on her,” Candace stated, stepping into plain view.

Robyn’s interest was piqued as she laced her fingers together and smiled at her niece. “Candace,” she said with an air of bewilderment. “I can’t believe it’s you.”

“Is that so?”

Robyn rose from her desk and walked over to engulf Candace in the fakest hug Candace had ever received. She didn’t even bother to squeeze her back even lightly.

Robyn pulled away with her hands still lingering on Candace's forearms. "You look well," she stated, staring the girl dead in the eyes. "It's good to see you again."

"I'm sure."

"Can I get you anything? Something to eat or drink?"

Candace shook her head. "This isn't a social visit."

Robyn's brow rose and she dropped her hands to her sides. "Leave us now, Leal. Thank you."

Leal didn't utter a word as she exited the office and closed the door behind her.

"So, to what do I owe the pleasure of this unexpected visit to my work place?" Robyn asked staring at her niece.

"I won't mince words," Candace stated.

"By all means, let's jump right into it."

"Lawrence is in trouble."

"What's new?"

"He's in jail," Candace said, ignoring her aunt's rude comment. "His bail is set at $50,000.00 and I can't afford that on my own."

"Ahhh," Robyn let out. "So you've come to me for a loan?"

"Yes," Candace answered, beginning to feel unsure of herself. "A small one. I mean, I'll pay you back as soon as I'm able. I have a job, but I have expenses and my boyfriend's daughter—"

Robyn held her hand up. "I don't need an explanation. You have a problem and you came to me for help. I get that. That's what family does."

Listening to her once again equate them as family irked Candace but there was nothing she could do or say because the truth was that she needed her in that moment.

Robyn walked over to her desk and sat on the edge of her, crossing her legs and staring hard at Candace. "The only issue is that I'm not too keen on giving out loans."

Candace rolled her eyes. "Don't do this. Do you know how hard it was for me to come down here and ask you for help at all?"

"Of course I do, darling. I'm sure that it was the last thing you wanted to do but I know that you're dedicated to saving your poor little delinquent, career criminal of a brother."

"He's not a career criminal! He's just a lost boy and as I remember correctly your influence placed him in such a position."

"I will not take credit for that boy's fallacies. I'm not one to shove a young person into the arms of the streets. If anything, I save them from the streets. Even you can attest to that via Leal." Robyn smiled mischievously.

"What you did was pushed her into the arms of any and every man that would pay top dollar for a lil' young thang."

"I saved her from a life of homelessness and drugs. I saved her from herself!"

"You saved her from the common pimps on the street that I give you credit for. But look around Aunt; you're nothing more than a glorified pimp yourself."

Robyn laughed. "A glorified pimp that you've come to for money."

Candace bit her lower lip. She wanted to tell Aunt Robyn to go to hell, but this was her only chance of helping Lawrence. "I need $40,000.00 to put up for his bail. And then we'll need his legal fees taken care of. We can set up a payment plan to go into effect as soon as possible."

Robyn considered it. "Okay. We can do that. But I'm not sitting around waiting for your little paychecks to clear and get my money monthly. You'll work your debt off until we're even."

"Excuse me?"

"Did I stutter?" Robyn snapped. "I'm not just handing you over money like that on the whim that you'll be able to repay with your pitling earnings. I believe that if you want anything in life you have to work for it. You're no exception."

"And by work for it you mean..." Candace waited for her to fill in the blank.

Robyn reached over and pressed a button on her phone. "Leal, bring me in a blank work agreement please." She tapped the button again and looked at Candace before plucking a sticky note off of the pad on her desk and jotting something down. "I mean, that you'll work for the $40,000.00, sweetheart. Like anyone of the other girls that want money from me, you'll be on call."

"Are you fucking kidding me?" Candace was livid. "I've told you on multiple occasions that I'm not loaning out my body, my kitty, or my time for your sick ass gain. Why are you always trying to force me into this business of yours?!"

Leal walked in without saying a word and handed the contract over to Robyn. In turn, Robyn handed her the sticky note.

"Face it, Candace," Robyn stated. "You were destined to be a part of the family business. You can't get away from your destiny."

"Bull shit."

"I've created a legacy here and I want my family to be a part of it. There's room for all of us to benefit if you'd just stop fighting the truth and see things my way."

"But I'm not benefiting from it. You're forcing me into bondage as a way to repay you."

Leal turned and left the room as quietly as she'd come.

Robyn scribbled a few words onto the document. "I'm not forcing you to do anything. Yes, this is our payment plan but only if you choose to do it. I'm not holding a gun to your head or making the decision for you. But, I believe that after you see how quickly the numbers add up, how quickly you can potentially earn...how quickly your debt will be paid off, you'll want to stick around to actually make a profit."

"I can't believe you," Candace seethed, her eyes welling up. "Your only nephew is behind bars and I'm trying to help him but all you can think about is making money off of using me. What kind of twisted person are?"

"The kind who's about her business. Besides, you came to me remember?" She waved the contract in the air. "What are you going to do?

Deciding that it wasn't worth the trouble, Candace shook her head and turned away. "Fuck you. I should have never come here." She headed for the door.

"That's your decision," Robyn called out. "But how are you going to save Lawrence with your pride all in the way? Sometimes you have to do whatever it takes to save the one's you love. You're the one always harping on you and he are all you have. What's he gonna do when his only source doesn't come through?"

Candace paused with her back to her aunt. Her heart ached at the mention of Lawrence's potential disappointment. She couldn't let him face his legal issues alone. She couldn't let him rot in jail until the system decided to give him a biased trial. She couldn't bear to think of what would happen to him behind those steel curtains. Candace loved Lawrence more than life itself and would give her own life in order to preserve his. If nothing else, Lawrence was her weakness and Aunt Robyn was preying on that.

Wiping her nose with the back of her hand and sucking up her tears, Candace turned back around and faced her aunt who was still holding the contract in her hand. She pursed her lips together wondering how Rico would feel knowing that his girlfriend was a call girl. How would she ever be able to explain things to him? She was in a bind and there were no other feasible alternatives. Robyn had what she needed and just like the devil, she was requiring Candace's soul in order to supply her with a way out of the mess her family was in.

Pushing her misgivings to the back of her mind, Candace walked forward, snatched the contract from her aunt, flipped to the back page, and laid it on the desk beside Robyn's round hips in order to place her signature on the dotted line. A tear fell from her cheek as she dotted the 'I' in her last name. It instantly smudged the letter but Candace kept going. She handed the form back to her aunt and spoke through clenched teeth. "This is only until I repay you for the $40,000.00 and I'll figure his court fees out on my own. This does not mean you owe me and I need that check today."

"You'll have it today," Robyn stated, picking up the agreement and smiling at it. "Your idea of repaying me immediately is on point. Expect a call by tomorrow evening." She smiled at Candace. "You'll see sweet pea. This can be good for everyone. Once you realize your full earning potential you'll be begging me to become a partner."

"Don't count on it," Candace responded, turning away and heading to the door. She couldn't get out of that office fast enough. Her chest was heaving and everything became a blur. Had she just signed herself over to Robyn after years and years of protesting?

As she headed towards the door to return to the lobby, Leal approached her from yet another office door.

"This is for you," Leal stated, startling Candace. She handed Candace an envelope.

Candace peeped inside to find a check for the full $40,000.00. Robyn had wasted no time in getting it to her. Apparently, she'd been awfully certain that Candace would succumb to her wishes.

"Welcome to the business," Leal stated sarcastically. "Isn't it funny where life brings you back to?"

Candace stared at her old friend for a moment. "You said you owe her," she said.

"What?"

"Robyn...you said you owe her because she saved you. But you don't owe her shit. She preyed on your vulnerability and suckered you into believing that the hell she placed you in was far better than any other hell you could have potentially suffered from."

"How can you be so ungrateful?" Leal asked.

"What?" Candace was astonished by what she was hearing.

"Robyn has been nothing but good to me and she had you and your brother living a decent life that you practically shitted on. Then you come back her and ask for a job only to continue shitting on her. Who does that? You never heard that phrase don't bite the hand that feeds you?"

"You're so off base."

"And you're so full of shit." Leal moved to turn away and then paused. "Don't fuck with Robyn. Do your job and don't create trouble for any of us and you'll be just fine. I don't know what you're used to or what's happened to you since your little accident and ya' military experience, but around here Robyn is the boss and if you shit on her she'll chew you up and spit your ass out." She walked off without another word.

Candace pushed the button and exited through the door to the lobby. Her life had just changed and there was no going back. Nothing would ever be the same. That's the way it was when you got caught up in Robyn's web. Leal was a clear example of that. The girl she'd once been cool with had more or less just threatened her on her aunt's behalf. Somehow, Candace couldn't help but feel responsible for what had happened to Leal.

"You good?" Rico asked, taking in the panicked look on Candace's face.

She nodded. "Let's go," she answering hauling ass to the door, ready to free herself of Robyn's spell and her office.

Nothing would ever be the same.

***

2006 - Atlanta, GA

Candace was riding shotgun in her aunt's pastel pink Cadillac as they cruised down a side street near Candler Road after leaving the mall. She'd gone along on a clothes run at Macy's as Aunt Robyn picked out a few pieces for her girls. She had a thing about her girl's looking like something and not coming off as common trash. It was astounding to Candace how her aunt could jazz up the fact that she was running girls by always trying to instill some kind of culture and class into them. As they sat at a red light, Candace noticed a familiar figure sitting by the side of the road balled up with sign in front of her.

"Leal," Candace said as she stared out of the window.

"What's that?" Aunt Robyn asked. "Speak up, child. What did I tell you about all that shy talking? Be demure only when the moment calls for it."

Candace pointed at the girl on the side of the road. "That's my friend. She hasn't been at school in weeks. Can I talk to her? Please?"

Aunt Robyn rolled her eyes but pulled over so that Candace could get out. It wasn't so much that she cared about her niece's friend; she was just never one to miss an opportunity to solicit new talent.

Candace ran over to the girl. "Leal! Leal! It's me, Coerce."

Leal's head shot up and immediately her eyes were filled with humiliation. She tried to lower her sign but it was too late. Candace had already read the plea for spare change.

"What are you doing out here?" Candace asked, taking in her unkempt appearance. "Why you ain't been in school?"

"Can't go to school if I can't even bathe and have clean clothes."

Candace was confused. "What are you talking about? What happened?"

"We got put out."

"Of your apartment?" Candace looked around. "Where's your mom?"

Leal shrugged. "Been gone a week before they put us out. Ain't no telling. Probably somewhere laid up with a needle in her arm."

Candace's shock was evident.

"Yeah, that's right," Leal said. "My mama's a junkie. So now you gon' go back to school and tell everybody that my mom's a J and I'm homeless, huh? You might as well. Don't matter no way. I'm not going back to school."

Candace kneeled on the ground and shook her head feeling remorseful of Leal's situation. "I wouldn't do that," she said. "I'd never spread your business like that, girl. I'm your friend. You don't have no family you could stay with?"

Leal shook her head and sniffed as tears began to fall. "It was just me and her."

Candace bit her lip and looked back over at the car where her aunt was waiting. She wasn't very sure of her own living arrangements these days given the stuff that her aunt made her do, but she was sure that Leal would be much better off in a warm house than living on the streets. "Stay here for a second," she said, jumping up and running back to the car. She snatched the door open and slid inside without closing the door.

"Are you done with your social hour now?" Aunt Robyn asked. "Can we please go so that I may get back to my

business or did you need me to drop you off to visit someone else?"

She sensed that her aunt was annoyed but she had to ask. "My friend's out on the street," she said.

"I can see that."

"She don't have no family."

"She doesn't have any family," Aunt Robyn said, correcting her grammar.

"Right. She got put out her apartment and her mom is missing...she's on drugs...I know it's a lot to ask especially since you're taking care of me and L, but do you think she could just stay with us for a little while? Just until she can find somewhere else to go?"

Aunt Robyn shot Candace a look that made the girl tremble. "You're asking me to take on another mouth to feed for free? Are you kidding me, little girl? Have you any idea how much it costs to care for one child much less three?"

Candace shook her head. "I know it's a lot, but please..." She looked over at her friend unable to phantom leaving the girl there and not helping her. "Please," Candace stated. "I'll do anything. We just...we just can't leave her here like this. There's no telling what'll happen to her."

Aunt Robyn liked the sound of desperation and someone admitting to being indebted to her. Yes, Candace very well would do anything in exchange for this huge favor she was about to do. She would begin working off her debt that very night. "Fine," Aunt Robyn huffed. "Get her. Hurry."

Candace stared at her aunt in disbelief. Was the woman sincere in helping another person? Not wanting to sit too long and give her a chance to change her mind, Candace bolted from the car and returned to Leal's side. "Come on," she said. "You can stay with us for a while."

"What?" Leal asked, looking at her friend as if she was speaking Greek.

"My aunt said you can stay with us. We're not going to leave you out here."

Leal didn't know what to do. Out of all the people that had passed her on the streets the last few days, especially those that recognized her, no one had offered her any help beyond a couple of bucks.

"Get up," Candace urged, holding out her hand to help Leal to her feet. "My aunt isn't a very patient person so you might wanna hurry up."

Leal hopped to her feet and followed her friend to the awaiting Cadillac. She slid into the back seat and closed the door softly before clicking her seatbelt.

From the rearview mirror, Aunt Robyn watched the young girl's movements and studied her facial features. Sure, she'd have to clean her up a bit but she had the budding frame that would bring her in quite a bit of cash, of that Robyn was sure.

Leal just sat there with her head down, not knowing what to say. She was grateful that she wouldn't be spending another night resting on concrete.

"Hold your head up dear," Aunt Robyn said to her.

Leal's head popped up and she locked eyes with Robyn in the mirror.

"No matter what we go through in life we must always keep our heads held high," Aunt Robyn stated. "Never allow the world to see you as beaten down and defeated. Once

you've noticeably relinquished your power then everyone will perceive you as weak and it will be so."

Leal nodded.

"What's your name, dear?"

"Leal."

"Leal, welcome to our family. Candace told me about your misfortune and I insisted that you stay with us."

Candace shot a quick look at her aunt in response to her lie.

"There's simply no way that I'd let such a pretty, young girl stay out on the street alone," Robyn went on.

"Thank you," Leal said her tone full of appreciation. "Thank you so much."

Aunt Robyn smiled. "You're more than welcome."

***

Candace entered the house and began to make the trek upstairs to her bedroom. A few of her aunt's girls were downstairs but she had no desire to converse with them. Before she could make it to her room, she saw her aunt's bedroom door open and out emerged Leal counting a handful of money. Leal closed the door behind her but was so engrossed in fingering the cash in her hand that she didn't even notice Candace staring at her.

"Where'd you get that?" Candace snapped, getting Leal's attention.

Leal looked up. "Huh?"

"The money, where'd you get it?"

Leal had been staying with them for nearly a month now and Candace was afraid that the girl had decided that stealing was the way she'd finance her future. The last thing she needed was for Aunt Robyn to find out Leal was taking her money. Candace was sure that she would end up punished for whatever dirty deeds Leal was guilty of.

"I got it from Aunt Robyn," Leal answered, looking at Candace as if she'd lost her mind for questioning her. "What's the problem?"

Candace was trying to make sense of it all. "You weren't in school today."

"Nice of you to notice," Leal said, walking by and heading to the room she shared with Candace.

Candace trailed behind her and slammed the door to her room shut. "Why weren't you in school?"

Candace had left earlier in the morning to walk Lawrence to his school just to make certain that he got there. Because her aunt never bothered to get up before ten in the mornings, there was no hope in getting a ride from her and she missed the bus every morning so she always walked to school. She simply assumed that Leal would ride the bus per usual and was surprised when her friend was seated next to her in homeroom that morning.

"I got more of an education staying outta school today than I've ever gotten," Leal told her, sinking down on her bed and stuffing her new found wealth into her pillowcase.

"What'd you do?"

"I did a favor for Aunt Robyn."

That was the second time that Leal had referred to Candace's aunt as Aunt Robyn and it was beginning to disturb Candace. Even worse, the prospect of what this secret favor could have been worried Candace. "What kinda favor?"

"Why are you sweating me about this?"

"Since when do we keep secrets from each other?"

"Look, it's not personal or nothing this is just business between me and Aunt Robyn."

"She's not your aunt!" Candace hollered. "Stop calling her that. She is not your aunt. She's my aunt and even I don't wanna claim her at times."

Leal stared at Candace. "What's wrong with you? You're lucky to even have family, someone who cares about you."

"Cares about me? Aunt Robyn doesn't care about me or you obviously." Candace stood in front of Leal with a crazed expression on her face. "You think I don't know what she does? What her business is? You think she just takes in all the strays off of the street because she's a nice old woman? You think those chicks down there just like being around her because she's helped them in some way? You think I don't know what kinda favor she had you do?"

"I don't know what's wrong with you but you're sounding crazy."

"She paid you to fuck somebody!"

Leal jumped up off of the bed and got in Candace's face. "You don't know what the hell you're talking about."

"Oh I don't? She didn't just give you that kinda money to take off school and go shopping for her. Aunt Robyn is like a female pimp and the chicks you see prancing in and outta here are her hoes. And you got ya' lil' money today so that makes you one of 'em too!"

Leal reached out and slapped Candace so hard that the impact seemed to resound off of the walls continuously. Candace instantly reached up and touched her face, reeling from the sting of the blow. Her eyes met Leal's as she glared at her in anger, yet she didn't say a word.

"For your information, she had me go with some guy she knows all over downtown today for his meetings and shit. I ate at the Cheesecake factory and went shopping with him at Lenox. When it was over, his car dropped me back off here. All I did was keep a dude company and got paid $400.00 for it. Ain't nobody fucking nobody." She closed the gap between herself and Candace. "She didn't have to put me on like that but she did it so that I wouldn't grow up to not have shit. I don't know what your beef is with your own aunt, but it ain't none of my problem. I'm good with Miss Robyn and if she asked me to wash some fat bastards clothes in a bathing suit in below freezing weather I'd do it 'cause when I had nobody she took me in."

Candace shook her head. "You think she's your saving grace now but you have no idea...no idea the kinds of things she'll have you do just for a dollar."

"Nuh-uh," Leal shot back. "I'm making hundreds of dollars, not just a dollar. You're just jealous. Think you're too good to use what you got to get ahead."

"I've got more than my pussy to get me ahead."

Leal looked her friend up and down and took a step back. "Well, good for you...the rest of us gotta get it how we live." With that, she turned away and exited the room, not wanting to argue with her friend any further.

Candace watched her go and massaged her face. What have I done, she thought? I pretty much handed Leal over to Aunt Robyn on a silver platter so she could turn her into a call girl. Candace wondered how many other favors Leal had done for her aunt before now and how many more she'd do before realizing that all the shimmered wasn't gold. But, there was nothing she could do. Aunt Robyn had Leal now and once her aunt caught someone under her spell there was no setting them free.

CHAPTER 8
2015 -ATLANTA, GA

L is lucky that I love his little spoiled ass, she thought as she pulled her car into the parking garage. A chill ran through her body, partly because of the sexy red VM collection cocktail dress she was wearing and partly out of fear for how the evening would end up. She'd told Rico that she had to run an errand for her aunt. It wasn't a lie, but she didn't go into detail either. She'd dressed in jogging pants and a t-shirt just to get out of the house. At a local Quik Trip, she changed into her dress in the bathroom. She hated the lying and sneaking around, but it was the only way that she could hide the truth from Rico and not have to face his possible disappointment. *I have to go knock this shit out super quick so I can get my baby out of there before he get into some more shit,* Candace though, wondering about Lawrence and his well-being. She was doing this for him. On everything she loved, it was her mission to make sure that he got out of this mess with as little repercussion as possible.

She entered the extravagant hotel and followed the instructions she'd been given earlier. Heading up to the fifth floor via the elevator, she got off and approached the requested door. Her red Christian Louboutin platforms had her standing tall, emphasizing her thick calves. She tried her best to look appealing and not let on that she was repulsed by the meeting in general. Gently, she tapped on the door and silently prayed that no one would answer.

"How are you doing? My, you are so stylish," stated the middle-aged man wearing the dark blue classic Ralph Lauren suit with a taupe & navy grid patterned tie.

Candace looked him up and down, and spoke quickly. "Thanks, I appreciate that."

"So can we try to match what you're wearing and what I'm wearing at one food some fine dining establishment sometime?"

Candace looked confused. Didn't he realize that this was a one-time arrangement and that if he intended to book her again he'd have to call the office? "First off, I don't even know your name. Second, you don't even know my name. Third, there are rules to this shit."

"I apologize for my rudeness," he stated. "My name is Michael Waters. Yours?"

Candace shook her head. "Unfortunately, you missed that opportunity. Besides, it's not important. For what you're paying, my name can be whatever you need it to be."

"Ahhh, so you're the girl."

Candace looked at him confusedly again. Michael handed her an envelope. She examined it and noticed that 'Monica' was written on the exterior. Candace shook the envelope and opened it to retrieve a door key. She looked up at Michael.

"Precautions," he stated and politely shut his room door.

Candace sauntered down to room 5010. She looked up and down the hall wondering what to expect next. This top secret shit was new to her. As she entered the room, she was wowed by the interior. It was a nice medium sized suite with a foyer. On the back right was a luxury D290 black and beige suede sectional and a glass table in front. From the sofa, her

John waved his hand for her to join him. He had a bowl cut that really looked like someone had placed one of grandma's soup bowls over his head and cut around it His face looked as though his nickname was Pudge or something. He couldn't have been any more 5'10 and about 280 lbs. As she neared him, her eyes fell upon his fat sausage hands. It looked as if he could have been a defensive lineman in high school.

Candace's thoughts began to run amuck as she sat beside him on the sofa. *I can't believe that this dude is this damn fat. What the fuck did I get myself into? I have an attitude right now. Let me try to find a way to slip out of this place. I can't do this. Let me find a way to get out of here.*

"Would you like champagne?" asked the middle aged white man wearing black suspenders and white shirt"

"No, I'm good," she answered. "Plus I don't know you well enough to even think about drinking champagne with you."

"Okay then. What do we need to do to loosen you up?"

"Just give me a minute." She was beginning to have second thoughts. "Can I go to the rest room and freshen up a little?"

"Give me a hug first." He looked at her with lustful eyes.

The thought of him touching her body with those chunky stumps made her nauseous. "Hold up. Let me freshen up first." She rose to her feet.

"Hold on now," the man spoke quickly, his forehead beginning to wrinkle up. "I didn't pay for you to just sit around, little bitch. Get your ass over here and let me rub that little juicy pussy."

"Don't freaking talk to me like that!" she snapped.

"You like this shit and you know it! I got you until you leave. Plus, I paid Ms. Robyn $5,000, so best believed I'm gonna get my $5,000 worth."

Before Candace could realize what was happening, the man charged her while mumbling obscenities under his breath. In the process, he knocked over the table in front of the sofa.

"Wait!" she pleaded, moving away from him. "J-j-just wait."

"Fuck waiting. I didn't pay my money to just wait. Now bring your dumb ass over here right now." His words were followed up by an abrupt slap to her face which was so mighty that it forced her back onto the sofa.

The throbbing pain forced her into reality and made it clear that and a note to the fat motherfucker was not playing. The moment she realized the severity of the situation she was in, Candace mentally reached back to a message she'd received from her basic survival school instructor while in the Army—live or be killed. There was no way she was about to let some mid-life crisis having, can't get a date, fat fuck of a John slap her around like some two-bit whore. With her anger at full mass and her adrenaline pumping, Candace bent her knees and forcefully kicked out her feet landing a heavy blow to his chest with her red and black pumps. The action rocked him backwards but not before he was able to land another blow to the right side of her face.

As he caught he breath from the kick to the chest, Candace had just enough time and distance for the clean break that she needed. She leapt from the sofa and ran towards the bathroom, slamming and locking the door behind her.

Mortified, she sunk to the floor and cried in the corner. *I didn't sign up for this,* she thought, cradling her knees.

Boom. Boom. The door rocked as if it was about to come off of the hinges.

"Get the fuck outta here, little bitch!" the fat fuck called out

"Are you going to be patient?" she asked through her sobs as her face throbbed. She didn't bother to wait for his response as he yanked her cell phone out of her purse. Her hands trembled. She thought about calling Rico and begging him to come to her rescue. But, that plan was no good because then she'd have to explain why she was half-dressed in the fat man's hotel room to begin with. She toyed with the idea of calling Robyn. After all, wasn't it her responsibility to make sure that her girls were safe when they went out on a run? But, knowing her aunt, Candace was sure that she'd die in that hotel room before Robyn even bothered to send someone her way.

Boom, boom, boom.

"Come out of there, little slut! Come play with daddy!"

Boom, boom, boom. "You're taking too long."

Candace closed her eyes and stuffed the phone back into her purse. She was on her own and was going to have to act accordingly. If she wanted to get out of the room alive and have the visit count towards her balance with Robyn, then she was going to have to get creative and find a way to deal with the fat, abusive asshole on the other side of the door.

Candace pulled herself up from the floor and braced herself. This was either gonna work out or go horribly wrong, but she couldn't sit in the bathroom forever. Quickly, she unhooked the strap of her purse and folded it, clutching it in her left hand with the purse tucked under her arm. Then, she ransacked the counter looking for anything that would serve her purpose. Settling upon a bottle of mouth wash, she unscrewed the top and turned to face the door. She was ready for war.

Bang, bang, bang. The horny bastard was relentless as he continued to beat on the door. Each thud made Candace jump but she was determined to turn this entire situation around. The military had taught her to be self-sufficient and instilled a keen survival sense in her. She was determined to come out victorious. Before he could assault the door further, Candace turned the lock and flung the door open. His fist was in midair, ready to pounce once again, and due to the target of his aim being rashly removed, the large man's body lurched forward in vain. This fallacy was done just in time for Candace to douse his face with the mint mouth wash which stung his eyes on impact.

"Fuck!" he screamed, rubbing his eyes profusely while fumbling backwards. "Fuck! You cunt! You burnt my eyes! You burnt my eyes!"

Capitalizing on her advantage, she dropped her purse and lashed out at him with the strap of her purse. She whipped him across the face twice as he whined about his eyes only adding to his injury.

"Owww!" he screamed, his pudgy body bopping up and down as he tried to move away from her. "Crazy bitch!" he called out, trying to reach out and grab the purse strap from her. But, the sting of his eyes wouldn't allow him the clear vision to see just where to reach out. "Bitch!" In his haste to get out of her way, he stumbled over his own suitcase position near the queen sized bed which in turn forced him onto the corner of the bed.

Candace stood over him, whipping at his hands and smiling at the way she'd turned him into her little fat bitch. He struggled to scoot back on the bed but was unable to free himself from her afflictions. Candace cracked her whip once more over his head and laughed.

"You like putting your hands on women you, huh?" she asked him. "You fat fuck! When I say be patient, I fuckin' mean be patient! Do you understand me?"

"Fuck you, you whore!" he spat out, tears dripping from his eyes as his vision began to clear up.

Candace held up her trusty bottle of mouth wash and glared at him. "I'll blind your ass with this shit if you call me another or whore or bitch! Now, shut the fuck up and listen. We both have an invested interest in this shit. You paid your money and want your services; I have a job and want my money. But neither of us is gonna get what we want if you fuck with me. The key to all of this is don't fuck with me."

"I paid my money," he replied. "I run the show."

Candace's brow rose. "Is that what you think? You paid to be entertained, you fat fuck, and I'm in charge of that entertainment." She lifted her leg and positioned her foot right between his fat thighs, dangerously close to his porky dick. "This can be pleasurable or painful. It's up to you."

The man remained silent. He thought about grabbing her foot and dragging her ass across the bed and the floor but the stir in his pants made him be still. He wasn't too fond of some black slut abusing him, but there was something oddly erotic about the way she was dominating the situation.

Candace slowly slipped her shoe off and began to massage his groin area through his pants with her bare foot. She at first she couldn't tell if she was rubbing pure fat or if his Johnson really existed. But, after a few moments of them having a stare off she soon felt him rise.

"There you go," she coaxed him. "If you play nice, I'll play nice, but this goes my way at my speed."

He simply nodded.

Candace swallowed hard as she realized what she had to do next. Even though she was in control, if she didn't give him exactly what he'd paid for then she'd be fucked. There was no way around it. She lowered her leg and slowly began to peel off her dress. Not a stitch of clothing existed underneath. She caught a glimpse of the fat man licking his lips as he stared at the curve of her breasts and the neatly trimmed hairs that covered her mound. She was disgusted watching him quickly discard his shirt and unzip his slacks. The sight of his male breasts only solidified her desire to not be touched by him. There was no way she was going to let his fat ass smother her.

"Take 'em off," she ordered, referring to his pants.

He wasted no time in ditching his slacks before reaching out to touch her swollen nipples.

Candace slapped his hand away. "No!" she snapped. "No touching."

"The fuck!" he protested.

"Since you like to hit women, they'll be no touchy-feely bullshit for you today."

"That's bullshit. I paid my money and I—"

"And I can just go if you don't wanna do things my way. I can just call the police and tell them you lured me up here and slapped me around. Is that what you want? Or do you wanna be fucked?"

The raunchiness of her last statement forced him into a horny bout of silence. He hadn't expected this kind of experience, but it was quite a change from the usual pillow princesses he'd hired from other agencies in other cities. He didn't put up a fuss, yet removed his plaid boxers and laid back on the bed, ready to see how she'd get him off.

Fuck, she thought as she turned to get her purse off of the floor and pull out a condom. Returning to him to place the condom on his pink dick, Candace had to keep herself from crying. This wasn't how she'd envisioned her life turning out. She prayed that her mother and father's spirits weren't in turmoil looking down on her as she performed acts of sin in the name of the mighty buck. It's for L, she told herself as she positioned herself on top of the horny fuck whose pre-cum was now dripping from her fingertips. He grunted as she wiggled about trying to get his dick in position to insert inside of her. With the way he moved about and moaned, she was sure that he was about to cum before she could even get it in good.

Oh yeah," he cooed, salivating and gyrating. "She was right about you...oh yeah..."

It'll be over soon, she thought as she felt him fill her. She stared at his round belly as it jiggled with each thrust of her hips. Eventually, her eyes roamed up to the ceiling. *Hurry up and cum,* she thought, ready to escape the room of ill repute and pray for forgiveness.

***

"What are you doing here?" Leal asked, answering Robyn's front door.

"Hello to you too," Candace said, pushing past her former friend. "Where is she?"

"Times have changed, Candace. We don't receive workers at the house anymore."

Candace shot Leal a dirty look. "Oh what? She's not personally coaching her girls on how to be ladies AKA whores at home anymore? My how we've evolved. Where the hell is she?"

"Look, you have no business here," Leal gritted. "And I'm not trying to be funny but this isn't the place for you. You made that painfully clear when you jetted way back when. Now, you've been given your money and you'll be contacted when your next assignment comes up. If I were you, I'd leave now before I'm forced to—"

"To what?" Candace snapped, stepping to Leal. "What are you going to do, Leal? Huh? You gonna hit me? Whoop my ass? Trust me, I've been through enough shit tonight and you'd just be lightweight."

Leal smirked. "We don't condone violence here. Or intruders. Please don't make me call the police. I'd hate to have to send you off to live in the county jail with your brother."

"His bail's posting in the morning, bitch. Speak what you know. I'm gonna ask you one more fuckin' time...where is she?!"

"And I'm going to tell you one more fucking time to get—"

"It's okay," a voice called out from the top of the stairs.

Candace whirled around to see her aunt decked out in a long white satin robe with her hair in full circles and jewels decorating her neck and ears as if she was preparing to go out at that late hour. Candace wasn't surprised that even in the comfort of her own home; the woman was full of her own self-importance and basked in her ill-gotten wealth.

"I didn't expect for you to ever return home, my dear," Robyn stated, descending the stairs. "I'm quite surprised."

"Yeah, you and me both," Candace shot back, moving to meet her aunt at the bottom of the staircase. "Look at my fuckin' face," she demanded; turning so that Robyn could see the bruise on her cheek.

Robyn seemed unfazed. "Looks like you've had an accident."

"Accident my ass. You sent me out to that crazy motherfucker and this is what he did to me."

"Did you finish the job?"

Candace stared at her in disbelief, but only for a second. "I don't know why I was caught off guard just then. It's just like you to be only about the bottom line."

"I run a business."

"You run a Mickey Mouse operation! With all the money you're raking in and some of the clientele you're servicing; shouldn't you have some kinda security for your girls? That man coulda beat the shit outta me tonight. I could have been killed working for your ass."

"What do you want me to do? I can't exactly offer you worker's comp now can I?"

Candace wanted to slap the smug look off of her aunt's face. She stared into her eyes and a brand new reality set in.

She could hear the man's voice clearly in her head. *You like this shit and you know it...she was right about you.* Candace became enraged. "You sick bitch! You told that fat fuck to beat me!" It all became clear to her. She lunged forward to grab her aunt but was stopped by a clicking sound that she was quite familiar with.

Candace turned around to see the butt of Leal's .9mm staring right at her. She shook her head and turned back to face her aunt. "So that's what it is? You fuck up my childhood, fuck up my brother's childhood, take advantage of us in our time of need, whore me out, set me up to get beat up, and then you have your sidekick ass goon pull a gun on me. What? You gonna order her to shoot me right here in your house? You're so good at covering shit up, Aunt Robyn, but tell me...how would you cover up murdering me in your own house?"

Robyn smiled sadistically. "I have my ways. It would behoove you to refrain from visiting my private residence again unless invited, especially at such an ungodly hour."

"Your prime working hours," Candace shot back.

"Much has changed, dear, but one thing is for certain. You do not want to fuck with me." Robyn looked past her niece. "Leal, please see our unwanted houseguest out."

Candace gave a curt smile to her aunt. "This shit isn't over. You think you're getting the best of me because of our arrangement but I promise you that I will get the last laugh." She turned to leave and caught eyes with Leal. "Nice to see that you're still her little bitch. I brought you in five g's tonight," she called over her shoulder as she moved towards the doorway. "Thirty-five more and you can kiss my ass."

***

"What the fuck happened to your face?" Rico was torn between being pissed and feeling hurt to see his woman hurt.

During the ride home, Candace hadn't thought much about the story she'd tell him. She spent the entire drive seething over her trifling aunt's behavior and piecing together a plan to fuck her up. But, now that she was home her immediate reality set in and she had to come up with something to satisfy Rico's curiosity.

"I got into a fight," she answered, walking into the kitchen and grabbing a dish towel to fill with ice. "It's not biggie."

"Yo, you look like you been in the ring with Tyson and you wanna tell me it's no biggie? Bullshit. Where'd you go?"

"I told you I had to run an errand for my aunt. I took her somewhere and dropped her back off." She looked down and was glad that she'd had the sense enough to remember to change back into her street clothes before returning home.

"So who you get in a fight with?" Rico probed.

"Leal." The answer came with ease since she had half the mind to beat the shit out of her classmate as well. Candace tossed three cubes of ice into her dish towel and took a seat at the kitchen table to hold the cloth to her swollen jaw.

Rico stared at her. "What the hell is going on? I don't get nothing but bad vibes from that stuck up ass bitch Leal and you ain't said much of nothing about this aunt that you don't really fuck with."

"We have a few differences," Candace told him. "Mainly she's a bitch and I'm allergic to bitch-ass-ness."

"You ain't even tell me what kinda business that is that she's running. Folk up in there all stuck up and shit...looking down their noses at folk."

Candace sighed. "It's a consulting firm. Basically, she provides people with the bullshit they need to boost their self-esteem." It was kind of the truth.

"Yeah? And where did you have to drive her to at this time of night that she couldn't take herself? Or her lil' assistant couldn't take her?"

Candace was tired and no longer wished to spin her web of lies regarding her involvement in Robyn's business. "To visit some family."

Rico's eyebrow raised. "Thought you said you didn't have no other family."

"I don't. Everyone's dead to me, except L. Even Robyn...it's just that we need her right now...Well, her money anyway."

Rico's little voice was telling him that something wasn't right, but he hated to believe that his future was lying to him. "Babe, you need more ice," he told her, grabbing a pack of frozen corn out of the freezer. "Here, try this."

Candace took the packet and pressed it against her skin, wincing from the pain. She looked up to see Rico walking out of the kitchen. "Where are you headed?" she spoke in a muffled tone.

"I'm about to roll one up. Why? You need something?"

She never done it before, her chosen vice was always liquor, but tonight she felt that she needed something a little more potent to take the edge off. "Let me hit it a few times."

"You sure, babe?" Rico was puzzled. He'd never once seen her smoke or even look interested in the pastime despite the hundreds of times he'd smoked in front of her.

"I just need something to calm this pain and get rid of this headache," she told him. "A lot of shit has happened and I just...I just want to escape it all for a little while."

Rico thought about it. "They not gon' be checking ya piss at work are they?"

She shook her head.

"Alright," he told her. "I'll be right back." He went off in search of his stash.

Candace exhaled and closed her eyes for a moment. Visions of Robyn were driving her crazy. She just wanted to permanently fuck the older woman up in a way that would make a lasting impression. The only thing that bitch cared about was her business. Candace had learned a long time ago that the best way to fuck with someone was to hit them where it hurt. The only thing that would make Robyn crumble was if she was stripped of the only thing that gave her power: the agency.

Candace rose and walked over to the counter to retrieve a bottle of Patron. She pulled the cork and took a swig of the smooth tequila. A smile spread across her lips as a plan began to materialize. If Aunt Robyn thought she'd gotten the best of her, the bitch had another thing coming. The war had just begun.

CHAPTER 9
TWO DAYS LATER

Robyn paced the floor for what seemed like hours. She was pissed. Who the fuck did the little bitch think she was playing with? I raised her when those good for nothing parents of hers died, she thought. I tried my best to get her to look at life for what it was...to set her up with an enterprise that would always be good to her so that she'd want for nothing. I tried to bring her in so that she could one day take over the legacy and she spat in my face. Robyn fumed as she stared out of the window of her office. She envisioned the look of hatred mixed with shame that was so evident in Candace's eyes as she'd stared her down the other night. That bitch thinks she's better than me, Robyn concluded. She cracked a smile. Dumb bitch! Doesn't she know that if it wasn't for me her ass would have been thrown into some foster or group home and not knowing what would have become of her life?

Robyn hated ungrateful people, especially weak and pathetic, ungrateful women. Candace was a weakling; she'd seen that from the first time she'd tried to put her to work. Sure, she survived the military and tours of duty but the demands of the Army had nothing on Robyn. She was a force to be reckoned with and as smart as Candace thought she was, Robyn was ten times wiser. Despite Candace's blatant disrespect and the numerous times that she'd declined Robyn's offers of employment, ultimately Robyn had gotten exactly what she wanted. And it was not coincidence. Robyn chuckled to herself as she thought of the thousands she'd put in to scratching the backs of so many who had helped her little plan come along. From the commander at Davis-Monthan Air Force base whose idea of a good time consisted of two busty blondes, neither of which were his wife, in exchange for assuring that Candace be made an example of right down to the little hood chick setting up L and his friend to take the fall for the altercation with her boyfriend.

Raising her hand to fondle her pearl necklace, Robyn couldn't help but to laugh out loud. It never ceased to amaze her what others would do to compromise their own lives just for the sake of a dollar or in the face of blackmail. Staring out of the window from her upper level suite in the shotty office building that most would have never looked twice at, she felt like the God of the hood, reigning over minions near and far; pulling the puppet strings and watching everyone else dance. She had power like no other. Pussy and money were her only two weapons. Armed with a shit load of both, she was able to do just about anything she wanted, including humiliating her ungrateful ass niece. Yes, Candace had fought tooth and nail to defy her, to do better than become just another one of her girls, but with a little help from her minions and Lawrence's innate habit of fucking up, she now had the pretty little ingrate right where she wanted her.

Robyn slowly eased into her burgundy, leather office chair and stared at her computer screen. Looking back at her was a spreadsheet of appointments for the following twenty-four hours. The wealthy bastard that she'd provoked to rough Candace up had requested her once again. Robyn knew he'd pay top dollar for her niece judging by the way Leal said his urgency had been in making the appointment. There was also a second date scheduled for Candace for later in that night. At that rate the girl would be done paying back the $40,000.00 in no time. But, Robyn no longer cared about the money. The thing between her and Candace was far more personal than the girl making good on her loan. It wasn't enough to bring Candace to her knees and force her into coming home and begging for money. It wasn't enough to humiliate the girl by forcing her to do that which she said she'd never do again and also having her beaten in the process. No, Robyn needed a way to wipe that petty little smirk off of Candace's pretty little face so that she would never again think that she was better than her. Candace needed to be humbled in the most brutal way possible.

Robyn tapped her manicured nails lightly against the receiver of her office phone before lifting it to place a call. If she knew nothing else aside from using pussy for profit, she knew how to make a person's life miserable. If Candace thought she'd been through hell thus far she had another thing coming to her. Shit was about to get very real.

***

Her body was tired and achy, her ass was sore from the relentless anal sex her recent client had insisted upon, and her mind was heavy. She'd snuck out of the house earlier while Rico was knocked out across the bottom of their bed. It helped that he'd recently returned home from a trip to visit Kelsey. She'd left work at the law firm just around lunch time to meet some dude and accompany him to some dumb as luncheon, pretending to be his fiancée. It was easy money, or so she thought. Once they were back in his limo destined for her drop off spot, the man had requested nothing more than some quick head in the back seat—spitting out his essence wasn't an option. It bothered her that she was missing out on steady money at work in an effort to pay back her sordid debt, but she had to make good on her word before setting her aunt in her place.

She pulled off her heels at the front door and gently closed and locked the door. Walking through the still darkness of the living room she made a mental note to shower in the guest bathroom so as not to disturb Rico.

"So what? You cat woman or something?"

The male voice startled Candace and she nearly screamed out in fright. Quickly, she flicked on the lamp near the hall entrance and turned to look in the direction of the sound. Laid out across her love seat was Lawrence with a smug look on his face.

"Why aren't you asleep?" she asked him, fidgeting with the overcoat that she was wearing.

"After you been locked away for a minute the last thing you wanna do is sleep since that's 'bout all you can do in jail."

"You were only there for a couple of days. Get over yourself."

"Yeah," Lawrence replied, sitting up. "Still...I got a lot on my mind." He eyed her suspiciously. "But you wanna tell me why you creeping in and out of your own house?"

"Last I checked I was the adult and I didn't have to explain myself to you."

"True dat, but inquiring minds wanna know." He cocked his head to the side. "And you smell funny."

"Excuse you?"

"Like smoke," he explained.

Her John had chain smoked three cigars while she'd serviced him over and over again during the night. It bothered her that the scent was strong enough for someone to detect with her simply walking by.

"Go to bed," she ordered, turning away.

"Sis, come on. The least you can do is be straight up with me. You creeping on ole boy?"

Candace shot back around. "No!" she hissed. "I'm not a cheater asshole."

"No? You sneaking out all times of the night with that long, hot ass coat on so I'm assuming you trying to hide your outfit. Only explanation I can come up with is that you either creeping or dealing. Which is it?"

"Fuck you for assuming the worse of me," she replied, pointing her finger at him. She thought of all the compromising situations she'd found herself in lately in the name of paying back the money she'd borrowed to help save his ass. "You don't know what you're talking about so just let it go."

"You came up off fifty g's for me, sis." Lawrence looked at her sorrowfully. "I been racking my brains trying to figure out how you got that kinda dough. I mean, I just assumed that Rico had it like that or some shit but then again if he did I'm sure we'd be in a bigger house in a different neighborhood."

"What's wrong with this house?" Candace asked, defensively.

"Nothing. I'm just saying, I don't really thing ya' boy's money is long like that. And then you working ya' day job and sneaking out at night like you got a lil side piece or a side hustle. I mean, how else could you afford my bail, not that I'm not thankful?"

She stared at him long and hard. It was eating her up on the inside to be keeping this secret. She knew that telling Rico could mean the end of their relationship, but telling Lawrence could cost her his respect. Candace wasn't willing to compromise that. Her lower lip trembled as she battled with herself over what to say.

"All the shit I done did, sis...you know you can tell me anything," he encouraged her.

She rolled her eyes up to the ceiling. "I borrowed the money...from Aunt Robyn."

Lawrence was silent but only for a moment. "You borrowed it from Aunt Robyn. Sis, I coulda kept my ass in jail before I woulda even suggested you going to that old crow. I mean, she just gave it to you just like that?"

"Not exactly."

"I bet you making you bend over backwards to pay that shit back."

Candace smiled. "Something like that.

"I'm so sorry sis. I never meant to push you back in her direction." He balled his left hand making a fist and punched the palm of his right. "Fuck! I'm so sorry."

Candace shook her head. "It's done now, L. It's done and I'm handling it." It was the way that she was handling it that had her wanting to lay down and die.

"Tell me what I gotta do," Lawrence pleaded. "Tell me what I gotta do to make this right."

"First off, stay the fuck out of trouble please. Go to school and come home. I'm worried about getting you off on this assault of an officer charge. The rest of it I'm not too concerned with. But I need you to stay outta the streets and focus on staying out of jail."

"And Aunt Robyn? You know she's a snake."

"I can handle Aunt Robyn. For all the treacherous bullshit she's pulled in her days, I'm gonna be sure to fix her right on up."

A smile crept upon his lips. "Ah shit. You working on a plan to get her ass ain't you? I want in on this man. You have no idea the shit she's done."

"No, I want you to stay clean. What did we just discuss?"

"But, sis!"

"No!" Candace snapped. "You focus on staying outta jail and I'll deal with Aunt Robyn. Okay?" She looked at him hard. "I said, okay?"

Lawrence nodded. "Aight."

"Okay then. Carry your ass to bed; you've got school in the morning." She turned and exited the living room, her mind once again fixated on Aunt Robyn. Don't worry little brother, she thought. I'm gonna get that bitch one way or another.

***

It was her lunch break and she knew she'd be a few minutes late returning, but this was an errand that simply couldn't wait. She entered the office suite and found Raul flipping through papers at the receptionist's desk. He looked up at her, rolled his eyes, and returned his gaze to his task at hand.

"What? No burly boyfriend body guard this time?" Raul sneered.

Candace smiled as politely as she could. "Nope, just me. Thought I'd come through and check to see if there were any upcoming assignments for me."

"You know how that work. The Girl Friday makes the calls or sends the texts. I'm just the paper pusher."

He sounded a little disgruntled and Candace liked the sound of that.

She leaned over the desk to get a better look at what he was up to. "What's all that?" She noticed the names of various catering companies at the top of several pages.

"Bids for the catering request."

"You planning a party?"

"Only the biggest bash of the summer, hunny," he sassed. "Ms. Robyn's birthday party."

This was news to Candace. "Oh?"

"Yeah, and The Girl Friday has me handling all of the invoices and doing the grunt work. They'll probably let me go before the party even gets here even though I'm doing all the work. You know I'm only a temp, right? Anyway, these heffa bitches don't know nothing about throwing together a shindig like Raul."

Listening to him refer to himself in third person almost made Candace giggle. "Well....between you and I...I did hear Leal say something about terminations."

Raul looked up at her in astonishment, placing his hand over his heart for dramatic effect. "No!"

Candace nodded. "She kept saying the temps, the temps but I didn't know who she was referring to."

"Catty bitches! Hard as I work, keeping these ladies in check, answering these phones, organizing their mail, maintaining this office and not to mention giving this soiree some class."

"Being unappreciated really sucks," Candace commented.

Raul looked down at the invoices and plucked one out. "Hmmm. This is the cheapest one. I'll just pick this one and hope like hell that the caterer drags the French bread along the floor before serving it." He laughed like a little school girl.

"Ummm...tell me, do the other girls typically come here during the day?"

"Mmmhhm. Some come to drop off their incentive percentages, some come to get their asses chewed out, some come to bring in copies of their health reports....that sort of thing."

"Incentive percentages?"

"Child, Ms. Robyn don't play about no money. If the girls get tips during their dates they have to bring her ten percent."

"Shut up!"

"Mmmhmmm, hunny. She prefers that no cash changes hands between the clients and the girls. She raking in as many coins as possible."

"I see. I didn't realize."

"Child, you ain't read your contract before signing on the dotted line?"

Candace raised a brow. "I gotta do better."

"Shoul' nuff. Y'all lil thangs might as well be handing out the cooch for free if you let someone take advantage of you and you don't know what's going on."

"And how does she know if the girls are pocketing their tips or not?"

"Secret shoppers."

"Excuse me?"

"Leal sets up fake Johns to test the girls. Says it keeps 'em honest."

Candace had heard it all. "You don't sound too pleased with the way things are done around here."

Raul shrugged. "I do my job and I do it well. Everything else doesn't concern me. But the fact that they'd just kick me to the curb at will, now that right there steams my broccoli. I got some ideas on how some things should go down."

Candace smiled. "Maybe we can help each other."

Raul looked up at her and considered the statement. "Hmmm. I heard tales about you. The prodigal child returns."

"Bullshit."

"Oh and she has a potty mouth. What you doing, hunny? Planning to overthrow the wicked witch of the SWATS?"

"And if I am?" Candace was taking a chance by laying her cards out on the table the way she was with the little gay man not knowing if she could truly trust him or not.

Raul leaned forward and whispered. "Mama likes a little scandal."

Candace beamed. Just like that, she had an ally. "Here's what I need. Get me her attorney's information. He's got to be a beast to keep her out of all of the hot water she's usually in and out of. Text me from your cell so I'll have your number and then I'll shoot you over some little tasks that I need you to attend to."

"And how's this going to benefit me in the end?"

"Oh honey, when I'm done with this place you'll never have to worry about employment again. You'll be my number one hitta...my ace...my go to."

"Basically I'ma run this bitch," Raul concluded.

Candace laughed. It wasn't taking much to pull him in her corner. "Like only you can," she co-signed. Things were looking up.

***

Unknown number: Hey it's me...this is my number. Lock me in, hunny.

Candace: Good deal! Here's what I need you to do. Start dropping a bug in the ear of the girls that you're sure would want a better deal outta their contracts. Let 'em know new management's offering armed protection, no claims on tips or gifts from clients, max limit of how many dates they're sent on in a week unless they request more appointments, and for good measure throw in vacation days.

Unknown number: Vacation days? Seriously? You know this ain't exactly a salaried position, right?

Candace: You got it or nah?

Unknown: I'm on it. BTW, you wanted the attorney's info right. I got that. The attorney's name is Benjamin Jackson, located somewhere in downtown Decatur.

Candace: You sure???

Unknown: Yes, hunny! You want the number and address?

A few minutes passed with no response.

Unknown number: ????

Candace: No, I'm good on that. Instead, shoot him an e-mail from Leal's account asking for an updated version of the Queen Bee's will. Find out how the business is set-up...and um...have him refer you to a criminal attorney. Can you handle all that?

Unknown number: You know this could get me fired before you swoop in and save all the hoes in Hoe-ville right?

Candace: I got you. Just be careful and I got you. Please trust me.

Unknown number: You better pray that you got all ya' ducks in a row little Miss Prissy, 'cause if I get screwed in the end...

Candace: LOL, somethin' tells me you like getting screwed in the end! Save it! I got you and that's my word.

Unknown number: LMAO, BITCH! I'll be in touch.

"Candace!" Rico hollered from his seat across the table from her. He banged his hand on the table top causing the flatware and dishes to rattle. His eyes looked like little slits as he glared at his woman.

Rattled from his abrupt outburst, Candace dropped her cell phone onto the table and looked up at in astonishment. "What?" she asked, unsure of why he was barking at her.

Lawrence sat quietly, moving his head back and forth between the two of them as if watching a volleyball match. He'd been watching as Candace fumbled with her phone for the last fifteen minutes as Rico had been trying to explain something to her about a procedure that his daughter would be having in the upcoming week. Candace hadn't even bothered to look up as the man spoke, much less utter a word to acknowledge that she was paying attention.

"The hell you mean what?" Rico gritted. "We sitting up here at the dinner table and I'm trying to talk to you but you been too busy attending to whoever the fuck keeps texting you."

"It's business," she replied nonchalantly.

"Business," he repeated, both hands lying flat on the table. "Business with who? From the office? They paying you over time now?"

"Not exactly."

"Uh-huh. Naw, it ain't them folk from the job. Must be ya' aunt right? Running you around town like her lil' bitch. Is that who it is, Candace? Is that cunt sending you orders again?"

Candace noticed the rigidity in his jaw structure and knew that Rico was pissed. She didn't want to further upset him considering she wasn't ready to give him full disclosure regarding her arrangement with her aunt. "It's nothing I can't handle," she assured him, picking up her fork and playing with her now cold mashed potatoes. "Go on, what were you saying?"

"Nah, it's okay. It obviously wasn't as important as whatever you were talking about on that phone."

"Come on, Rico—"

"Come on Rico what?" he challenged. "I barely get to have more than two words with you these days because of your work schedule and my schedule and then you running around doing secret missions for this infamous ass aunt of yours."

"Infamous?"

"Tell me something...why wouldn't you let me meet ya' family, Candace? What? You ashamed of me? Of her? Or is it that there's really no aunt?"

Candace laughed. "You're sounding a lil crazy now bae with your whole conspiracy theory you got going on."

"What the hell am I supposed to think when you're acting all shifty and secretive?"

"I'm not."

"Like hell you ain't. You think I don't notice the change in you? Hell, you want even let me touch you! You come home all beat the fuck up but don't wanna tell me much of nothing 'bout what happened."

Lawrence stared at his sister with his mouth open waiting for an explanation. So many thoughts were running through his head but with Rico sitting there he couldn't voice even one of them.

"I told you what happened," Candace said. "Can we just drop this and try to have a cordial dinner."

"Nah, we don't talk no other time so we talking now. No more bullshit, Candace. Give me the real. What the hell's going on?"

Candace swallowed hard and weighed her options. As mad as Rico was at that moment the last thing he needed was to be given the truth. She looked into Lawrence's pleading eyes and saw that he too wanted to hear all of what she was holding back. But she couldn't do it. For the love of her family, she simply couldn't tell them everything—at least not yet.

"I just have a lot of stuff on my mind," she said slowly. "Trying to keep up at work, trying to keep Aunt Robyn off my ass about the money we owe her, and trying to get representation for, L."

At the mention of his sister's last concern, Lawrence lowered his head. He felt bad for putting his sister in a position to have to lie to her dude, to stress over his fuck-ups and well-being, and to be in debt to their conniving aunt.

"Those texts were about the lawyer," Candace went on. "I'm just...I'm just trying to handle everything. That's all."

Rico looked at her long and hard. He knew this woman well enough to know that she was lying. Whatever she was keeping from him she clearly had no intentions of confessing it. He didn't know what hurt worse—her lying to his face or her feeling as if she had to do whatever it was she was doing alone. He tried to dismiss the feeling that she was cheating on him. That would have explained so much but it just didn't seem to fit with her character. Frustrated, Rico banged the table once more, rose from his seat, and walked out of the kitchen without a word.

For a moment, brother and sister sat in silence. Both simply stared at their dinner plates considering their own thoughts. In the distance, they could hear Rico rummaging around through the house.

"I'm sorry sis," Lawrence said softly. "You do so much for me...you always have...and I always find a way to fuck things up for you."

"Watch your mouth." It was all that she could say as she picked up her phone to re-read her recent conversation. Her head was still reeling from the bit of information that she'd received.

"I mean, here you are doing what the hell ever and ruining your relationship just to try to help me." His eyes misted over as he looked at Candace. "We were supposed to be there for each other but all I did was let you down and make things worse. I'm sorry." He took a breath. "Don't get the lawyer," he said.

Candace shot him a confused look. "What?"

"That's just gon' make you be into her for more money 'cause I know we can't afford it especially with Rico's daughter going back in the hospital. Yo, I assaulted that cop so I'll have to take that charge. Don't worry 'bout the lawyer. I'll just get a public defender and be done with it."

Candace frowned. "Are you crazy? That cop provoked you and you were already out of your mind at the moment. Besides, you willing to take the rap for those other charges too? I'm not letting you spend the rest of your teenage years and young adult life in prison for some shit you didn't do, L. I'm not doing it."

"You can't take no more money from her, Ce-Ce! I can't let you keep putting ya' life on pause or messing up your good situations just because of me."

Candace considered her newfound information once again, a new plan formulating in her mind. "Stop worrying about me. When I tell you that I got this, I mean that I've got it. I need you to trust me."

"How the hell can I trust you when I don't even know what it is you're doing?" he snapped. "How can I trust you knowing that you're fooling around with Aunt Robyn and knowing the kinda bullshit she be on?"

Candace stared at her brother while pointing her finger in his face. "If I tell you about your language one more time, this verdict and jail sentence will be the least of your worries."

Lawrence opened his mouth to pop off but thought better of it and remained silent.

"Now, I'm getting you this lawyer and I won't be owing Aunt Robyn one red cent for it."

"How you gon'—"

"Don't question me. Just trust me. Please."

Lawrence remained silent for a moment. "What about Rico? He ain't gon' just trust you for too much longer sis. You gon' have to come up off the truth at some point."

Candace nodded. "When the time's right I'll fill everyone in on everything."

"Yeah...I just hope it's not too late when you do."

Candace felt the exact same way.

***

Candace was extremely focused on the document presented on her screen. She'd gone over it and over it and was completely bewildered over how astute her aunt really was. For the past few years she'd actually been passing her escort service off as a true business, an actual consulting firm. Pleasure Principle Consulting was set up as a limited liability corporation, had a federal tax identification number, and was actually paying taxes. Candace could imagine the number of people in high places that Robyn had on her payroll ensuring that her fraudulence never made headlines. She was doing a booming business and Candace knew firsthand how stellar her attorney was so she was pretty sure that Robyn was living the good life and had little to no legal worries.

She re-read the final clause of her aunt's will before hitting the reply button. The changes had been made and now it was time to put the legal wheels of her plan into motion; the physical aspect would occur later.

"Ms. Williams!"

Candace rolled her eyes and quickly checked her tone before responding. "Yes, Ms. Shirley?"

"Ms. Williams, you are going to have to do whatever personal task you're engrossed in during your lunch break. I shouldn't have to tell you about office protocol. Weren't you in the military? Didn't they teach you better than this?"

Ms. Shirley was a pain in the ass and Candace's patience was often tried by her snarky remarks. In the short time that she'd been there she realized that it wasn't a personal thing, she was just a bitch in general, but everyone seemed to accept her attitude. Not wanting to lose her job, Candace tried her best to keep her cool. Truthfully, if she just ignored the woman the days went by smoother. She had far greater problems in her life than to be fazed by the old, bitter woman's nasty attitude.

"I'm actually proofing a document for Mr. Jackson," Candace replied, being sure to give her supervisor a phony smile.

"Is that so? I've never seen you so focused on a work task before."

"Shirley, that's not nice," K.C. called out as he strolled out of his office. "Why are you giving our little worker bee here such a hard time?"

Ms. Shirley snarled at Candace and then looked to her superior. "Just making sure she's on task. That's all."

K.C. put his hands on Ms. Shirley's shoulders and gave her a two-minute massage. "Candace is the best paralegal we've ever had. I can vouch for that. Come on, give the kid a break. If not because she's so awesome, then do it because I'm so awesome and you like me."

Ms. Shirley smiled. Candace shook her head and continued sending her e-mail message. The only time she ever saw her supervisor smile was with K.C. was around buttering her ass up. She was pretty sure that Ms. Shirley had a crush on the man.

"I hope you weren't goofing off for real after I just saved your butt," K.C. teased Candace once Ms. Shirley returned to her office.

"Never that," Candace said with a smile.

K.C. smiled at her adoringly. Candace couldn't lie; the man had a beautiful smile and great charisma.

"I was wondering if you'd like to have lunch with me today," he stated.

Candace thought about it. Things with Rico were shaky but that was all her fault. Even still, she wasn't the type of woman to go around cheating on her man. But, K.C. was her superior—well, her boss's boss—and it would really be more like a business lunch than anything. She weighed her options and figured the free meal wouldn't kill her. Plus, it would be nice to break up the monotony of her troubled life for a moment.

"Sure," she replied.

"Any place in particular?"

"Hmmm, there's this burger joint on the Southside that sells the fattest, greasiest burgers ever with home fries."

"Sounds like clogged arteries to me."

"Sounds like you wanna go to lunch alone to me," Candace joked back.

K.C. covered his heart with his hand. "Ouch! It's like that? Fine, Heart Attack Restaurant it is. Be ready to roll out at twelve on the dot, young lady."

"Yes, Sir," Candace replied, returning her attention to her computer just as her cell phone began to buzz in her desk drawer. “Shit,” she mumbled. She wondered for a brief second if Leal was calling to send her on a run, but then realized that the woman generally texted and didn’t call.

Looking down at the CALLER ID quickly, she realized that it was her newfound ally. She answered hurriedly. “Now’s really not a good time for calls. Texts or e-mails are better.”

“Duly noted, hunny. But I just want you to know that you’re asking me to commit fraud by forging ole girl’s signature.”

“Where’s the trust? I know the best lawyer in town, worst case scenario.” She giggled a little.

“Oh you laughing bitch, but I’m the one assuming all of the risks here.”

“For now,” Candace stated. “And let’s not forget that I’m the mastermind. If anything I’d get a bid for conspiracy or some shit. But that’s not going to happen.”

“You better be glad that I’m man-less and bored with life right now otherwise I’d have to tell you to kick rocks.”

“You’re the best. Sign the papers and fax ‘em over to the number that I gave you now please.”

“Yes your highness.”

“Ugh! Don’t call me that. Makes me think you’re equating me to that bitch.” Candace heard movement coming from the open door of Ms. Shirley’s office. “Okay, gotta go. Remember, no calls. Texts or e-mails.” She disconnected the call before her ally could utter another word.

Twenty minutes later the fax machine buzzed. As she would have on any other day, Candace retrieved all of the incoming faxes from that morning and sorted them out by recipients. She made copies just in case anyone desired them, including a special copy for herself on one particular fax of interest. Then, she placed everyone's documents in their corresponding inboxes situated near her desk. A smile brushed across her lips as she returned to her seat and thought about the future. Things looked bleak now but she was about to come into a great deal of money and all of her troubles would soon be handled.

***

Her work day had flown by following the first of many lunches with K.C. It was great to be able to talk to a guy and not have to lie to him about anything and not have him coming on to her blatantly. Sure, Candace knew that K.C. was crushing on her but he wasn't disrespectful about it. After work, Candace hurried across town to get to Robyn's office before Raul left for the day. Maybe it wasn't the best idea for her to keep sniffing around her aunt's domain, but Candace didn't care much about pissing the old woman off these days.

"Oh, look who came to visit," Raul quipped the moment he saw her enter the office suite.

In her hand she carried a large gift bag and on her face she donned a huge smile. "You getting smart? You want me to just take my lil' gift back?"

Raul smiled. "No, no, hunny. We like gifts." He held his greedy little hands out eagerly.

Candace handed over the bag and watched as he peered inside.

"Ooh, no you didn't!" He pulled out the cream and brown Michael Kors bag and posed with it. "You know I'm gon' be too cute rocking this around town."

Candace laughed. "Just a little incentive for all you've done for me."

He eyed her. "Bitch, can you afford this?"

"Don't look a gift horse in its mouth, Raul. Where're your manners?" she snapped back. "Just don't let your employer find out where you got it from."

Raul busied about packing up his belongings for the day. "No matter. She's not here anyway. Had some early dinner meeting with some guy from out of town. Nice looking man too. Mmmhmmm, he looked like he could be your type."

"And what would you know about my type?"

"You like 'em buff with a wild side to 'em, hunny. A dude that looks like he'd click on stupid the second somebody even looked at you the wrong way."

Candace smiled. "Maybe."

"Well, well, well," Leal, piped in as she approached the desk from the back offices. "We're seeing an awful lot of you these days. How have your appointments been going?"

"I get 'em in, get 'em off, and get on. Isn't that how it goes?" Candace asked sarcastically.

Leal looked over at the package sitting on Raul's desk. "You been shopping on your lunch breaks again?"

"Does it matter?" Raul shot back. "Or are you just mad because I didn't bring you anything back?"

"Down boy!" Leal warned. "It was just a question."

Raul grabbed his things and headed for the exit. "I've got places to go and things to do. Goodnight, ladies." He left without looking back.

Leal walked over to the bar counter situated in the tiny waiting area of the suite. "Can I offer you anything?"

"No thanks. I was just dropping by to see if there were any assignments up for grabs," Candace lied.

"You know that I'd text you if we had anything for you."

"Well, I'm trying to pay my debt off as quickly as possible and though you're sending me some, I feel there could be more."

"Ambitious are we?" Leal smiled as she reached into the cabinet of the bar and pulled out a half drunken bottle of Jose Cuervo. She poured up two shots and looked over at Candace. "Have a drink with me."

"Y'all just have this sitting out like this for anyone to drink up?"

"Considering we typically only take visitors by appointments we're not really concerned about anyone cleaning us out. Besides, Robyn likes to make sure that her visitors are as comfortable as possible when they come."

"As liquored up as possible," Candace retorted, remembering how she'd come to have her very first drink as a teenager. "Probably in order to impair their judgment as she screws them over."

Leal took a breath and held a shot glass out to Candace. "Drink," she insisted.

Temptation got the best of her and Candace snatched the glass from her former friend's hand. "In honor of what?" she asked.

"New beginnings."

"Excuse me?"

Leal stepped closer Candace. "I don't know why you're so hot with her after all of these years but I am warning you...no, begging you, to leave it alone. Robyn will fuck you up, Candace. You and I both know what she's capable of."

"Do we? Why don't you enlighten me to what it is that you know exactly."

Leal shot her a pensive look. "Don't act coy with me. You know damn well that Robyn has pull. She's not one to be fucked with. And frankly, I'm not one to sit around and watch those I'm loyal to being fucked with."

"And you think I'm fucking with her?"

"Showing up at her house and getting buck? Being straight out disrespectful after all she did for you. Yeah, I think you're purposely trying to piss her off."

"Hmmm, and here I thought you really knew some shit."

Leal squinted her eyes. "I know that Robyn will make sure that L's ass rots in jail meaning you would have whored yourself out practically for free after your monetary debts paid off. I know that when someone rubs her the wrong way she has no problem setting them straight. You don't fuck her over and live to tell about it. Your parents are proof of that."

Candace's interest was piqued. "What?"

Leal realized her blunder and shook off her nervousness. "Uh...drink up, love. Today's an opportunity to start fresh and toss your grievances to the side. Don't keep pressing her buttons, okay?" She downed her liquor and sat the glass on the countertop of the bar.

Candace stared at her, reeling back the urge to strangle the bitch and force her to explain herself. But she didn't need an explanation; not really. Putting two and two together she was beginning to understand more than she could have ever imagined. Quickly, she threw back her shot, grimaced, and placed the glass next to Leal's. "Don't you worry about my grievances. You just worry about sending out your little appointment messages. I've got this." She turned to walk away and then stopped abruptly. "And the next time you pull a gun on me be ready to use it."

"You think you're so much better than everybody don't you? You think you intimidate me, Candace? I have everything you wish you had...money, my own child, not some hot-headed brother that I had to take responsibility of...power...your aunt's respect."

Candace laughed. "We'll see how long that lasts. I'm going to remember this shit, Leal. Trust. The way you've turned on me...I'm going to remember."

"Take a picture, it lasts longer."

"Very mature."

Leal shook her head. "Sure you don't want another shot before you hit the road?" she asked with a smirk. "I seem to have heard something about you being fond of drinking while intoxicated."

"Fuck you."

"That can be very dangerous." Leal smiled. "Drive safely, hun."

Candace dashed from the suite knowing that it was the best thing to do. Had she stayed a second longer, Leal would have been one dead bitch.

***

It was a Saturday afternoon and Candace was exhausted. Between working at the law firm during the day and handling her appointments every few nights out of the week, she was just about ready to call it quits. But, she couldn't do that. She was on a mission and her debt to her aunt would be over before she knew it. Meanwhile, she was working her plan to get even. Either one, one of the two things would work out and provide her with a little relief from the hectic double-life she was now leading.

Things were bad with Rico. They went whole days without speaking and she couldn't even remember the last time they'd had sex. It was just as well; if he entered her she feared that he would be able to tell that she was getting some action from elsewhere. She was so deep into the whole Madam/escort thing now that there was no way she could come out with the truth and expect him to actually stay with her. He would go berserk and their relationship would be as good as dead. It was already halfway in the grave now as a result of her secretiveness and the distance that was growing between them.

On the up side, a criminal attorney had contacted her regarding Lawrence's case. The referral that she'd had her ally put in for had actually worked out. Though they'd discussed his fees, Candace still wasn't sure how she was going to finance Attorney Blight's appointment to Lawrence's case. She had an idea, but hadn't yet figured out how to put it into play. Still, he was being patient with her on the strength of the relationship that Attorney Blight had with Robyn's attorney. So far, things were okay.

As she cruised towards the hotel where her next appointment was waiting, Candace heard the low hum of her cell phone. Quickly, she answered, recognizing the ringtone. "Long time no hear," she answered.

"I could say the same for you," Allison replied jovially in her ear. "How you doing out there with the new boo?"

"No complaints," she lied.

"You haven't had any run-ins with that crazy aunt of yours have you?"

Candace veered her car to the right to pull into the hotel's parking deck. "Nope. Everything's okay. I mean...Lawrence has a little issue, but I'm working on that."

"Oh no! That boy's not getting into trouble again is he? Girl, you just can't seem to get a break."

"It's fine. He's fine, I'm fine...we're all fine."

"And Rico's daughter?"

"Uhhh, she's having another procedure done this week. Fingers crossed that this will be the last one and that it'll work out the way they're saying it will."

"Poor thing."

"How's life at the base?"

"The same."

Candace frowned as she parked her car. Her silence resonated with Allison.

"Uh, you know what I mean, girl," Allison stated. "We're just doing our regular ole work and dealing with political bullshit. But I miss you. I miss you being here."

"I miss you too," Candace said softly.

"How's the job? Kayden's not giving you a hard time is he?"

Candace smiled. "Not at all. K.C.'s great. It's that witch that supervises me that makes me wanna scream." She laughed.

Allison chuckled. "Well, don't hurt nobody."

"I won't."

"Look, don't be a stranger okay? I really miss you, girl. Just because we aren't in the same city anymore doesn't mean that you have to distance yourself."

Candace thought about it. With all that was going on she really hadn't given much thought about her friendship with Allison. Life simply got in the way of any of the things that she would have normally done if she wasn't in such a fucked up situation. "Ally, I'm sorry. I'd really like to stay on the line and play catch up but there's something important I've got to tend to."

"Okay. I understand."

"No, you really don't. And one day I'll try to explain it to you, but right now...I gotta go."

"Tell Lawrence I said hi, okay? Take care of yourself, Candace."

"I will. Kiss the baby. Bye, girl."

Tossing her phone into her purse, Candace exited the car and headed for her destination. After a short elevator ride, she approached the appropriate door and let herself in with a room key that had already been given to her. As she walked into the room she noticed a dark-haired girl sitting down on the floor sipping on some champagne as a short gentlemen kissed her hand.

"Welcome," the man said, leering at Candace with dirt thoughts filling his head.

"Thank you for inviting me," Candace responded. "It looks like you've got quite an intimate party going on here. You're Oscar I presume?" she asked, drawing from the information that had been provided to her.

The man was 5'8 with light grey eyes which were squinty, almost shut, sandy brown hair, and a European accent. "Yes, yes. Welcome to the party, Ma'am. You were taking a little bit too long so Alex and I kinda got started without you. I hope you don't mind." He let out a squeaky laugh.

Candace made eye contact with Alex and the girl quickly rose to her feet to make a formal greeting. "Hi, I'm Alex," she said with a French accent.

Candace knew that she was another one of Robyn's girl's. She was pretty sure that the young thing was using her real name as well, something that Candace never did with her Johns. "Hello, how are you? I'm Monica," Candace replied.

Candace studied Alex for a moment. Alex stood about 5'9 and was noticeably fit. She wore some sexy cream white jeans and a red laced belly shirt that hug her 36C breasts and made each of them scream to be instantly released from their incarceration. The girl was very sexy and appeared to be relatively young. If her skill matched her appearance she was sure to be every John's fantasy.

"I see y'all have alcohol," Candace observed. "Pour me a glass." The order was given to no one in particular but she knew one of them would jump.

Oscar hurried over and poured Candace a glass of champagne. He then refilled Alex's glass. "Do you ladies need anything else?" he asked.

The two ladies looked at one another as Candace spoke. "No, I'm good."

"Me too," Alex said, following suite.

"Okay then, ladies," Oscar said, sitting the bottle of champagne down on the table and rubbing his hands together. "I'm a pretty straight forward guy. I'm not here to waste your time. I'm not here to waste my time. I paid your employer $10,000 earlier today for this meeting and I don't want to waste a second of my time or a dime of my money going back and forth over my wants and desires. So, tell me right now if you aren't down with what we are about to do tonight so that I can free you of your obligation and make the necessary arrangements to get my money back."

Each woman took a seat on the couch to solidify their intent upon staying.

"Very well," Oscar went on. "I'm sorry if I come off a bit brash. I guess I get that from my German side of the family. But anyway, I like my money and I like pussy. Both are equally important to me. It's fair to say that I know no limits when it comes to my two favorite subjects."

Alex fidgeted and the movement didn't go unnoticed.

"Are you disturbed by this, Alex?" Oscar asked.

"No, no...it isn't that," she answered naively. "It's just that...What exactly are we going to be doing tonight? I'm not going to lie to you, if it has something to do with cocaine, then I will call my Uber car and head home now."

Candace took a sip of her champagne and made a mental note to be sure to give the girls coaching before unleashing them into the realm of escorting. A call girl should never tell the John what she will or won't do unless she's established some dominant role in the relationship. There wasn't anything remotely dominant about Alex.

"No, no, no! I'm not that guy," Oscar assured her. "Don't get me wrong, I like to party but not that type of party. If I can't break it up, chop it up, cut it up and roll it up," he stated, impersonating Mystical, "then I don't fuck with it, babe. Anything else, ladies? Any other misgivings or concerns?"

"No. We're good," Candace answered as she sipped from her glass and looked over at Alex.

"Now that we have gotten that out the way, I think there's too much fucking tension in here right now. Either of you guys smoke weed?"

"Yea. You got some?" Candace answered quickly. Anything would be good to help take the edge off considering what she assumed was about to happen. She'd pressed Leal for more work to get the debt over and done with but she hadn't expected to be thrown into some orgy type of situation. Still, she was a professional and would play the role with ease, unlike Alex. A little weed mixed with the alcohol would only make the task easier.

"That's what I'm fucking talking about." Oscar pulled out his stashed and lit up a pre-rolled blunt. He took two puffs before passing it to Candace.

Candace pulled twice from the L and then handed it over to Alex whose eyes engorged quickly and then returned to normal at the sight of Candace's scowl. Alex took the joint and puffed a little too hard on it causing her to cough.

"Take it easy, Mama," Oscar coaxed her. "Drag slow."

Candace didn't say a word.

Alex got over her coughing spell and by the time the blunt was in its third rotation, she was at ease. Oscar turned on Pandora and sat in an armchair across from the girls.

"Alex," he said, watching Candace finish off the blunt. "Why don't you put your mouth around Monica's left tit?"

Candace noticed how it took Oscar no time at all to jump right into his perverseness.

"What kind of question is that ma? That's like going to war without your helmet and

Alex leaned over and slid the straps of Candace's tank top down to free her braless breasts. She lowered her head and took Candace's left nipple into her mouth just as instructed. Oscar watched with a smile. Getting into it, Alex squeezed Candace's right breast and a small moaning sound escaped her throat as she devoured Candace. Candace watched Oscar's facial expressions as he stared at the display of foreplay. She tossed the butt into a nearby ashtray and pushed Alex off of her.

"Hey!" Alex cried out.

Oscar moved to the edge of his seat and was about to protest but was stopped when he saw Candace peel off her shirt and then snatch off Alex's top as well. Alex's tiny, pert breasts looked like little plums. She had nipple piercings that instantly turned Oscar on.

Candace then started to suck on Alex's right breast in a circle motion around her barbell nipple ring before showing the left breast equal attention. The sensation forced Alex to release a long, loud moan.

"Oh God!! Oooohhh, oui, oui, oui," Alex cooed, half in English and half in French.

"Damn, Monica, you seem like you've done this a few times." Oscar spoke with excitement in his voice.

"Maybe once or twice," Candace responded as she took breathes in-between flicking her tongue against Alex's piercings. She looked over at Oscar and winked.

"Ohhhh, ça fait du bien," Alex continued to cry out in French as she felt her panties moisten. She'd never been with another female and Candace was turning her out right in front of their client. She looked up at Candace and spoke in a throaty tone. "Monica, you know I'm going to get you back right?"

"We will see," replied Candace as she laughed. She was unfazed; to her this was all just acting. She continued to lick and suck on Alex's nipples while squeezing her own.

Alex closed her eyes and moaned deeply. "Mmmmm."

"Oooohhh." A long moan came from Oscar as he squeezed his hands in-between his legs in excitement. "You ladies are the shit," stated Oscar as he pulled on yet another blunt dangling from his lips that neither of them hand seen him light.

Feeling daring, Alex flipped Candace over onto her back and began to kiss her passionately, squeezing her breasts, and gyrating against her leg. Soon, Alex beckoned for Oscar to join the party. As her tongue began to run vertically down Candace's stomach, Oscar seized the opportunity to replace where Alex's mouth had been by taking Candace's breast into his mouth.

Candace moaned. "Ooohhh....oooohhh."

Candace could feel Alex pulling down her mini skirt and then pushing her thongs to the side. As Oscar toyed with her breasts, Candace couldn't concentrate due to the sensation that Alex was causing down below. She began to squirm the feel of Alex's warm breath over her clit.

"Monica, I told you I was going to get you back," Alex teased as she started to kiss on Candace's inner thighs before flicking her tongue across Candace's clit.

"Oh my gosh!" Candace's breathing became irregular at the thought and feel of what Alex was doing.

Her gasps for air only made it more exciting for Oscar as he freed himself of his pants to give his erection room to stand out. He jacked his dick as he continued to suck on her large melons while watching the timid one burying her face between Candace's legs.

Candace was in heat, but it was interfering with her airway. "Y'all about to....make me..." She could barely get her words out as her hips gyrated against each stroke of Alex's novice tongue. "I-I-I'm gonna die. Ohhh, damn that shit feels so goodddddd."

Alex licked and sucked harder on Candace's pussy while Oscar matched her actions by sucking and licking Candace's breasts harder. From top to bottom, Candace felt as if she was about to explode.

"Alex!" Candace cried out. "Alex! Alex! Stop! St-st-stop! I'm about cum."

"Cum, baby," Alex encouraged her.

"No, Stop!" Candace wanted to curse her body for actually enjoying the threesome. "I'm about to cum!"

"Cum on my tongue, baby," Alex murmured as she inserted her tongue inside of Candace's drenched opening.

"Oh no...oh no! I'm about...I'm about. Oh my God!" Candace's legs began to shake uncontrollably as she tried to use her hand to move Alex's mouth from her pussy. But it was useless.

Alex was intent upon getting Candace to gush in her mouth and she got exactly what she asked for. Oscar pulled back and watched in amazement as Candace screamed out her pleasure and Alex tongue fucked Candace straight through her climax. Turned on, Oscar abandoned his post, ran around to get behind Alex, and began to fuck her from the back.

"Oh!" Alex called out, feeling the impact of his rather large dick.

"Fuck, this pussy is so good!" Oscar screamed as he stroked in and out of Alex's petite body.

Candace got in an upright position and fondled Alex's breasts as their John gave the younger girl the business.

"Right there baby, right there, baby," Oscar coached as Alex threw her ass back against his thrusts. "Oh yeah, just like that."

It didn't take long for the man to orgasm as he body shuddered in quick jerks. He held Alex's waist tight as he spilled all of his love juices over into her body. Candace shuddered at the thought, making another mental note to mandate the girls to take condoms on every run with them in the future.

Recovering from his orgasm, Oscar pulled out of Alex and collapsed onto the floor. He looked down at his expensive time piece and sighed. "Damn, that was fun. It was nice having y'all here but I'm going to need you to get out before my wife and family comes back from their shopping and lunch date."

Candace stared at him in disbelief before hopping up to retrieve her clothing. Alex fell right in line with her. That was the kind of shit she had to deal with; cheating ass, horny men doing her up and whisking her off before the love of their lives found out about their bullshit.

CHAPTER 10
CURRENT DAY

Fuck, Candace thought, her mind a blur of thoughts about her past and how she'd ended up playing call-girl. It was as if life had spiraled out of control and she was grasping at straws trying to get things back in order. With purposeful steps, she made the trek to her car from the office building. She had at gig across town in two hours that had been set up days ago. The hotel key had been passed along to her by Raul upon a visit to the office. It seemed that Robyn was enjoying having her holed up in various hotel rooms like a real common whore these days. But it was fine with Candace; anything to get her balance depleted or least keep Robyn off her ass until the real moment of truth.

Tonight was going to be a little different for Candace. She had two appointments back to back. Before, the thought of servicing two strangers would have made her vomit. But, she was used to doing all kinds of foul things now. Nothing Robyn and Leal threw at her surprised Candace anymore. Her phone buzzed again as she pulled into rush hour traffic. She looked down and decided to ignore the text. Leal was getting on her damn nerves with her multiple check ins. She knew where she was going and what she was supposed to be doing; she didn't need the head Madam's flunky babysitting her.

It took nearly forty-five minutes for her to make it to the St. Regis Hotel. The valet relieved her of her car and she sashayed into the foyer and towards the elevator with her

Louis Vuitton tote bag dangling from her shoulder. She rode to her appointed floor alone, got off and headed for the room that had been booked for her. Upon entering the deluxe suite, Candace smiled. The décor was so simplistic yet soothing in nature with its taupe and mineral color scheme and the ebony wood furnishings. The overall feel of the hotel itself was majestic. If only this was a social visit and not an illegal work arrangement.

In the bathroom, she found all that she needed to enjoy a quick yet soothing bath in the deep soaking tub. Even the scent of the amber and honey bath wash made her feel as if she was in another world. After drying off, she pulled a thin gray slip dress from her bag and wiggled her body into it. She pulled her hair back into a messy bun and checked her reflection in the bathroom mirror. She remembered a time when her work attired consisted of a uniform and hat and not a slinky nightgown. Her morals had done a complete about face and she was no longer the woman she'd been a year ago. It was funny how time changed a person's circumstances, beliefs, and behavior.

From the crack of the bathroom door she heard the open and close of the hotel room door. She glanced down at her cell phone which was resting on the counter. It was 6:54 P.M. Her first guest of the night was a little early.

"Hello?" a male's voice called out. "Monica?"

It was her 'stage-name' if you will and the Johns were becoming accustomed to asking for her by name now. Better she use a fake name verses her real name. No one needed to know who she really was.

"I'll be right out," she shouted, still looking at her face in the glass. She wondered just how long it would take for him to handle his business and get out. Her next guest was scheduled to arrive at 8:00 P.M. and she didn't have time for this current appointment to overlap. The sooner they got it over with the better.

"Take your time. You know, I was anxious to meet you," the man spoke loudly. "I've heard great things about your...uhhhh...services if you will. I'm looking for someone on a permanent basis really. Someone who can...ummmm...meet me weekly at prearranged location. I'm all about your comfort and making sure that it's a mutually pleasing agreement."

As the man continued speaking, a since of familiarity filled Candace. Something about the sound of his voice made her feel as if she knew him. Then again, after a while all of the Johns seemed the same to her. She took a deep breath and mentally prepared herself to handle yet another client. She exited the bathroom to find him helping himself to a drink at the fully stocked bar. She considered having one herself but decided she'd much rather remain sober. She surveyed his frame from behind and marveled over how well-built he appeared from that angle. She smiled, wondering to herself what a man with such a nice voice and body would be doing ordering up a high-priced escort.

"Thanks for your patience," she said sweetly, standing near the plush, queen sized bed.

The blinds covering the doors of the balcony were open and she looked out at the view of the hustle and bustle overlooking West Paces Ferry. The room reminded her a little bit of the hotel suite she and Lawrence had stayed in during their mini-vacation. She missed that time period where they had been free and able to live life without lying, scheming, and being in someone else's debt.

"Patience is a virtue," he told her. "Can't be without those."

She found it odd that a man paying for sex would be lecturing her about virtues, but she remained silent.

He mixed his rum and cranberry juice, took a swig while simultaneously turning around, and then spat out the liquid as his eyes looked her over and his brain made the connection. "Oh my God!" he spoke in a quivering tone as he sat his glass down. "You're not...Y-y-you're not Monica."

Candace was frozen by her shock. Of course he sounded familiar; why wouldn't he when she heard his voice every single day? It made sense now. Of course he'd be getting special, high-quality fucks in expensive hotels since he was making sure that Aunt Robyn stayed out of the legal hot seat. Candace's blood boiled as she thought about the probability of her aunt knowing just what she was doing when she approved the appointment for her. *Bitch*, Candace thought.

Mr. Jackson, one of the partners at the firm where Candace worked by day, stared at her in disbelief. "Candace?" He called her name as if he wasn't sure whether or not she was truly there. "What are you doing here?"

I believe the true question is what are you doing here?"

He considered it and knew that he would have to work quickly to spin this whole thing in a positive direction. "I...I uhhhh...It's not what you think."

Seeing how nervous he was, Candace realized that she'd ultimately been placed in a position of power. Aunt Robyn had miscalculated. Somehow she must have thought that forcing her to screw her boss was going to fuck her over but in the end it actually gave her the upper hand. "Oh, but I'm pretty sure that it's exactly what I think. I mean, you said it yourself, Sir. You said that you're looking for a permanent girl to meet you weekly to ummmm...to do what? Suck your dick? Ride the shit out of you? Fuck you like you've never been fucked before?"

Mr. Jackson shook his head. "I wouldn't...no, no, no. I'd never go so far as to—"

"As to what?" Candace challenged. "Pay for sex? But isn't that what's happened? You paid Robyn to have one of her pretty little flexible eager to please call girls meet you here in this lavish room so that you could live out your little fantasy of fucking some exotic looking chick, right?" Candace folded her arms, daring him to call her a liar.

"But...But I didn't pay for anything. It was a favor....I mean, this is all a misunderstanding. I was just looking for companionship. But I swear that I didn't pay a cent for sex."

Candace was seething. Aunt Robyn was even more of a bitch than she'd thought. They'd sent Candace out on this appointment and the dude wasn't even a paying customer. The thought of being loaned out for free grated Candace's nerves. She'd never be able to pay back her debt with her aunt cheating her out of paying appointments. "You know exactly what Robyn does. You've been her attorney for years. I know what I was told to do...I was paged to come here and fuck you however you wanted in exchange for payment to my Madam. I have a contract stating that I'm Robyn's call girl and any law official or media reporter would be more than glad to hear me out."

Mr. Jackson raised his hand in the air and stepped forward. "Whoa, whoa, whoa! Let's not bring anyone else into this, okay? I told you, there was a misunderstanding."

"I understand exactly why I'm here, Mr. Jackson. But here's what you need to understand, contrary to whatever my aunt was thinking I don't fuck for free."

"Jesus, Robyn's your aunt?" he shouted, running his hand over his head and connecting the dots. Candace Williams. He'd recently seen her name on papers pertaining to Robyn's estate but hadn't put two and two together. Then he realized what the pretty girl had just said. "B-b-but, I'm not asking you to fuck." He laughed nervously. "No, no, no. I'm not asking you to fuck for free at all. I mean, I'm not asking you to fuck at all."

"Okay, fine then...I don't meet men in upscale hotel rooms for free under the pretense of servicing them. This visit, however nonsexual it may or may not be, comes with a price, you feel me?"

She was blackmailing him and he knew it. His temples began to pulsate wondering what the paralegal could possibly wish to extort from him. He wanted to kick himself for taking Robyn up on her offer. He knew that it was too generous to be true, but she'd offered so many times over the years and his dick was so dry from the lack of sex he was getting at home that he'd been desperate to do something to remedy the situation. Now here he was with his reputation on the line and a paralegal holding his horniness over his head.

"What is it?" he asked. "You want me to promote you? Give you a raise? You want a special bonus? Just name it so that we can put this whole thing past us."

"You were asked refer an attorney to me for my brother, Lawrence Williams."

"Yes, yes. And I did that. The guy was supposed to contact you directly."

"He did. He assessed my brother's case and told me his fee but I'm not going to pay it."

"Okay," Mr. Jackson replied, looking confused. "Why not?" he asked, taking the bait.

"Because you are. Tomorrow, in full. Otherwise, I go to the press and tell them how you're helping Robyn cover up her brothel as a freaking consulting business and that you are one of her top paying Johns."

"But you can't do that!"

"I can and I will unless you do what I ask. Deal?"

He considered the alternative. He couldn't afford to lose his wife, his clients, his business and the stellar reputation that he had for himself in Atlanta. Society would chew him up and spit him out if ever they found out about his shady business practices, not to mention soliciting sex. Mr. Jackson lowered his head in shame and nodded. "Fine, fine," he agreed. "I'll have the money wired over to him tomorrow."

"I'm going to need you to forward me an e-mail confirmation of that," Candace replied. "You can just send it to my work e-mail." She smirked. "In addition you will make certain that your little buddy gets my brother off on all charges, including the assault charge...no matter what."

Mr. Jackson looked at the expression on her face and it didn't take long for him to grasp her meaning. "You...you're talking extortion? You want me to pay off somebody? The jury? The judge."

"Whomever." Candace didn't even blink an eye as she made the order.

Mr. Jackson shook his head. "You're trying to pull me into some deep shit, Candace."

"You're already in deep shit."

He couldn't argue. "I don't think you'll have to worry about paying off the judge. Judge Bennett is trying your brother's case. He's in your aunt's pocket so you shouldn't have a problem there."

"Excuse me?"

"He's on her client list. I'm sure if you hit him with the same bullshit you're hitting me with then you won't have a problem."

Candace nodded. This just couldn't get any better. She was beginning to appreciate the close knit circuit her aunt had built for herself. "That's your task. Make it happen."

"I could get disbarred for this if anyone found out."

"Mmmhmmm. But where was your conscience when you were doing Robyn's bidding for her and keeping her ass out of jail? You could also get disbarred if anyone found out about your little plan for tonight and ongoing."

He stared at her. "Fine," he said. "I'll do it and then we'll be good right?"

Candace shrugged. "Unless I can think of any other way that you could be of good use to me."

"Come on. Let's not drag this out."

"You're the boss at your office, Mr. Jackson," she stated, heading towards the door. "But here, in this situation, I'm in control." She opened the door and turned to smile at him once more. "So until next time my love."

"Son of a bitch!" another male's voice called out from the hallway.

Candace turned her head but was unable to do anything to stop Rico from barging in and sucker punching Mr. Jackson right dead in the nose. The older man stumbled backwards onto the bed and blood began to stain the beige bedspread as Rico pounced on him and continuously punched the man in the face.

"Rico, no!" Candace shouted, running over to the scene and struggling to pull her boyfriend off of her boss. "Please! Stop it. Baby, stop! Listen to me!"

Rico climbed off of the man who was now cowering in the middle of the bed. He shook his wrist feeling the soreness of his knuckles and the swelling of his hand. He turned and looked at Candace, his chest rising and falling with anger. "I trusted you."

"I can explain," she said lowly, afraid that his aggression would now be directed at her.

"All this time you been creeping, lying, and shit. You been out here fucking this old cat. What the fuck's wrong with you bitches? You got a good man at home trying to provide for you but you'd rather have your fuckin' cake and eat it too."

"It isn't like that!" Candace cried out again.

"No? You up here in this fancy ass hotel. You fuckin' half-dressed looking like you came straight out the pages of Playboy, and you in here with this dude talkin' 'bout 'til next time."

"It's an assignment, baby," Candace said. "A job. I'm working. I swear it."

"That's what you calling it now? This ain't no after-hours law firm shit, Candace."

Now wasn't the time to mention to him that Mr. Jackson actually was the big boss at the firm where she worked.

"Unless you a hoe or something now, ain't no such thing as working when you laid up in some hotel."

The room fell silent. Mr. Jackson stood at the foot of the bed afraid to make a move towards the exit. In one evening he'd gotten blue balls since clearly he wasn't going to get any pussy, he'd gotten blackmailed, and then he'd gotten beat up. All he wanted was to get far away from St. Regis and pray to God for allowing him to make it out alive.

Candace looked down at the ground for a moment and then back up at Rico with a guilty expression. She clasped her hands together and tried to find the words to save her ass before it was too late.

"Sneaking out at night," Rico said abstracting. "Coming home smelling like smoke...What? You thought I didn't notice? I'm a smoker, babe. Getting beat up, running errands for your aunt at night. You whoring? Is that what the fuck you're doing now?"

"I...I can explain."

"Explain what? Why you letting random men run up in your every other night for money? What the fuck are you thinking? I was gonna marry you! I wanted you to meet my daughter! I moved you out here with me and then you go out and become a hoe!"

"Stop calling me that."

"What am I supposed to say, Candace? Huh? Ain't that what you doing?" He pointed to the shaking Mr. Jackson.

"Ain't that what you just did with ole' boy? Whored yaself out?"

"Rico, if you'll just listen to me."

"I don't want to listen to you. I been trying to talk to you for a minute now but all you cared about was your secret lil' hustle. Jesus...is it your aunt? Are you in business with that bitch now because none of this shit was happening before we went to see her?"

Again Candace was silent.

"Fuck!" Rico called out. "What the fuck kinda family do you have man? Who the fuck decides, hey let me go be a hoe?"

Candace couldn't take it any longer. "Fuck you, Rico! I'm not a hoe! I'm doing it for L! We didn't have the money to get him out of jail or to cover his legal fees. You couldn't handle it because your money's all tied up in Kelsey's medical fees and I didn't have it either so I figured out a way to make it happen. You wanna crucify me for that, fine! But I worked this shit out and I'm handling our finances better than you'll ever know. You can either trust me on that or keep standing there and judging me, but fuck you for looking down on me when I was only trying to take care of my brother!"

Rico didn't have a rebuttal. She'd said a mouthful and he was sinking it all in. His eyes ventured over to Mr. Jackson who was staring at the two of them awkwardly. "Get the hell out," he ordered the man.

Mr. Jackson didn't need to be told twice. He hightailed it to the open door feeling relieved. Candace was right behind him.

"Don't forget," she told him. "Nothing's changed."

He simply nodded and approached the elevator directly across from the hotel room. The bell dinged and the door opened before Mr. Jackson could even press the down button. He stepped to the side to allow a handsome, muscular gentleman to exit before hurrying inside and frantically pressing the closed door so that he could get far away from St. Regis.

Candace was once again dumbfounded as she stood rooted to the spot. Their eyes met as he approached the door with an awkward look on his face. She wanted to sink right through the floor in order to avoid the next big fall out that was about to occur, but this was no cartoon; this was real life and all of this bullshit was truly happening.

"What are you doing here?" she asked breathlessly. She'd been so sure that she'd never see him again.

Their chance meeting months ago had been surreal—to say the least—but meeting again clear across the continent couldn't have possibly been a coincidence. Was God playing a cruel joke on her? What had she done in her past lives to be so traumatized now with all of this mess that was being placed on her?

"We never got to finish what we started," he told her, reaching out and touching a lose strand of her hair. "So this time I figured I'd make sure there were no interruptions."

"What?" she asked, confused by his statement. "What are you talking about?"

"You don't come cheap, beautiful." He leaned forward to kiss her.

Candace took a step back and slapped his face. "You bastard!" she called out.

"What the hell's going on?" Rico asked, standing behind her.

"Who's this?" Sean asked, stroking his face.

"Her man. Who the fuck are you?"

"Her paying customer for the next two hours, motherfucker."

Candace was sick to her stomach. She'd been setup. She didn't know how Robyn had managed to pull it off, how she'd gotten in contact with Sean, but she'd created an entire plan to humiliate her within one night. Candace looked at Sean in disgust. "I can't believe you."

Sean laughed. "Me? Imagine my surprise when I got a call from some old chick telling me that the woman I thought I was in love with once could be mine for one whopping fee. She visited me at the hotel that weekend and told me that I could have you whenever I wanted if I was willing to put up the money. She called me a few days ago and told me when and where I could find you. I didn't believe it and you damn sure wasn't trying to explain yourself. I assume that you bailed on me that night because you had a paying fuck to attend to."

"Go to hell!" Candace shouted.

"Right after you my dear. I couldn't believe that the pretty smart woman I knew would ever go into the sex-trade business. So I paid her...I had to see for myself...and here you are with not one, but two men leaving your suite before I come through."

"You're so fuckin' off base," Candace told him.

"Aye, you need to leave partna'," Rico said, pushing his way in front of Candace.

"But I paid my money like everybody else," Sean lightly protested.

Rico stepped closer to the man with his fists clenched.

Sean noticed the violent rage in Rico's eyes and decided to cut his losses. "Fine," he said. "I already know what it's hitting like anyway. Too bad I couldn't really get my money's worth, but I'm glad I didn't waste my time or energy on some whore." He threw his head up at Rico. "Take it easy, homeboy. She's all yours."

Sean turned away, approached the elevator bank, and pressed the down button three times. When nothing happened, he threw the couple a quizzical look and quickly decided to take the stairs.

The moment the other man was out of eyesight, Rico turned to face Candace. She was shaking with betrayal, humiliation, misery, and anger. A man whom she'd felt connected to, felt like she once had a kismet alliance with, had pretty much made it known that he had paid for her services. Right to her face Sean had regarded her as nothing more than a whore. Hoe: it was what Rico had been calling just before the whole encounter with Sean. Tears burned her eyes as she realized how the men she loved, at one point or another viewed her.

"You got a whole lot of explaining to do," Rico said through gritted teeth,

Candace nodded and wiped away her tears. He was right, but where was she to begin?

CHAPTER 11

"Leal, come to my office now please."

The request was abrupt and to the point. Within seconds, Leal was standing in front of Robyn's desk with a notepad and pen just in case something important was about to be said.

"Everything in place for the party?" the Queen Bee asked.

Leal nodded. "Yes, all the contractors have been paid, the girls you wanted invited have been invited, the top picks from the client list have been invited, and we have the roof top secured for the evening. Everything's good to go."

"Perfect." Robyn leaned back in her chair and patted her bouncy curls. "I deserve this."

Leal looked down at her hands nervously. She had a lot on her mind. Lately, she hadn't been feeling her best and she really needed some time to rest. Robyn had her running around the clock. Not that she wasn't grateful to her for keeping her laced with cash and changing her lifestyle drastically, but it seemed that all the woman cared about was making money and breaking hearts. Leal was certain that even Satan let up some times.

"Hey, I need you to make contact with Judge Bennett's office and handle what we talked about earlier," the boss instructed. "Make sure that he knows I'm not playing with him and that if he fucks this up I have the AJC on speed-dial. Even if you gotta show him the pictures of him and whatever bitch he ordered up last month. Do what you have to do. I want that boy's ass to rot in prison."

It was a sadistic request but who was Leal to argue? She needed her job so that she could continue making her money, the money which helped to fund her heavy medical expenses, her kids private school, and the nanny that looked after her children when she was too busy working or too sick to so much as hug them.

"Got it," Leal answered.

"Also order me some lemon pepper wings with fries from Atlanta's Best Wings. Hurry up; I'm hungry as fuck right now."

Just as Leal walked out to do as she was told, the office phone rang. Robyn looked down and saw that it was her home number on the screen. She snatched up the receiver before anyway at the front desk could answer it.

"I told you never to call me from the house phone," she snapped in a whispered voice.

Leal pulled the door up but not before she'd heard the woman's panicked statement. Who could be calling her from her house phone? Intrigued, Leal entered her office and gently eased her phone receiver from the cradle. She typically knew everything that was going on in Robyn's life; they rarely kept secrets. She was interested in knowing what was going on.

"That's how you speak to me now?" a male voice stated. "I'm just saying, you ain't gotta talk to me like I'm one of your lil' punk ass clients or something."

"No, no. I didn't mean it like that," Robyn said. "It's just that I told you it's too risky for you to be calling me from the house phone. No one needs to know where you are during the day...no one needs to know who you are."

"Well ya lil' gay homie at the front desk wouldn't put me through earlier when I called via private number from my cell."

"Raul?"

"Yes. He kept telling me that you were unavailable."

"I'll deal with his ass."

"I shoulda dealt with his ass before."

"That's all neither here nor there. What are you doing?"

"Nothing, I've been just chilling at the crib. Waiting on you to get here so we can finish what we started this morning before you went to work."

"Mmmm mmmm. Sounds good to me," Robyn said as she licked her lips. She loved the way he put it on her with his young ass. She hadn't had meaningful sex in eons but the moment she found his brazened chest, thick dick, strong personality, and beautiful smile she knew that she couldn't let him slip thru her fingers. "How's the baby doing?"

"She's doing alright. Just laying here on my lap. We have to go to the doctor later today to get a checkup, but everything else appears to be normal. She's actually been asking about you."

"Well, tell my baby that I will there as soon as I handle business here. I have to solidify some things but after I get confirmation of what I need then I'll slide home to see my three babies."

Still eavesdropping, Leal threw her hand over her mouth in shock. Baby? Or was it babies? Where the hell did Robyn get children from and how on earth did it ever get past her?

"By business I'm assuming you're talking about this shit you got going with Candace and L," the man concluded.

"'Cause we all know you don't do much at work but order Leal's simple ass around."

"I delegate," Robyn corrected him. "That's what you do when you're the boss."

"What are you about to do?"

"Why the sudden interest in how I handle my family? I'm not telling you shit for you to go back and tell that little slut of a niece of mine. You think I'm stupid? I'm not about to be the topic of your pillow talk any more than I already am."

"Really, boo? Haven't I shown you that I'm only loyal to you? You told me to charm her ass, I did that. You told me to get her back to Atlanta, I did that. You told me to encourage her to come to you for help, I did that. You told me to act like I'on know what's up, I do that. So... shut the fuck with that stupid shit."

"You mean to tell me that in all the time you've been keeping up this charade that you haven't developed feelings for the little bitch?"

"Nah. I'm true to one and one only. Long as you keep taking care of Kelsey and keep her whore ass mama away from her then I'm good."

Robyn cringed. Was that really his bottom line? She'd been financing his daughter's medical care with the Emory Health Care Team since her illness was discovered. But long before then, she'd officially adopted the child as her own once she was born to one of Robyn's hardest working call-girls who unfortunately was also an addict. When he, the child's father, approached Robyn and begged her to free Heather from her contract she came up with a better plan: for an exuberant amount of money, she gave him a better life in exchange for his and Heather's consent to adopt Kelsey. High and stupid, Heather signed away her rights and continued working her appointments until she was found in a back alley apparently having overdosed on cocaine.

Robyn brushed off the memories of her conniving deeds. "I'm sorry, sweetheart. I'm just having a stressful day. The party's this weekend and then I'm dealing with this...situation...Ugh...I hate ungrateful people. I wouldn't even be bothered with any of this if Candace and L weren't so damn ungrateful and disloyal. But not my Kelsey. I know she'd never turn on Mommy."

In the background Robyn could hear a light whimpering sound.

"Uh, that's Kelsey," he said. "I gotta go."

"I'll be there soon, but if I don't make it before two then you guys should go ahead and clear out. Wouldn't want to walk in with Leal later and risk running into you."

"Aight, I got you. See you later."

"I love—" Robyn's statement was cut off by the sound of the dial tone. She stared at the receiver and then quickly put it down feeling ticked that he'd cut her off when she was attempting to be affectionate. Brushing it off, she turned to stare out of her window and await news from Leal.

***

Leal was stunned. Gently, she returned her receiver to the cradle and simply stared at the phone. Her brain was busy connecting all of the dots and eventually her stomach began to turn from her realizations. Robyn was obviously a lot grimier than she'd ever thought. True, it was bad that she'd set her own niece up to have the love of her life catch her in the act of whoring. It was despicable that she'd set her nephew up to go to jail and then planned to bribe the judge into making sure that he served hard time although she'd forced Candace into an escort contract to pay his bail. It was even disheartening to know the role that Robyn had played in Candace and L's parents' demise, a secret that had been revealed on a night when Robyn had had far too much to drink during one of her depressed stupors. But, knowing this now...hearing how she'd been pulling so many strings and toying with Candace's happiness all this time was just like pouring lemon juice in a wound. When Robyn set out to destroy someone she really went for the jugular.

Leal shook her head as she hurriedly placed the call to Atlanta's Best to put in Robyn's order. With that task down, she sent over a quick e-mail to the judge's chamber with images attached. It sickened her to know that she was continuously doing the bidding of a woman with little to no scruples. The reality was that if she were to ever go against Robyn's wishes or disagree with her at any time, it could very well be her life that the woman turned upside down. Morally, Leal was repulsed. She was beginning to hate herself for shunning Candace and the role she was playing in screwing the girl over. But, with her own issues she was just too far in now to get out. Sadly, she needed Robyn—well; she needed the money that Robyn paid her. There was no way that she'd be able to afford her expenses on some meager salary offered to her for some office job.

The truth was that she had no skill outside of running the escort service and being an escort herself. But even more to the point, once anyone learned that she was HIV positive, a gift given to her by a former, regular John and one of the reasons why Robyn had given her administrative duties thus pulling her off of the call list, she'd be out on her ass with nowhere to go. Yep, Robyn had a hold on her much like everyone else she screwed with.

***

His conscience had been fucking with him for some time now and Robyn's question had struck a chord with him that he couldn't ignore. The shit was foul and he was tired of being and in thick of her constant dirty deeds. He picked up his cell and hit the speed dial option to reach a familiar number.

"Hello?" Candace answered eagerly.

She hadn't heard from him since the day he'd left her in the hotel suite. When he'd told her to explain herself, all she could give him was that she was doing what she could to help Lawrence. She couldn't bring herself to tell him her plans to fuck over Robyn because the fact that she was escorting alone was far too much to deal with. She figured she'd tell him everything in increments eventually, but her heart was broken when he'd walked away from her. She was sure that their relationship was over. She couldn't blame him. Now that he was calling after two days, hope sprung eternal and she grasped the phone tightly as she prayed for the right words to say to bring her love back to her.

"How you doing?" he asked as if they'd just spoken the day before.

"Miserable from missing you."

"Yeah?"

"I'm so sorry, baby. I really am. I mean, I can't tell you how sorry I am. I should have been upfront with you from the beginning, but I didn't think you'd understand. I mean, I'm sure it's really a difficult thing for anyone to accept...and I...I didn't want to lose you. But if you just give me—"

"Do you love me?" he asked, cutting her off.

"Yes," she said without hesitating, speech slurred and all. "Yes...yes, I do."

"Are you drinking?"

"Wouldn't you be?"

She had a point. He leaned his head back against the pillows on the bed that now seemed foreign to him. He'd become accustomed to lying beside Candace, holding her, smelling her, seeing her beautiful face. The farce had eventually become his reality and now his loyalties were switching up and he wasn't sure how things would turn out in the end.

"Look, I think we've both been keeping some secrets that the other may or may not understand. But if you love me like you say you do then maybe we can sort it all out and move past it." He took a breath before jumping in further. ""'Cause I love you, Candace, and I swear I don't wanna see you living a life of hurt."

Candace was confused. "Wh-what's going on, Rico?"

"There's something I need to tell you but you gotta promise me that you'll hear me out and not hang up, aight?"

Candace grabbed her bottle of Ciroc and took a swig. It was way too early to be drinking but she'd skipped work, finding it pointless to go at this point, and needed to wallow in her own misery for a while. "Okay," she said, uncertain of what to expect to roll off of his tongue. "Give it to me."

***

The light drizzled danced on the windshield as they sat in her car in a parking lot a block away from Robyn's office building. She handed him a Ziploc bag of white powder.

"Bitch, what's this?" he asked.

"Make sure her drinks stay laced with it all night," she instructed.

He shook his head and flipped his bone straight hair shoulder. "Oh no ma'am. I'm not playing pusher. What's this? Crack. No, no. You got me all the way fucked up."

"Stop being so dramatic. It's not crack you nut. It's crushed up oxycodone. A whole prescription's worth. I get it for my migraines. Anyway, it's enough for a bitch to overdose on."

His eyes danced with understanding. "Ruthless bitch!"

"You better know it." She had no emotion. With all the ammo she had fueling her hate, there was nothing left to feel except for triumph once the bitch was extinct.

He held the bag in his hand and surveyed the fine powder. "You worked hard on crushing this up, huh?"

"I had a little time and frustration to work with."

"You know that bitch had the audacity to fire me the other day over some damn phone call shit? Leal came behind her and told me to ignore her, that they needed me, but I don't need this fickle bullshit in my life." He smiled at the powder. "My spirit says she's the devil hunny." He laughed. "And the devil does indeed wear Prada. Mmmm Mmmm. Scandalous."

"We good?" she asked, ready to get on with prepping herself for the upcoming event.

"Yep. We're good."

"No fuck ups."

"Oh, hunny. Have I failed you yet?"

She thought about it. Because of him she was able to quickly secure the documents she needed, which rested right in her purse, to give her controlling reign over Pleasure Principle. In addition to those papers were also confirmation e-mails of L's attorney being paid in full and the arrangement with Judge Bennett, pictures and all, making everything on her end good to go. That last tidbit of information had made its way to her personal e-mail from a surprising source, but she'd had it confirmed by Mr. Jackson himself and was pleased to know that Lawrence would not see one day inside of a prison.

"You're the best," she told her ally. "Thanks for trusting me."

He smiled. "Oh suga, thank me with some real benjamins once you take over."

"Consider it done."

***

"Another drink, Madam?" Raul offered Robyn a full glass of champagne.

She eyed him suspiciously knowing damn well that she'd fired him earlier in the week. Still, she drained her current glass and then took the one he was handing her. She was already beginning to fill lifted and festive. There was no sense in tearing him a new ass right then and there. It was a party—her party. She'd let his ass enjoy the luxury of being in her presence before crushing his spirits on Monday. She sipped from her glass and turned away from him without so much as a thank you.

Looking around at the crowd, she smiled. The weather was holding up beautifully and the roof top deck of her office building was splendidly decorated with cream-colored table clothes covering circular tables with matching sashays on the white wooden chairs. The posts were covered with strings of clear lights creating a mystical affect in the light of the evening sky. Her cream colored dress with the golden undertones complimented the décor perfectly. Her makeup was flawless and her weave was laid to perfection. Watching as her special selected guests drank merrily and helped themselves to the buffet offered by the caterer, who'd fucked up her menu choices, made Robyn proud. This was her legacy, her world, her doing. She controlled it all. There wasn't a person in attendance that didn't owe her something, be it her girls or her clients. As for the public officials that were present, she paid them handsomely in order to keep her business operating with no problems. From police officers to judges, right down to military personnel and politicians, she had all of their numbers. Her two weapons of choice spoke volumes no matter who you were: pussy and money, no one could resist one or the other.

"Enjoying the party?" Leal asked, coming up behind her.

"Quite. Thank you, dear."

Leal could tell by the goofy grin on her face and the slur of her speech that Robyn had had one too many drinks. "Perhaps you should slow down." She motioned towards the glass of champagne.

"It's just champagne," she replied. "It's a celebration. My celebration. What's that bullshit the young people are saying these days? Turn down for what?" She laughed and lightly stumbled backwards.

Leal rolled her eyes. She paused for a second and figured that this was a good time to try to lobby for a break. "Listen, Robyn, I really need a little vacation. My body's exhausted and—"

Robyn waved her off. "Take vitamins. Our business doesn't rest so neither do we." With that, Robyn walked off and hooked her arm around that of the police chief for the Atlanta Police Department.

Leal watched her employer in disbelief. Even drunk the woman was a bitch. It had taken years for her to finally see Robyn for who she was and she didn't like it one bit. But, even worse, she hated the person that Robyn had forced her to become. All partied out, Leal turned around, sat her half empty glass of champagne on a nearby table and headed to the door to exit the roof top party just as a few drops of rain kissed her face.

Robyn mixed and mingled with her royal subjects as she privately considered them trying her best to ignore the droplets that seemed to start falling out of nowhere.

"Ma'am, we're going to move the buffet inside now," the head of the catering service advised.

Robyn squinted feeling as though she was seeing double. Around her, guests were starting to head to the exit.

"Where's Leal?" Robyn asked.

"Who?" the caterer asked.

"Leal! My assistant!" She huffed upon getting no response. "Fine, fine. Move the stuff inside. Go on."

The hustle and bustle around her had Robyn swaying as she looked on. Earlier she'd felt some kind of way by not having Rico attend the party with her. Sometimes she really loathed living in silence. He was the steadiest relationship she had and it was a shame that she couldn't share their love with the world. After all, he and Kelsey were the only people that truly loved her. Everyone else in the world simply feared her. While she loved the power that gave her, there were moments when all she wanted was to be normal and loved.

"Here, Madam. You look like you could use this." It was the gay guy stuffing another drink in her hand.

Robyn took it and took a gulp as he headed for the door behind everyone else. Sighing, Robyn followed the crowd being last to make it to the door. Before she could cross the threshold, she came face to face with the last person that she expected to attend her soiree.

"What are you doing here?" Robyn asked, glaring at the woman who had caused her so much heartache over the years.

"I'm a part of the company," Candace said, steadily moving forward causing her aunt to step backwards back onto the roof top. "Why wouldn't I be here?"

"Shouldn't you be somewhere resting up for your next appointment? It can't be easy for a double working girl like you to keeping going from day to day."

"And what would you know at all about my daily life struggles?"

Robyn sipped from her glass and smiled. "You think you're struggling now? You ain't seen nothing yet dear."

"Hmmm," Candace let out. "Educate me."

"Life will educate you. I've done all I could."

"I'll say. That was some plan you had there, Aunt Robyn...setting me up to get caught up with Sean...forcing me to have to fuck my boss for money only to fuck me out of the payment in the end."

"Whatever do you mean, dear?" Robyn asked, laughing cynically. "A man paid for a fuck and I gave him you."

"Bullshit! You sought Sean out to humiliate me. But I'm over that." Candace moved closer to her aunt as rain drops bounced on the concrete of the deck. "My beef with you is far greater. This isn't about you whoring me out for free or humiliating me. This is about loyalty."

Robyn stumbled as she laughed in her niece's face. Her champagne spilled over the side of her glass as she lost her balance. "You silly girl. What the hell do you know about loyalty? I went out of my way to care for you and your brother...to give you a better life. And how did you repay me? You spat in my face and turned your back on me. You know nothing about loyalty!"

"So in exchange you decided to ruin our lives?"

"You made your own choices in life." Robyn sneered at Candace before sipping from her glass. "Live with it."

Frustrated and wanting nothing more than to wring the woman's neck, Candace reached out and grabbed a crystal vase that served as a centerpiece on a nearby table. Before she could think, she hauled the glass across the short distance. Robyn dodged the incoming object and the vase crashed just at her foot, a shard of glass managing to spring upward slashing her calf.

"Crazy bitch!" Robyn called out. "Leal!" she screamed, looking around and realizing that no one was there. Her eyes darted to the door across the floor and behind Candace. There was no way that she'd be able to run past her psycho niece and exit without being caught. She was too old for physical altercations. This was what she paid others to do: handle her dirty work for her.

"Leal's gone," Candace said. "It's just you and me. I just wanted to pay you a visit to let your old, twisted, fucked up ass know that the game is over! You think you got the best of me? You think you won the battle, Aunt Robyn? Maybe you did come out on top in a few rounds, but bitch... I've won the war!"

Robyn had no clue what Candace was going on and on about. "All of this over an appointment or two?" Robyn asked, trying to make light of whatever had Candace so enraged.

"Fuck your appointments."

"You watch your tone with me. Let's not forget who holds the upper hand here," Robyn threatened. "Y-y-you owe me! I saved that worthless brother of yours w-w-with my money!" she spat out.

Candace shook her head. "You drunk cow. You saved him huh? Is that why you tried to blackmail Judge Bennett into making sure that he got a maximum sentence and a conviction that you set him up to get?" She saw the guilt flicker in her aunt's eyes and knew that she'd hit a nerve. "What? You thought wouldn't find out? Just like you thought I wouldn't find out about you ribbing Sean up to bid on me? Or how about you keeping tabs on me in Arizona and putting Rico in place to sweep me off me feet and play me? Oh yeah, bitch. I know it all. Even how you got me fired."

"I-I-I don't know what you're talking about," Robyn insisted, suddenly feeling woozy and vulnerable since she was alone with her niece who looked like she'd come for blood.

"I bet you don't. You wanna talk about loyalty? Everybody you thought had your back has turned on you," Candace told her, taking a step towards her aunt. "They're tired of your manipulative bullshit."

Robyn thought about Rico and it all made sense. He'd been missing for the past couple of days and she hadn't heard a word from him since their phone conversation about her plans for Lawrence. Robyn's eyes shut for a moment and the rain began to fall more steadily on her closed lids. She thought he loved her, but the truth was that he was no different from the others. "Kelsey," she murmured, thinking about the child that legally belonged to her. Her daughter was all she had now and apparently Rico thought that he could just take her away. He had another thing coming to him.

"You don't have to ever worry about my man and his daughter again," Candace said.

"Your man?" Robyn repeated, opening her eyes and blinking profusely.

"That's right. Oh you thought you could control his feelings too? Sorry to inform you that you were sadly mistaken."

"You can't take my life!" Robyn screamed. "That's my daughter and my man!"

"Trust me, where you're going you won't need family."

"And just where do you think I'm going?"

"To hell!" Candace gritted, coming face to face with her aunt.

Robyn couldn't breathe. She didn't know what her niece was capable of and it was clear that she herself was in no position to squabble with the woman. Hurriedly, she increased the gap between them and backed up closer to the railing at the edge of the roof top.

"And I'll meet you there!" Robyn retorted. "Always thinking you're so much better than me. Remember, I made you a whore and that's all you'll ever be. A drunk whore. A broke, drunk, whore. I tried...I tried to give you so much more. I tried to be your family...to teach you...to show you how you could be something. But you're an ungrateful piece of shit and you'll die with nothing, just like your mother."

Candace balled her fists and her eyes turned to slits. "Don't you dare disgrace the name of my mother."

Robyn laughed nervously before chugging back the remainder of her champagne and tossing the glass to the ground carelessly. Her usual lady-like demeanor was coming undone in her frantic moment of intoxicated raw emotion. "I tried to tell Patricia that she was wasting her entire life being married to a...a janitor," Robyn spat out as if the word alone left a bad taste in her mouth. "He could barely keep the rent paid while she busted her ass at some desk job. I tried to get her to partner with me...I tried to get your mother to see that she could be and do so much more. And what did she do? Turned her back on family. Wouldn't let me have a relationship with you and Lawrence. Told me I was a bad influence. Even agreed to testify against me once when I was being brought up on pimping and pandering charges."

Candace glared at her aunt and listened. She watched as the older woman's body swayed unsteadily while she suffered from verbal diarrhea. Listening to Robyn insult her dead mother only made Candace angrier with each word that left her mouth.

"That's when I learned that these hoes ain't loyal," Robyn said, laughing at her own colloquial statement. "I tried to help you, tried to help her...I helped Rico and Leal and look at you! You all turned on me."

The rain began to fall harder and Robyn flung her arms open as if she was embracing the free-flowing water. "You all fail to realize that I run this!" she screamed out. "I run this!" Her eyes zeroed in on Candace's as she blinked away the rain drops that clouded her vision. "But you'll all learn what happens when you turn your backs on me. I despise disloyalty. Your mother and father, may they burn in hell, are a testament to that."

Suddenly, Candace recalled a flippant statement that Leal made the day that they'd had a drink at the office. She picked up a shard of glass from the ground and charged her aunt whose back was immediately pressed up against the railing. Behind her the lights of the cityscape shined brightly through the sheets of rain that beat upon their heads. Candace raised the glass to her aunt's neck as the woman stared at her with large eyes.

"What did you do to my parents you crazy bitch?" Candace demanded an answer.

With liquid confidence running through her bloodstream Robyn smiled as if her life wasn't being threatened. "They had an accident," she answered slowly and softly. "A very expensive accident...they learned a fatal lesson to never fuck with me. Fuck them and fuck you!"

Tears welled up in Candace's eyes at her aunt's confession. Her entire life had been fucked up since her parents' death and now it turned out that Robyn was at the root of it all. Everything that hurt her, everything that pushed her to drink, everything that stressed her out, and everything that depressed her was caused by Robyn. Looking at the woman made Candace go into an emotional rage.

"AHHHHHHHHHHHHHHHH!" she screamed through her tears, feeling her chest tighten as her lungs struggled to fill with air. "You...y-y-you killed them! Y-y-you killed my mom...my dad...How...h-h-how could you do that? How could you do that?" Quickly, she raised her hand and whipped the shard of glass across her aunt's face. "I hate you!" she screamed.

Immediately, Robyn's hand flew up to her face and she stumbled causing her to grab the rail to balance herself. She looked down at the long distance between the roof top and the ground. Her head was spinning and her face was burning from the fresh slit on her cheek that was rapidly leaking blood, which was being washed downward onto her beautiful dress with the help of the rain. Her face turned towards Candace who was clutching her chest and breathing uncontrollably with death in her eyes.

"Join the club," Robyn seethed.

"I hope you burn in hell while I take everything you've ever thought was yours," Candace said. "Your business, your home, your man."

"You can have the pathetic dick, but you'll never have what I've built."

"You've always underestimated me. I have a piece of paper that names me as your power of attorney, another the bequeaths everything to me in your will, and another that I got drawn up earlier making ME Kelsey's legal, adoptive mother. Checkmate bitch."

Robyn shook her head. "Liar! My girls will never work for you! I've been good to them and Benjamin wouldn't dare legalize you to take over my estate."

Candace gave her aunt a crazed smile. "Oh but he would and he did! As for the girls, I think they're much fonder of my ideas and leadership than your dictatorship. You lost, Robyn. Burn in hell."

Robyn was speechless. The world seemed to be spinning out of control around her and for the first time she realized that she was drunker than she'd ever been. She wasn't in her right mind. She couldn't have heard Candace correctly. She couldn't be losing everything. It wasn't possible. She tried to clear her head quickly to make sense of the situation. Candace had mentioned a will, but the will was of no consequence if she wasn't dead. Robyn laughed. "Silly bitch. What are you gonna do? Kill me? The only way you can take my legacy is in my death. I'll have my will switched back before you can blink an eye."

"Will you?" Candace lurched forward as if she was going to push her aunt, yet didn't touch her at all.

Robyn's eyes grew huge realizing that her demented niece was actually about to push her to her death from the seven foot office building. Her heart rate quickened, her eye sight became even more blurred, and she could feel the wind whipping past her face as she lost her footing the haste to move out of Candace's reach. The air around her was cool as her body tumbled haphazardly over the railing and gravity proved its existence. Her screams were loss in the mix of traffic noises and the soundtrack of the current storm. In the moment that she fell freely through the air in the wind it all became clear to her. In the end, everyone was loyal to themselves and the moment they felt threatened, unhappy, or that something better was in store they'd simply toss you away without a care.

Candace watched as her aunt forced herself backwards and then as she fell to her death on the concrete sidewalk below them. Quickly, she placed the glass she'd been clutching into the waistband of her miniskirt and turned to exit the rooftop. It was over. She never again had to worry about Aunt Robyn wreaking havoc on the lives of those she loved or forcing her to do things that compromised her character. She didn't owe the woman anything else. She was free to love and live the way she wanted to. She'd saved Lawrence and prayed that he'd now fly on the straight and narrow given all that she'd done to give him a second chance in life. She had work to do to repair her relationship with Rico because despite their fucked up start and foundation, they loved each other undeniably. Everything was falling into place and she was now much wealthier than when she'd woke up that morning.

As she descended the stairs from the roof another set of feet trotting upward. Before reaching the level where Pleasure Principle was located, Candace came eye to eye with Alex and a few of the other girls who had once been in Robyn's employ.

"Oh my God," Alex called out. "Someone said they heard screaming outside and there's a crowd downstairs...What happened up there? Candace! What happened?"

Candace's mind was all over the place but she knew that she had to be careful how she answered the question. Or did she? She now had an attorney, a judge, and a whole slew of horny yet powerful men on her client list who were practically indebted to her for her silence and confidentiality. Candace smiled, realizing the power she now held. "I just became the boss bitch," she answered moving past the girls and stepping into boss mode.

They weren't ready. At all.

****THE END****

ORDER FORM
DIAMANTE' PUBLICATIONS, LLC
P.O. BOX 1034
Stone Mountain, GA 30086

Name (please print):__________________________

Address:______________________________________

City/State: ____________________________________

Zip: ____

QTY	TITLES	PRICE

ORDER FORM
DIAMANTE' PUBLICATIONS, LLC
P.O. BOX 1034
Stone Mountain, GA 30086

Name (please print):______________________

Address:______________________

City/State: ______________________

Zip: ______________________

QTY	TITLES	PRICE
	FLATLINED 1	$20
	FLATLINED 2	$20
	LADY GOONZ	$15
	LADY GOONZ 2	$15
	GHETTO GOSPELS 1	$12
	GHETTO GOSPELS 2	$12
	TRIPLE CROSS	$15
	BRIDAL BLISS	$20
	CRUMBLING DOWN	$15
	KHARMA'S CHILD	$15

ORDER FORM
DIAMANTE' PUBLICATIONS, LLC
P.O. BOX 1034
Stone Mountain, GA 30086

Name (please print):________________________

Address:________________________________

City/State: _____________________________

Zip: ______________________________________

QTY	TITLES	PRICE
	KHARMA DEADLY DEMISE	$15
	DOPE	$15
	LACED PANTIES	$10
	THE POWER OF V	$15
	UNBREAKABLE TIES	$15

Shipping and handling: add $3.00 for 1st book. Then $1.00 for each additional book.
Please allow 2-4 weeks for delivery

Stay Tuned as Diamante' Publications has plenty more heat for you

Join our mailing list
diamantepublications@gmail.com

To see what's releasing next, read a sneak peek or win great prizes

YOU CAN ALSO VISIT US AT
www.diamantepublications.com

Made in the USA
Columbia, SC
03 April 2024

33948788R00150